PRIME SUSPECT

Ashlee paled under her self-tanner. "Uh-oh."

"What do you mean, uh-oh?"

"Well, I didn't say anything to the cops, but . . ." Her voice trailed away.

I leaned across the table. "But what?"

She still wouldn't meet my gaze as she traced a chip in the surface of the table wood. "We argued in his truck on the drive to the fairgrounds. Then when we got there, we were still fighting all the way across the parking lot. And I yelled at him in front of a bunch of people."

I thought about that for a moment. "Totally understandable. The cops would expect you to chew him out."

Ashlee shook her head, tendrils of blond hair waving around her face. "I don't care so much that I got all huffy in front of his stupid friends. It's what I said." Tears pooled along her lower lids as she finally met my gaze. "I told Bobby Joe I was going to kill him . . ."

Books by Staci McLaughlin

Going Organic Can Kill You

All Natural Murder

Published by Kensington Publishing Corp.

All Natural Murder

Staci McLaughlin

KENSINGTON PUBLISHING CORP.

http://www.kensingtonbooks.com

KENSINGTON BOOKS are published by

Kensington Publishing Corp.
119 West 40th Street
New York, NY 10018

All Kensington Titles, Imprints, and Distributed Lines are available at special quantity discounts for bulk purchases for sales promotions, premiums, fund-raising, and educational or institutional use. Special book excerpts or customized printings can also be created to fit specific needs. For details, write or phone the office of the Kensington special sales manager: Kensington Publishing Corp., 119 West 40th Street, New York, NY 10018, attn: Special Sales Department, Phone: 1-800-221-2647.

Kensington and the K logo Reg. U.S. Pat & TM Off.

ISBN-13: 978-0-7582-7501-1
ISBN-10: 0-7582-7501-3

First Mass Market Printing: February 2013

10 9 8 7 6 5 4 3 2 1

Printed in the United States of America

To Michael, Jacob, and Connor, with all my love.

1

A gust of warm, dry air swept onto the porch step and swirled around my sandals, tickling my toes and sending a shiver up my calves as I tilted my head for a good-night kiss.

A shriek sounded from inside the house, followed by a bang. I jerked my head toward the front door, recognizing the sound as coming from my sister, Ashlee. I turned back to Jason, noticing how the touches of gold in his reddish-brown goatee glinted in the porch light.

"Everything okay in there?" he asked me.

No way was I letting Ashlee's latest emotional meltdown interrupt my big kiss with Jason. Who knew when our next date might be?

"Nothing we need to worry about."

Jason reached over and tucked an errant chunk of blond hair behind my ear, sending a ripple of excitement down my back. "Sorry your bowling score wasn't any higher tonight, Dana," he said.

I felt my face heat up and hoped it didn't show in the

dim light. "The strobe light blinded me. I couldn't see the pins."

"Must have had your eyes closed to score a seventy-four."

"Hardee har har." I just hoped he didn't print my score in the local newspaper. As the lead reporter for Blossom Valley's only paper, he sometimes had to get creative to fill the space. "I'll wear sunglasses next time. Be prepared to quiver in your bowling shoes when I approach the lane with my mighty ball."

Jason moved closer, his ironed Ralph Lauren dress shirt almost brushing the front of my lacy sweetheart top. "You've got me quivering right now."

A smile played across my lips as my hand found Jason's, his long, slender fingers intertwining with mine. "Where were we again?" I closed my eyes and leaned in.

Another bang, this one followed by an undecipherable shout from my sister. The moment evaporated faster than a slushie on a hot summer sidewalk. Whatever Ashlee was mad about tonight, it sounded like a doozy.

I dropped Jason's hand and dug my keys out of my jeans pocket. "Guess I'd better go in."

"Sounds like someone needs help." Jason half-turned toward the door, obviously torn between going in with me and escaping while he could.

"Only a licensed therapist can provide the help that Ashlee needs." I stuck the key in the lock. "Thanks for a great night."

"I'll call you, arrange that bowling rematch." He offered me a wink and a smile with that promise, then stepped off the porch.

I shot a quick glance at his butt before I entered the

house. The front hall was silent, save for the ever-present ticking of the grandfather clock. I checked my teeth in the hall mirror and noticed I had spinach lodged over a canine. Great. Maybe Jason had missed that.

A ripping sound off to my left reached my ears, followed by muttering. I walked toward the living room and stopped at the entrance.

Glossy photos were strewn across the tan carpet, most torn in half. Ashlee sat cross-legged in the middle of the wreckage, her normally brushed and styled blond hair, three shades lighter than mine, hanging down from an untidy bun, tear tracks evident on her flushed cheeks.

"Ashlee, what's wrong?" I asked, pretty sure her crisis involved a man. Ashlee went through boyfriends faster than world champion competitive eater Joey Chestnut went through a plate of Nathan's hot dogs.

She lifted her head at my voice, her clenched fist squeezing two halves of a photo. "Bobby Joe is such a pig. He's been cheating on me!"

I raised my eyebrows. Ashlee and Bobby Joe had been dating since they'd met at the cricket-chirping contest back in May. Though I figured their relationship wasn't going to be long-term, I'd assumed it would at least survive through the upcoming Fourth of July weekend. Nobody likes to watch fireworks alone.

"Are you sure? Did Bobby Joe tell you he cheated?"

Ashlee sniffed, her face a portrait of wounded pride. "He told me. Right after I found the evidence, the big coward."

My mind flashed to lace underwear stuffed in the glove box of his truck. Or maybe a bra tangled around a wrench in the oversize toolbox he carried in the truck bed. "What evidence?"

"Text messages." Spittle flew from her mouth along with the words.

I screwed up one side of my mouth, not hiding my doubt. "That's your big evidence? Text messages?"

Ashlee grabbed another picture, this one showing Bobby Joe holding a large striped bass, and ripped it in half with a vicious yank. "I don't need more proof than that, especially when I read about what a great time the tramp had last night and how she can't wait to see him again. You know, I'd heard Bobby Joe cheated on his last girlfriend, but he said he'd grown up."

Great, my sister had been dating a serial cheater. I bent down and gave her an awkward, one-armed hug. "I'm sorry he turned out to be such a jerk. I know you really cared about him."

"Yeah, I guess. 'Course he was starting to be a drag. You can only go four-wheeling so many times." Ashlee shrugged my arm off her shoulder and attempted to smooth down her hair. "It's just that I've never been cheated on before. These things don't happen to me."

I resisted the urge to mention that she dated most men for two weeks or less, not giving them much time to stray, but now didn't seem like the time. "Anything I can do to help?" I asked instead.

"No. I can't believe I started going to the gym to get in shape for that bum. What a total waste." Ashlee stood, photos falling from her lap like tiles from a roof during an earthquake. "I gotta update my Facebook page. Change my status to 'Single.'" She stomped from the room.

I used my hands to sweep the pieces into a pile and dumped them in the wicker garbage can that sat next to the beige and brown floral couch. With my limited number of ex-boyfriends, I had little advice to offer

Ashlee. Luckily, her prognosis was most likely a battered ego rather than any actual heartbreak. She'd line up a new boyfriend by tomorrow and forget Bobby Joe's betrayal in a week.

I headed to my own bedroom, pushing Ashlee's troubles from my mind. A smile formed on my lips as I remembered my evening with Jason and stayed there as I drifted off to sleep.

The alarm screeched at six the next morning. I shot an arm out from under the sheet and slapped at the cheap plastic box until I was rewarded with silence. With a groan, I tossed back the covers and stumbled out of bed. I took a quick shower and donned my summer uniform of khaki walking shorts and a navy blue polo shirt with STAFF stitched on the back that everyone now wore at the O'Connell Organic Farm and Spa, a long way from the blouses and skirts of my marketing days at a computer software company.

It had been four months since I'd moved back home after a lengthy stint of unemployment down in San Jose, thanks to a layoff where I worked. With my mother still grieving my father's unexpected death, I'd convinced myself she needed someone around to keep an eye on her. Sure, Ashlee still lived at home, but she was out most evenings and at work the rest of the time. Plus, she might move out one of these days, and then Mom would be completely alone.

The one big downside to living at home was that since my father had died of a heart attack, Mom now insisted that we abolish all processed and sugary foods and stop frying our dinners, which meant no more kids cereal in the mornings, no more fried chicken for

Sunday dinners, and no more giant bowls of ice cream during *Scream* movie marathons. Now it was whole-wheat pasta and poached fish, with fresh fruit for dessert. As if adjusting to life back home wasn't hard enough, I didn't even have any chocolate fudge brownie ice cream to ease the transition. At least not without a disapproving glare from my mother.

Casting aside my musings, I headed for the kitchen to face breakfast. Box and gallon jug in hand, I sat at the oak table under the watchful eyes of the family por-traits that lined the wall and swallowed my bran cereal without really tasting it, not that there was anything to taste. I pushed the empty bowl away, gulped my orange juice, and glanced at the clock. Only 6:30. Mom and Ashlee were still asleep. Who knew how long Ashlee had stayed up last night, changing her Facebook status and tweeting about her suffering? She might be in bed for another hour or two, but I preferred to start my day early.

Besides, Esther might need help with the chickens.

I grabbed my purse, locked the front door behind me, and slipped behind the wheel of my Honda Civic. Already, the sun beat down on the roof, warming the car like a hothouse, a precursor to another scorching day. The weatherman called for this heat wave to con-tinue through the July Fourth weekend, but I was keep-ing my fingers crossed that his satellite was broken and a cold snap was imminent. A girl could dream.

Easing out of the driveway, I waved to Mr. McGowen, who had been tinkering in his yard every day for the last thirty years, and drove the few blocks through the downtown. The owner of the Get the Scoop ice cream parlor was already setting out the patio tables and chairs in front of his plate-glass window, business so booming with the current stretch of hot weather that he'd started opening for breakfast. Only a handful of cars were parked in the Breaking Bread Diner lot, though I knew from experience the place would get crowded as the morning wore on. Having the best omelets in town always guaranteed a hungry crowd. Since there was no commuter traffic, I traveled Main Street in less than a minute and was on the highway, headed for the farm.

When I'd moved home, the *Blossom Valley Herald* want ads had listed few jobs, exactly zero of them involving marketing. But then Mom had met Esther, owner of the new O'Connell Organic Farm and Spa, at a grieving spouses support group, and Esther had hired me to promote the place, although the job had quickly evolved into a Jill-of-all-trades position. When I wasn't marketing the farm, I helped the maid clean the cabins, the cook serve the meals, and Esther tend to the animals. I was just happy to be employed, something that had been in jeopardy back in May after a guest was murdered on opening weekend; that had almost closed down the farm.

Two months later, with the killer behind bars, the farm and spa was finding its footing again. In fact, all ten cabins were booked for the long weekend, ensuring me plenty of work around the property.

Traffic was light, as it tended to be on Thursday mornings, or any morning for that matter. I took the freeway off-ramp for the farm and bounced down the lane. Time for repaving. I passed the sign for the farm and slowed as I approached the small lot. I parked near the side path that led to the kitchen. A pickup truck with oversized tires and a compact car already filled two spaces.

Sparrows chirped in the nearby pine trees, a melody

to accompany the staccato crunch of my sandals on the gravel. I stepped onto the dirt path next to the vegetable garden, admiring the plump Brandywine tomatoes, a deep red against the lush green vines. A cucumber peeked out from beneath a broad leaf. Zennia, the spa's health-conscious and adventurous cook, would no doubt snag that cuke for a lunchtime salad. Little did that vegetable know that its fate was already decided and the end was near.

I wound around the camellia bush, passed the pool, Jacuzzi, and patios, and entered the kitchen by way of the herb garden.

Zennia stood at the counter, layering homemade granola and Greek yogurt in a parfait glass. She straightened as I entered, her long black braid with a few strands of gray sliding over her shoulder and hitting the counter, almost dipping into the yogurt container.

"Morning, Dana." She added a handful of granola to the top of the parfait, then grabbed her honey pot and held the drizzle stick aloft.

I nodded at her dish. "Looks delicious. Wish I hadn't wasted all my stomach room on boring old bran cereal." I grabbed a blackberry from the bowl on the counter and popped the fruit into my mouth.

"Hope you didn't fill up too much. We're having curried lentil burgers for lunch."

My stomach seized. Where did Zennia find these recipes? Torture Cuisines R Us? I forced a smile. "Great." Before my expression faltered, I snatched one last blackberry from the bowl and headed down the hall.

In the office, I plopped down in the desk chair, punched the power button on the computer, and swiveled idly, studying the room as I waited for Windows to load. The wall closest to the door held an overstuffed book case, and extra books were stacked on the faded green carpet. A metal guest chair sat between the book case and the door. Against the opposite wall, there was a wooden filing cabinet under the window and a floor lamp in the corner. Pictures of the farm in earlier years, along with a handful of family photos, filled the walls.

When all the icons had appeared on the desktop, I checked my e-mail, then wrote the day's blog. Today's topic covered the benefits of watermelon, celery, and other foods that could rehydrate your body during a heat wave.

After posting the blog to the spa Web site, I logged onto Facebook and read the latest news. Ashlee had changed her status from "In a Relationship" to "Single," and posted, "Cheaters suck! You stink more than your bad breath, Bobby Joe!!" Sheesh. At least she was being mature about the whole thing.

I closed the Web browser and returned to the kitchen. Two more parfaits had joined the original at the counter. Zennia stood nearby, drying the now-clean blackberry bowl.

"Need help serving breakfast this morning?"

Before she could answer, Esther huffed and puffed her way into the kitchen from the hall, her denim shirt with the embroidered kittens misbuttoned. Her gray curls drooped in the morning heat, and her plump cheeks were flushed.

"Goodness gracious, those ducklings have escaped," she gasped.

"Again?" I said, trying to remember if this was the second or third time this week. The newest additions to the farm, the ducklings weren't the first animals to escape their pen, but they were definitely the most frequent offenders. "Esther, I know you want the guests to see the ducklings the minute they park so they'll be in the right mood for their farm stay, but don't you think those ducks are more trouble than they're worth?"

Esther finished catching her breath. "Sure, they run away a lot, but they're so darn cute. And the kids love them so."

I didn't point out that we'd had no more than three kids stay with us. Besides, she was right: the ducks were pretty cute.

Esther patted my arm. "You're always such a dear, Dana. Would you round them up with me?"

I looked at Zennia to see if she needed my assistance with breakfast, but she waved her hand in a shooing motion.

"Call me quackers, but I'll help," I said.

Zennia chuckled as I walked out the kitchen door, Esther shadowing me through the herb garden. No little ducks were hiding under the mint leaves. I stopped at the toolshed for a cardboard box, then wandered by the pool area.

The surface of the water was as smooth as the patio tables. I craned my neck to peek under the chaise longues in case the ducks had decided to seek refuge from the summer heat, but the space was empty.

I suspected the ducklings were entertaining the pigs again, but I held out hope they'd still be waddling down the sidewalk and we could intercept them. No such luck. One glance at the pigsty showed little yellow feathers coated in mud and only God knew what else, although I had a pretty good idea.

I placed my hand on the top railing. The fence

around the sty was the same style as the slat fence around the pond out front. Three rails with large gaps in between. "Ever think of enclosing the ducklings in a more escape-proof fence? Maybe add a bottom board to keep them in?"

"I couldn't do that to the precious little things," Esther said. "Then they'd feel like prisoners."

"We could give them an hour of yard exercise every day. Isn't that what they do in real prisons?"

Esther tittered. "Oh, Dana, you're a hoot."

I hadn't actually been kidding, but apparently Esther wasn't keen on fencing in her pets. I scanned the area near the gate for the rubber boots that usually sat there, but the boots were missing. Someone had probably left them at the chicken coop or off in the vegetable garden. Those boots had a habit of walking away.

With a resigned sigh, I slipped off my sandals, opened the gate to the sty, and placed one bare foot in the muck. Mud and mystery objects, cool and slimy, squeezed between my toes. I shuddered as I added my other foot to the mixture, ready to catch those fuzzy felons and get out of the pen.

Wilbur, an occasional escapee himself, snorted at me. The four other pigs started a backup chorus of squeals and snuffles. Joy.

I grabbed the least muddy duckling, careful not to squeeze too hard, and handed it off to Esther, who dipped the duck in a nearby bucket of water and placed it in the cardboard box. I grabbed another duck, and we repeated the process.

By the fifth bird, my hands and wrists were covered in mud, the brown goo inching toward my elbows. The sixth pooped in my hand, but really, what difference did it make at this point?

I looked around the pen for the final escapee, not seeing any yellow peeking through the brown. The pigs had quieted down and were huddled in a group at the far side of the pen, watching the day's entertainment. If I didn't know any better, I'd swear Wilbur was smirking as he watched me play the farm's version of hide-and-seek.

Movement caught my attention across the pen. A brown blob crept toward the fence and the freedom beyond the rail. I jerked my head toward the duckling to point him out to Esther. She nodded her head in return, just as I heard the opening bars of my cell's ringtone coming from my pocket.

I raised my gunk-covered hands and continued to listen as Coldplay got louder, wondering who was calling at this exact moment. Oh well, if it was important, they'd call back.

I took two steps toward the moving blob, the pigs shuffling and snorting in nervous anticipation. These pigs really needed more excitement in their lives.

Chris Martin started singing again. I abandoned the errant duckling and slopped over to the gate, ignoring the sucking sounds from my feet. I snatched a nearby rag from a fence post, rubbed my hands mostly clean, and gingerly slid my phone from my pocket. The display showed my home number. Ashlee should be at work by now, leaving only Mom to call me here. But she was old-school when it came to interrupting someone's workday. This might be serious after all.

I pressed the green button and held the phone to my ear, crinkling my nose at a whiff of pig smells. The duckling popped his head up from the mud, and I eased toward him.

"Dana," Mom said, her voice clearly strained, "I need you home right now. Your sister's in trouble.

"What's wrong with Ashlee?" I asked, the grip on my phone tightening as I ran down a mental list of possibilities. Had she crashed her car again? Been fired? Gotten in a fistfight down at the Prescription for Joy drugstore over the last tube of Cotton Candy lipstick?

"It's Bobby Joe," Mom said, the words spilling out so fast, I expected them to drip from the receiver.

The duckling moved closer, and I lunged for it. With my attention half on the phone, I lost my balance and went down on one knee, using my free hand to break my fall. Mud shot up and splattered my shirt. Perfect.

Behind me, Esther gasped, but I was too embarrassed to look at her.

"Dana, are you there?" Mom asked in my ear.

I focused back on the conversation, a little crankier thanks to the mud decorating my shirt. "Is she still upset about Bobby Joe? She told me last night they weren't even serious. Tell her to find some new guy at work today, and she'll forget all about Bobby Joe."

The pause on the other end made me wonder if my cell service had cut out, something that happened often at the farm.

Then I heard Mom again, her voice practically a whisper.

"He's dead."

By reflex, I grabbed my St. Christopher medal, a gift
from my father that I had worn around my neck every
day since his death. I stared at Esther, not really seeing
her as she clutched her box full of ducks. I forgot all
about the mud and poo bits smeared on my hands and
clothes, the sweat trickling down my temples.

As if from a distance, I heard Esther say, "Dana, what
is it?"

But the phone and my mother's last words were all
I could focus on. "What do you mean Bobby Joe's dead?
How?"

"Murdered. At the fairgrounds. The police asked
Ashlee all sorts of questions about what they did last
night, what time she got home, if anything out of the or-
dinary happened." I heard a sob.

"Hang on, Mom. I'll be right there." I clicked off the
phone and jammed it in my pocket.

Bobby Joe.

Dead.

My mind couldn't grasp the finality of that. How

could he suddenly be gone? Murdered, of all things. And now the police were talking to Ashlee.

Esther watched me, her grip on the cardboard box so tight that the corners were bending. A bright yellow head peeked over the top, the cheerful color a sharp contrast to the dark news I'd just received.

"Everything all right, dear?" Esther asked. "You look like someone dropped your basket of eggs."

I wasn't familiar with that exact phrase, but I understood her meaning. "Family emergency. I need to get home."

She bit her lower lip, worry etched in the lines of her face. "I can catch the last duck. You go on home. I hope it's nothing serious."

Murder was about as serious as it got, but I didn't want to take the time to explain what had happened. I slogged out of the muck, stopped at the garden hose to wash off, and slipped on my sandals. Then I jogged through the kitchen with barely a nod to Zennia, grabbed my purse from the bottom drawer of the office desk, and jotted down my departure on my time card. Before I reached the lobby, I'd already extracted my keys from my purse.

Gordon Stewart, the spa's manager, stood at the front desk, pounding on the computer keys like Victor Borge on the piano. His fingers froze when he saw me with my purse and keys in hand.

He consulted the gold watch peeking out from the sleeve of his suit jacket, then frowned at me. "Going out?" he asked, his tone stern.

Every muscle in my back stiffened. Even though Esther owned the place and was technically my boss, Gordon managed the day-to-day operations and devoted most of that time to shadowing the employees and offering suggestions on how we could improve at our jobs. I was one of his favorite "works in progress," as he liked to call me.

"Family emergency. I'm leaving for the day."

I grabbed the doorknob, but Gordon spoke before I could make my escape.

"Unacceptable. We've got a big holiday weekend, and guests arrive tomorrow. You're supposed to help Esther finish the decorations, I'm not sure all the rooms are ready yet, and you need to reply to any comments on the farm's blog today. We can't afford to have you dodging your responsibilities here."

Dodging my responsibilities? Could he be any more dramatic? "Right now my responsibilities are at home. I've already asked Esther and updated my time card. I might be back later, but I'll have to play it by ear." I jerked the door open, walked out, and pulled the door closed behind me, but not before a "Now wait . . ." escaped through the gap.

Too bad. My sister needed me.

Luck was with me as I raced down the highway. The California Highway Patrol officer, notorious for ticketing anyone going over sixty-five on this stretch, wasn't lurking behind his usual billboard. As I pulled up to the house, I found Mom's car backing out of the garage. She must have spotted me in the rearview mirror, because she immediately braked and shut off the engine.

I climbed out of my car as she exited hers, and we met in the driveway, Mom's freshly curled silver hair gleaming in the bright summer sun. Even in this July heat, she wore brown slacks and a red sweater set. I felt hot just looking at her.

Mom encircled me with a hug. "Dana, thank goodness you're home. I don't know what to do about Ashlee."

I gave Mom a squeeze and let her go. "Don't worry, we'll figure this out. The police can't possibly believe Ashlee had anything to do with Bobby Joe's death. Is she inside?" As I asked the question, I realized her car was gone, which meant she was too. "She didn't go back to work after being questioned, did she?"

Mom shook her head. "That nice policeman who asked her all the questions wanted her to go down to the station. I was on my way there now to see what was taking so long."

I forgot to breathe as Mom burst into tears. She pulled a handkerchief from her pocket and blotted her eyes as I placed a hand on her back and reminded myself to inhale.

"The police station? Did they arrest her?" An image of Ashlee behind bars, wearing blue denim and trading cigarettes for playing cards, sprang to mind. I needed to stop watching those old *Charlie's Angels* reruns.

"Not yet. They wanted to get her fingerprints, something to do with comparing them to ones they found in Bobby Joe's pickup truck."

"And she went? Without asking a lawyer if that was a good idea?"

Mom twisted the handkerchief, her eyes growing large. "Do you think that was a mistake? The police were so polite, and they said people get fingerprinted all the time for this kind of thing." She wound the handkerchief tighter. "Are they going to lock my baby up?"

I eased the handkerchief from Mom's grip and gently wiped at the mascara streaks on her cheeks.

"I'm sure she hasn't been arrested," I said. "But we should call a lawyer. Do you know one?"

"I already called Harry Wilson, your father's old attorney, and asked that he go down to the station in case Ashlee needed him. After what you've said, I'm glad I did."

"Me, too."

Mom moved toward her car. "Now, I really need to get down there. Ashlee needs me at a time like this."

I walked over and grabbed the passenger-side handle. "I'll go with you. She needs all our support right now."

I climbed in the car and clicked my seat belt while Mom backed out of the driveway. The drive to the station was brief and silent. I glanced at Mom and saw her chewing her lip as she clenched the steering wheel.

In the lot, Mom parked and hopped out of the car. I practically had to jog to keep up with her as she hurried to the entrance of the single-story brick building. "Slow down," I said. "I'm sure she's fine."

"I'll believe that when I see it," Mom said, yanking one of the double glass doors open.

She didn't have long to wait. Ashlee stood in the lobby, still dressed in her vet smock from when she'd been at work. She'd piled her blond hair atop her head in a loose knot, her Coach sunglasses perched in front. She was talking to an older gentleman in a tailored suit that did a good job of hiding his paunch. Beside him, another man, also in a suit, listened to the conversation.

Ashlee spotted us and breezed over, as though she was window shopping at the mall, not down at the police station at the request of the cops.

"Mom, Dana, what are you guys doing here?" she asked.

Mom ran to Ashlee's side. "Thank God," she said. Mom squeezed Ashlee so hard, I heard her squeak. She stepped back, keeping her hands on Ashlee's shoulders. "What happened? Did you talk to Harry?"

Ashlee gestured to the two men. "He's right there." I had to assume Harry the lawyer was the one in the better-fitting suit. She dropped her voice to a whisper. "I'm not sure how good he is. He doesn't even own an iPhone."

Apparently the best lawyers had only the hippest phones. At least in Ashlee's world.

"Harry is a well-respected attorney in this town," Mom said, keeping her voice low to match Ashlee's. "I wanted his advice on how you should deal with the police."

As if sensing the conversation was about him, Harry shook hands with the other man and headed over to us. "Dorothy, so wonderful to see you again. It's been far too long."

"Harry, thank you for coming down here so quickly. Can you tell me what's going on?"

He glanced at his watch, a silver number that probably cost more than a month's salary at the farm. "I'm afraid I'm due in court soon. I'll try to call you later today and fill you in, but I can assure you there's nothing to worry about." He walked toward the door, Mom plucking at his sleeve as if that might stop him.

"Let me walk out with you. I had a quick question," she said.

The other man walked up to Ashlee. "Thank you for coming down here, Ms. Lewis. Your cooperation is appreciated."

Ashlee reached up and patted her hair. "Anything for the local law enforcement."

I'd swear if she batted her eyelashes any faster, he'd have to issue her a ticket for excessive speed.

I stuck out my hand. "I'm Ashlee's sister, Dana. What can you tell me about Bobby Joe's death?"

We shook while I studied his large brown eyes and tan face. He was borderline handsome, but his buzz cut made his face look too severe, probably to keep the criminals on their toes.

"Detective Palmer," he said, giving me an amused smile. "And I can't tell you anything about Bobby Joe's death."

"Of course not. I just wanted to let you know that Ashlee was home last night, you know, whenever Bobby Joe was killed."

Ashlee swatted my arm. "I already told him that."

"Good, that's important." I offered Detective Palmer my most winning smile, hoping he'd let the tiniest of details slip. "Do you know what killed him? Or who?"

Detective Palmer reached into his jacket pocket as though he might show me the murder weapon right here and now, but when he brought back his hand, all it held was a pack of gum. He extracted a stick, unwrapped it, and stuck it in his mouth, his movements slow and deliberate.

"You sure know a lot about the business of murder. Why is that?"

"I don't like to brag." Well, maybe a little. "But I helped the sheriff's department solve a murder a while back. You should call Detective Caffrey. He'd vouch for how helpful I was."

The amused smile returned as Detective Palmer chewed his gum, and I felt the first inkling of doubt creep its way inside my gut.

"Detective Caffrey is my cousin, and I remember him telling me all about you. Helpful wasn't the word he used."

I felt the skin on my face prickle and knew I was blushing. "He must have been talking about someone else."

"Must have been." He winked at me.

Ashlee pinched the back of my arm, and I yelped.

"What are you doing, Dana?" she hissed. "I want to go home, now."

"Fine. Let's go." If this detective didn't want my help, just as his cousin hadn't, then I'd go home. His loss.

I marched out of the station with Ashlee right behind. I held the door open while she turned and offered Detective Palmer a little wave and a toss of her head.

Mom was walking back toward the station but stopped when she saw us.

"Are you all finished?" she asked Ashlee.

"Sure, it was no big deal. I'll see you guys at home." She turned toward her salsa-red Camaro, but not before I saw her lips tremble. She could pretend all she wanted, but the trip to the police station had shaken her.

I almost offered to drive her but knew Ashlee would reject the offer. Instead I climbed back in Mom's car, and we trailed her home. She flipped a U-turn and pulled up to the curb, her tires rubbing the cement. Mom parked in the driveway. The trip had been too short for the air-conditioning to do any good, and I was sweating when I got out.

As we headed up the walk, Mom said, "I didn't have much time with Harry. What did he tell you at the station?"

"He said I shouldn't answer any questions without him there," Ashlee said over her shoulder as she stepped onto the porch. We all moved into the house, the sudden drop in temperature an immediate relief. "By then, it was too late," she said. "I'd already told the cops everything. I mean, why not? I didn't do anything."

Mom smoothed down the sleeve of Ashlee's vet smock. "Of course you didn't."

I wasn't exactly an expert, but all the lawyer shows warned against talking too much. "With Harry there, he could at least tell you when the police are asking you a question that seems totally innocent but that might somehow incriminate you. You wouldn't even know you were doing it."

Ashlee curled her lip at me. "Don't be silly, Dana. I'm too smart for that."

I didn't bother to object, though it was sure tempting.

"What else happened at the police station?" Mom asked, plucking at Ashlee's sleeve. Usually Mom wasn't so touchy-feely. I sensed that she wanted to convince herself that Ashlee was really here and that they hadn't forced her to remain behind at the station in one of their holding cells.

"What that cutie of a detective said would happen. Took my fingerprints. That was it." Ashlee held up her hands. "That reminds me, I need to clean up." She stalked off toward the bathroom, her leather mules slapping against the linoleum.

Mom watched her go, gnawing her bottom lip again.

"How about I fix you some lemonade, Mom?"

She placed a hand on one temple. "No thank you. I

do believe I'll go lie down for a little while. This whole situation has given me a headache." She went down the hall.

My heart twisted. Mom had been through so much with Dad's death, and now this.

Left alone, I went into the kitchen. Now that I'd mentioned the lemonade, I wanted a glass for myself. I wasn't usually much of a drinker, but considering how this day was going, I thought about adding a splash of vodka. Not that Mom allowed alcohol in the house now that we were super-healthy eaters. Or trying to be.

I pulled a glass from the cupboard and set it on the counter as Ashlee emerged from the bathroom, drying her hands on a towel.

"I still don't feel clean, but I guess that'll have to do," she said.

I retrieved the lemonade pitcher from the fridge and poured a glassful. "Have a seat. We need to talk about last night."

Frowning, Ashlee sat down and watched as I slid into a chair across from her. She eyed my glass. "Where's my lemonade?"

"In the fridge. Now tell me everything that happened on your date."

"Why?"

I grabbed a napkin from the holder and wiped the condensation off my glass and the tabletop. "Because *I* know you didn't kill Bobby Joe, and *you* know you didn't kill Bobby Joe, but the police don't know that."

"They do, too. That cute police officer told me all their questions were routine, like taking my finger-prints, and that I should relax and answer." Ashlee had taken down her hair from her earlier knot. Now she poofed it up in the back as she talked. "You know, I might ask him out after they catch Bobby Joe's killer. I'd do it sooner, but that might be a bit tacky."

I stared at her. Surely Ashlee was adopted. No way were we related. "Your boyfriend just died," I said.

"Ex-boyfriend." She examined her fingernails.

If I hadn't been looking at her, I would have missed the tear that ran down her cheek and clung to her jaw. She was still trying to act like she wasn't upset, but she couldn't bottle it up forever.

I took a long drag of lemonade to clear my head. "Anyway, you can bet the police told you not to worry. They tell everyone that in the hopes that someone will get too relaxed and let something slip."

"He was way too hot to lie to me."

God, give me strength. "Please, Ashlee, tell me what happened. Let's figure out if the police would be suspicious of anything you did."

Ashlee gave a big dramatic sigh. "Fine, whatever." She leaned back in her chair and crossed her arms. "Bobby Joe picked me up about seven, and we went and saw that new action movie, the one with all the racing cars and girls in bikinis."

"When did the movie let out?" I felt like I should be jotting down her information, but I didn't want to leave the table and give her a chance to escape.

"Nine, I guess. It was mostly dark by then." She reached over and grabbed the *Glamour* that had come in yesterday's mail and started browsing.

"And then?" I prompted before she could get distracted by the latest hair-care article.

She flipped the magazine closed. "Bobby Joe was all jacked from the race cars in the movie and started talking about his big monster truck rally this weekend. I told you about that last week, remember?"

I stared at her blankly.

She jutted her chin forward and let out another sigh, clearly disappointed in my bad memory. "A bunch of other drivers are coming in from out of town? And actual scouts?" My face must have still offered nothing because she threw up her hands. "God, Dana, you never listen to anything I say."

I had a vague memory of Ashlee whining about how her holiday weekend was ruined because she'd have to spend it at the fairgrounds, watching Bobby Joe in some sort of competition. "Wait, I remember you mentioning something."

"Nice try. Anyway, he wanted to go down to the track and check out what the other guys were planning. He's been working on some new routine for weeks that he was keeping as a big surprise from me, but he still wanted to make sure no one had anything close. We stopped for gas on the way, and that's when I saw all his texts."

"What did you do, hack into his phone?"

"No, you big snot." Ashlee squinted her eyes, her poofy hair looking more like a near-sighted cockatoo than an angry sister. "His phone kept buzzing, so I was going to shut it off. But when I picked it up, I saw all these messages." She raised her voice in a sing-song lilt. "Oh, Bobby Joe, you're so hot. Oh, Bobby Joe, I can't wait to hook up with you again. Oh, Bobby Joe, you're such a man."

Something heavy sat in the pit of my stomach as I looked at my sister. "Did you tell the police about this?"

"Of course. They need to know what kind of guy Bobby Joe was."

"And did you use that voice? The one that says, 'I am so mad that my boyfriend cheated on me'?"

Ashlee flitted her eyes away from my gaze. "I might have. Why?"

I gripped my glass. "Because you've handed the cops your motive. Your boyfriend happens to be murdered the same night you find out he's cheating? What are the odds?"

Ashlee paled under her self-tanner. "I-I didn't think about that." She swallowed so loud, I could hear her. "Uh-oh."

The object in my gut expanded in size and doubled in weight. "What do you mean, uh-oh?"

"Well, I didn't say anything to the cops, but . . ." Her voice trailed away.

I leaned across the table. "But what?"

She still wouldn't meet my gaze as she traced a chip in the surface of the table wood. "We argued in his truck on the drive to the fairgrounds. When we got there, we were still fighting all the way across the parking lot. And I yelled at him in front of a bunch of people."

I thought about that for a moment. "Totally understandable. The cops would expect you to chew him out."

Ashlee shook her head, tendrils of blond hair waving around her face. "I don't care so much that I got all huffy in front of his stupid friends. It's what I said." Tears pooled along her lower lids as she finally met my gaze. "I told Bobby Joe I was going to kill him."

3

Ashlee swiped at the tears. "Everyone must have heard me threaten to kill Bobby Joe. Do you think someone will tell the cops?"

I stood, too tense to remain seated. I rubbed my forehead with one hand, but the thoughts in my brain didn't get any clearer. "I'm sure you're exaggerating about what you said. But we should ask that lawyer, Harry. He might suggest you tell the police yourself, before someone else mentions it."

Ashlee jumped up, the tension contagious. "Oh God, I'm going to be arrested." Her voice rose in pitch. "I'm too pretty to go to jail. Someone will want me for their girlfriend."

Leave it to Ashlee to turn a serious situation into a preposterous one. The three-year age difference between us now felt like three decades. "Don't overreact. You were mad at Bobby Joe. Everyone says things they don't mean when they're angry. The cops will be interested in a lot more than your little outburst."

I tried to recall my first week at the O'Connell Organic Farm and Spa, when one of the guests had been murdered, and the steps the detectives had taken to find his killer. I snapped my fingers.

"Do the police have the murder weapon, whatever it is? Maybe it has prints on it, and that's why they wanted yours for comparison. The cops will know you didn't kill Bobby Joe as soon as the results come back."

Ashlee rubbed her bottom lip with her thumb. "You think so?"

Actually, I didn't. I wasn't even sure how Bobby Joe had died, but any killer who watched TV would know to wipe off his prints. I nodded anyway, wanting to calm Ashlee down. "I'm sure they'll figure out who the real killer is in no time."

Ashlee smiled, the tears already drying on her cheeks. "I bet you're right." She touched her hair and frowned. "I need to take a shower. That station gave me the willies with all those criminals. Who knows what cooties jumped on me."

According to the *Herald*, the biggest criminal so far this week had been some kid who'd tried to rob the Hole in One doughnut shop with a water gun and a ski mask. His math teacher had been buying a newspaper at the same time and recognized his voice, and the kid had burst into tears and cried for his mommy. Not exactly scum of the earth. Of course, now the major criminal in town was whoever killed Bobby Joe, but he obviously wasn't down at the police station yet if the cops were talking to Ashlee.

She went into the bathroom, and a moment later, I heard water running. I wandered aimlessly around the kitchen, straightening the dish towel, putting the chef's knife back in the block, anything to keep busy.

I could go back to the spa and put in a few more hours. I could definitely use the money, and Ashlee really didn't need me here. The police hadn't arrested her. Maybe this whole thing would blow right over.

The doorbell rang before I could decide, and I went to answer it.

Jason stood on the doorstep in a white dress shirt and crisp chinos. My heart flip-flopped as he smiled at me, his green eyes brighter than usual in the light of the summer day.

I took a step back. "Uh, Jason, hi." Wow, what a fantastic opening line. I'd been on a date with the guy last night, and here I was acting like we were practically strangers.

His smile faltered. "Dana, this is awkward."

I studied him, unsure of what he meant, until he held up his spiral notebook, the one he kept in his pocket at all times as the *Herald*'s lead reporter, in case a major story broke. With a rush of insight, I realized one had.

"I'm covering Bobby Joe's murder," he said. "I've been talking to the cops all morning, and now I need to interview Ashlee. Sorry."

I shook my head, disgusted with how dense I'd been. A crime as big as murder would be headline news in Blossom Valley. And, my sister, as girlfriend of the victim, would be part of the story.

Jason took a quick step forward into the house, as if afraid I'd slam the door in his face. "I need to nail down the events of last night. I'd like Ashlee to tell me exactly what she and Bobby Joe did before he was killed."

Was it too late to throw him out? I liked Jason. A lot. But I wasn't sure I wanted him questioning my sister. "She had nothing to do with his murder. She must have been home long before he even died, remember?" My words picked up pace. "You heard her here in the house when you dropped me off. I already told that detective that. Did you?" I stopped for breath and looked at Jason, waiting for him to back up my sister's alibi.

Jason put one hand on my shoulder, still holding his notebook in the other. "I know Ashlee would never kill anyone."

"And you told the cops she was here last night?"

"They didn't ask, and I'm not sure it matters."

My breath caught as hope soared through me. "What do you mean? The police know who did it already? Did they arrest someone after they talked to Ashlee?"

We'd left the station only a short time ago, but maybe another detective had been off arresting the killer.

"Afraid not. I meant the coroner has narrowed the time of death to between eleven and one. Ashlee had plenty of time to leave here and go kill Bobby Joe." Jason watched my face as it melted with disappointment. "Not that she would have," he added belatedly.

My knees trembled, and I suddenly wanted to sit down. I always mocked the damsel in distress who swooned at bad news, but I now understood what she was feeling. My sister didn't have an alibi for when her boyfriend was killed. On the same night she discovered he was cheating on her.

"What about the murder weapon?" I blurted out, remembering my comments to Ashlee a few minutes before. Maybe the police had found fingerprints, slim as the chance was.

"Killed by a blow to the head with a tailpipe."

"You can kill someone with a tailpipe?"

Jason ran a hand through his reddish-brown hair. "If you hit him hard enough. And his wallet held a few bucks, so robbery wasn't the motive. Looks like a heat-of-the-moment killing."

Another mark against Ashlee. Call me stubborn, but I was going to find a ray of sunshine if I had to search through fifty rain clouds. "Any prints on the pipe?" I pressed.

"Nope. Wiped clean."

So much for that theory.

I heard a noise in the hall and turned to find Ashlee behind me, toweling her hair off. Her bare legs stuck out of a pair of artistically frayed denim shorts, her pink T-shirt declaring, "I'm a Babe."

"What's this about prints?" she asked, giving her hair one last good rub before running her hands through it to separate the tresses. I noted that she'd applied mascara before emerging from the bathroom.

"Jason was telling me that the police didn't find any on the murder weapon." I tried for casual, but my voice sounded tight.

"What?" Ashlee shrieked. She glared at me. "You told me they'd find prints. That I wouldn't be in trouble anymore."

"Calm down," I said. "I'm sure the police know you're innocent."

Jason cleared his throat, and I whirled around.

"What?" Every muscle in my body tensed in anticipation of his answer.

"There is one more thing." He fiddled with his notebook and stared at a point over my shoulder, avoiding eye contact. "Two witnesses at the fairgrounds last night have already told the cops that Ashlee threatened to kill Bobby Joe."

I felt like I'd been slapped. Ashlee had said she'd told Bobby Joe she'd kill him, but I assumed she'd been embellishing what she'd said. But people, real people, had seen my sister threaten her boyfriend right before he was murdered.

Behind me, Ashlee let out a wail. I rushed over and put an arm around her shoulder. "The police will solve this."

"No, they won't," she blubbered, hugging the towel. "No one ever gets murdered in this town, except for that one time at your spa. And you're the one who caught the killer." Ashlee sniffled. "You know, that's not a bad idea."

I saw where she was heading and cut her off. "Forget it. The police will do their job."

She slipped out from under my arm and faced me. "You have to help me, Dana. You have to solve Bobby Joe's murder before the police throw me in the slammer. I know you can do it."

I shook my head, but it was an automatic reflex. I was going to help my sister.

What else could I do?

4

I managed to hustle Jason out of the house after only a handful of questions. As I closed the door and leaned against its wood surface, I could hear Ashlee crying in the living room and went in.

She was curled up on the end of the couch, covered by a cream afghan even though the room was already so warm that I felt like going outside and running through the sprinklers. Her cheeks were wet with fresh tears.

I sat down on the other end of the couch. "Don't cry. So the cops didn't find any prints. So a few people heard you yelling at your cheating boyfriend. A jury won't convict you on that."

She bolted up on the couch, the afghan falling to her waist. "A jury? You think it'll get as far as a jury?"

Oops. Bad timing for that phrase. "No way. The police won't even arrest you. You have nothing to worry about."

But did she? The Blossom Valley police department, such as it was, had little experience with murder. Even the murder at the farm had been covered by the

Mendocino County Sheriff's Department. The local police hadn't seen a murder in years.

Of course, Ashlee had a way of magically skipping through life while being showered with good luck and smiles. The police would no doubt trip over the solution without even trying, and she'd be cleared.

Still, did I really want to bet my sister's future on a group of officers who spent most of their days handing out speeding tickets to unsuspecting tourists driving through town on their way to the ocean? Probably not. I'd solved one murder a couple months back. Maybe I could at least look into this one, provided I could still do all my work at the farm. Esther was counting on me to help make the guests' stay memorable for the big holiday weekend. We needed the repeat business to guarantee the farm's survival.

I took a deep breath and hoped I wouldn't regret my next words. "Ashlee, I promise I'll see what I can find out about Bobby Joe's murder."

Ashlee grabbed my hand with a gasp, not one to tone down the drama. "I knew you would."

The tears instantly stopped falling. The sniffles and runny nose vanished. Had I been played?

"Don't get too excited. I can't guarantee I'll find out anything that will help."

Ashlee tidied the afghan around her waist. "You'll solve the whole thing. You'd never let me down."

Gee, no pressure there.

I leaned forward and grabbed a pen that was sitting on the coffee table, along with the tablet Mom used to make her grocery lists. "Okay, tell me about Bobby Joe. Why would anyone want to kill him?" For a moment, I wondered if this was how Jason felt when he was conducting an interview.

Ashlee recoiled at the question. "I would never date anyone people wanted to kill. What kind of girl do you think I am?"

Considering Ashlee had dated an ex-convict, a guy who peddled Gucci knock-offs from his Web site, and pretty much any other guy who asked her out, I opted not to answer her question.

"Look, the police don't think he was killed during a robbery. And random auto parts must be all over that fairground during a truck rally. Whoever killed Bobby Joe probably grabbed the tailpipe on the spur of the moment. We need to figure out who was angry with him and what set the killer off. Was Bobby Joe still working at that gas station?"

Ashlee nodded. "For now. Until he hit the big time with his monster truck career."

I held my pen over the tablet. "You mentioned a competition this weekend. Was he really that good?"

"The best. You should have seen him jump those cars and whip around the track. He would have been famous. And I would have been right there with him, like those Nascar wives you see on TV."

I put one hand over the other so I wouldn't slap my forehead in disbelief. Or slap my sister. "Did you forget the part where he cheated on you?"

Ashlee waved her hand in dismissal. "We would have worked through that. Our love ran deep. I bet we would have gotten married if he hadn't been killed like that."

Oh no, here we went. Last night, Bobby Joe was a tool. Today he was a marriage-worthy monster truck master, cut down in his prime. Tomorrow, he'd be in line for sainthood.

"What can you tell me about this girl he was cheating with?"

Ashlee played with a pom-pom on the fringe of the afghan. "She must have been some hussy who got him drunk and took advantage of him, that's all I can come up with."

"Does this hussy have a name?"

"Melissa, Martha, Maria. Yeah, Maria sounds right. Bobby Joe said he met her at the Breaking Bread Diner. She waitresses there."

I jotted down the name, not hiding my smirk. "The diner doesn't serve alcohol."

Ashlee stopped fiddling with the pom-pom. "What?"

"You said she must have gotten Bobby Joe drunk for him to cheat on you. The diner doesn't serve alcohol, remember?" I really shouldn't tease my sister at a time like this, but sometimes these opportunities jumped out, and I couldn't stop myself.

Ashlee tried to stamp her foot on the floor, but it got caught in the afghan, and she almost fell off the couch. "Maybe she got him all hopped up on too much caffeine. Bobby Joe wouldn't cheat on me without a good reason."

She looked genuinely hurt, and I felt a pang of guilt for picking on her. "You must be right. In fact, I was thinking this girl might have killed Bobby Joe in a rage if he refused to see her again because he cared so much about you."

Ashlee nodded eagerly. "I bet that's it. Anyone who would cheat with a taken man is the kind who would kill him."

I didn't really think this other woman killed Bobby

Joe, but she might be able to provide a few more details about someone who would. All Ashlee would give me were wonderful memories and a glorious, unrealized future. She seemed to have forgotten all of Bobby Joe's shortcomings now that he was dead. His other friends might remember him differently.

Tomorrow, before I headed to work to finish all the Fourth of July preparations, I'd wake up early and stop for a breakfast of fluffy pancakes with golden syrup and fatty butter.

At the Breaking Bread Diner, of course.

The diner was packed at six-thirty the next morning. The people who lined the counter acted like they'd been up for hours, all cheerful and alert. I waited at the wooden hostess stand while the waitress led the couple in front of me to a table.

The inside of the diner sported a tractor theme, with photographs of John Deeres and wheat fields filling the walls. Criss-crossed sheaves of dried wheat hung on the wall over the pie display. Toy tractors lined the shelves positioned high on the walls, and a giant tractor wheel sat on a wooden platform in the back corner.

The waitress returned and grabbed a plastic menu from the holder on the side of the stand. "Just you?"

Wasn't I enough? I wanted to ask. Man, I needed coffee.

I nodded.

"Booth or counter?"

"Actually, I was hoping to sit in Maria's section." I crossed my fingers and silently prayed that Ashlee had remembered the correct name.

The waitress scanned the dining area.

"Looks like we have one table free. Follow me." She wound her way past several diners slurping up their eggs, buttering their toast, and salting their hash browns.

I suppressed the urge to skip as I trailed after her, astounded by my good luck—Ashlee had not only remembered the name, but this was Maria's shift. Surely that was a good sign.

When the waitress stopped at the only vacant booth along the back wall, I plopped myself down on the Naugahyde seat, wincing as my bottom smacked the hard surface, and looked around. Which waitress was the evil temptress who had lured my sister's boyfriend over to the dark side?

I could rule out the woman who had seated me since she would have admitted her name when I asked to sit in Maria's section. While the plump woman in her late sixties handing off a plate of waffles to another customer was attractive enough, Bobby Joe didn't strike me as the type to woo the geriatric crowd.

Then I noticed a petite, trim Hispanic girl about Ashlee's age, with a curly mass of hair piled on her head and gold hoop earrings dangling from her lobes. My first thought was that she was almost too short to retrieve the dishes from the pass-thru counter, so this job must be ridiculously awkward for her. My second thought was that she was much too tiny to beat Bobby Joe to death with a tailpipe. Unless she'd kicked him in the shins first and knocked him down.

She stood near the swinging kitchen door, deep in conversation with a man with short brown hair and glasses. I couldn't be sure, but I'd guess the two were arguing as they leaned in close to talk. Every few seconds, one or the other would look around to see if anyone was watching.

Whatever the guy was telling the girl, she wasn't happy about it. He held up a smartphone and pointed at the screen, but she shook her head, lips pressed together. He swiftly typed on the keypad and raised the screen again, but the girl turned away. The guy slapped his hand on the wall so hard that several diners looked over. When he noticed the attention he'd drawn, he dropped his hand and stalked out of the restaurant.

Interesting.

Even from a distance, I could see the girl's cheeks grow pink. She moved to the beverage station but didn't fill a glass, push a button, or wipe down the machine, making me wonder if she was trying to calm her nerves before returning to work.

I glanced back toward the door and saw the man through the window as he crossed the parking lot. He climbed into an olive-green Ford pickup. The truck had a bumper sticker that I couldn't read from this distance. My gaze went back to the waitress.

She smoothed her uniform with both hands, then pulled an order pad and pen from her apron pocket as she walked to my table.

She stopped before me, head bowed. "What can I get for you?" She didn't make eye contact.

Up close, I noticed the sallow hue to her skin, the bags under her eyes big enough to hold a week's worth of clothes, the marks dark like bruises. Someone was having trouble sleeping.

"Are you Maria?" I asked.

Her gaze flitted from my face to the carpet and back several times, ultimately settling on the carpet with its gold and green pattern. Kind of shy for a waitress. "That's me. Do I know you?"

I opened my mouth and then shut it. I hadn't

thought up anything to say. I'd been so sure that Maria wouldn't be working today or that Bobby Joe had lied to Ashlee about where he'd met his mistress that my only focus had been to find this mysterious Maria. Now what?

Maria looked up at me, probably wondering what was taking me so long to answer such a simple question.

"Uh, no, uh, one of my friends said you were a super waitress and that I should ask for you next time I ate here." God, what a lame story.

Her eyes popped open, and she smiled. "That's sweet. What's your friend's name?"

Good question. What was my imaginary friend's name? "Um, Ashlee?" Oh, right, that wasn't a friend, that was my sister. The one whose boyfriend supposedly cheated with this wisp of a girl. My bad.

Maria tapped her pen on her lip. She shook her head, the hoop earrings swinging like a trapeze act. "I don't remember an Ashlee, but we get lots of people in here." She pointed at the menu with her pen. "Are you ready to order?"

I hadn't bothered reading the menu, I'd been so busy thinking up lies. I abandoned my plan to order pancakes and went with a smaller breakfast. "Coffee and a bagel with cream cheese."

"Great."

She retrieved the plastic menu with her left hand, a flash of color catching my eye. A simple gold band sat on her finger. My mind hummed as I thought of the implications. Was this really the same Maria who was cheating with Bobby Joe? Had her husband found out and killed him? Is that the man she'd been arguing with when I'd sat down?

Maria headed toward the side counter that held the

coffee dispensers and extra cups and plates. I watched her go, then straightened my silverware and tried to think of a way to work the conversation around to Bobby Joe. Not the easiest job in the world, considering I barely knew him, didn't know Maria at all, and had no reason to make chitchat with a waitress at 6:30 AM on a Friday morning. But now that I'd spotted a ring, I had to find out if this was indeed the same Maria. Maybe she and her husband were separated. Maybe she was a young widow who was still grieving and that man I'd seen her talking to wasn't her husband after all.

I sensed movement to my right. The waitress who had originally shown me to my table held up two carafes, separated by the big smile on her face.

"You want your coffee leaded or unleaded, darling?" Her perkiness hurt my ears.

"Leaded."

She set the orange-topped carafe down, flipped my cup over, and poured coffee from the second carafe, then moved to the next table to offer a refill.

Over by the counter, two waitresses stood near the pass-thru window, chatting, but Maria wasn't one of them. And she wasn't waiting on any other tables either. Probably taking a bathroom break. I took a sip of coffee, grimaced, and added a packet of sweetener, still stumped about how to get Maria to open up to me.

Maybe I should have said Bobby Joe was the friend who recommended Maria as a waitress, but that would have set off all kinds of warning bells. Then again, if I asked her about her affair with Bobby Joe, the bells would be clanging pretty loud.

The same waitress who had poured my coffee appeared again, this time carrying my bagel and a sealed packet of cream cheese. She plopped the plate on the table with a clank.

"You need anything else, hon?"

I stared at the slightly burned bagel, wondering if my plans had gone up in smoke. "What happened to Maria?"

The waitress shrugged. "Not sure. All of a sudden she wasn't feeling so hot and asked me to cover her shift."

She'd definitely appeared tired when talking to me, but not sick. What had sent her hightailing it out of here so fast?

Was it something I said?

Or something the man arguing with her had said?

5

I scraped the burned edges off my bagel, slathered on the cream cheese, and gobbled up my breakfast, anxious to get to work. I'd already wasted enough time at the restaurant, especially since I'd found out absolutely nothing. Except that Maria had apparently been struck by a spontaneous case of stomach flu.

With a last gulp of coffee, I tossed a couple dollars on the table, paid my tab at the door, and hopped in my Civic. The morning heat was stifling. I flipped on the air conditioner as I eased out of the parking lot. Summers in Blossom Valley often reached ice-cream-for-dinner temperatures, but this latest heat wave was almost unbearable.

At the farm, I parked on the side closest to the pond and made sure all the little ducklings were paddling in the water. At least I wouldn't be on duck roundup this morning.

The lobby was empty, the rustle of the potted ficus leaves the only movement as warm air drifted in the door with me. The blue-and-white checkered love seat and matching blue wing chairs patiently waited for guests to sit and browse through the activity brochures spread out on the side table.

I went down the hall and hung a left into the office. While I waited for the computer to boot up, I read the book spines in the bookcase by the door. Esther was always adding new titles to her eclectic collection. I spotted *Learn Mandarin in Minutes,* the latest purchase, and wondered how long it would be until she was speaking Chinese. Of course, she'd purchased a book on learning hip-hop a while back, and I had yet to hear her rap a single verse.

After checking e-mail, I typed up the spa's daily blog. When the farm had first opened and I'd started the blog, I'd heard nary a peep in reply, leading me to believe that no one ever read the thing. But then a few comments started to trickle in, and now I had a steady group of readers, some former guests, others random people. I tried to put in extra effort now that I knew my posts weren't merely disappearing into cyberspace.

With the hot weather, I'd focused the week's topics on staying cool, keeping pets comfortable, and eating rehydrating foods. I'd use today's entry to describe how to read sunblock labels, verifying both UVA and UVB information.

I worked steadily for twenty minutes, while occasional sounds drifted in the open door. Based on the clink of silverware on dishes, Zennia was prepping breakfast, the one meal of the day when the food she prepared was what most folks would consider normal. Homemade granola, yogurt parfaits, and omelets from eggs produced by the farm's chickens were all part of her repertoire.

I read through my blog one last time, posted it to the spa site, and headed down the hall to see if Zennia needed help.

Today, she wore a yellow tank sundress, the light cotton material brushing the floor, the tips of her Birkenstocks peeking out as she moved.

She was slicing peaches on a cutting board and paused to wave the knife at me. "There you are. You know, you sped out of here so fast yesterday that you didn't get to try my new recipe for natto."

"What's natto?" I asked a little fearfully. I never knew what to expect from Zennia's cooking.

"It's made from soybeans that have been fermented with special bacteria that provide lots of healthy probiotics for your digestive system."

Finally, a benefit to Ashlee being taken downtown for questioning. I'd avoided natto. "Gee, Zennia, sorry about that. Family emergency and all."

She pointed over her shoulder at the fridge. "Don't worry. I saved you a bowl. It's there whenever you're hungry."

With a bowl of natto waiting for me, I might never be hungry again.

Zennia set the knife on the cutting board and wiped her hands on a dish towel. "I heard about Ashlee being involved in that man's murder. How is she holding up?"

For a moment, I wondered how Zennia had already heard, but then I remembered her nephew worked for the sheriff's department. Besides that, in a town of only five thousand residents, everyone had most likely heard about Bobby Joe by now. And everyone knew Ashlee was his girlfriend.

"She's doing okay," I said. "But she wasn't really

involved with his death. I mean, she was home long before someone killed him."

Zennia hung the dish towel back up. "Of course Ashlee had nothing to do with his death. Everyone knows she's sweet as agave nectar."

"Thank you, I appreciate you saying that." At least I could count on Zennia's support. I could only imagine what the other residents of Blossom Valley were saying.

"If you're not busy this morning, Esther mentioned that Heather's home taking care of a sick child, so she might need help with the rooms."

"Okay, I'll check with her." I hadn't seen Esther in the house this morning, but maybe she was out on the grounds somewhere. The farm had acres of woods and trails, a hot springs, vegetable gardens, and the guest cabins, and I often went hours without seeing my boss. I headed out the back door of the kitchen in search of Esther and any work she needed me to do around the farm, admiring the deep green of the basil as I passed through the herb garden, its scent reminding me of Mom's spaghetti sauce.

A man, presumably one of the guests, swam laps in the pool. As I walked by, the tattoo of a pelican popped out of the water with each stroke of his arm, making it appear as if the bird was diving for fish. He reached the end of the pool and turned in my direction, catching me in mid-stare. He appeared to be in his mid-twenties, and he spent a lot of time outdoors if his tan was any indication. I smiled and nodded hello before hurrying my steps toward the main path.

The ten guest cabins were on my left, but every door was closed, with no maid cart in sight. Esther must not have started cleaning yet. I followed the paved path toward the vegetable garden, wishing I'd worn a hat to block the sun.

In the distance, I spotted Gordon, the manager, dressed in a suit and standing among the tomato plants. As I approached, he scowled at a plant and kicked the dirt. A cloud of dust puffed up, then settled on his shiny leather shoes. His frown deepened. I noticed his clipboard, a constant companion, tucked under one arm. I'd never managed to see what he wrote on those pages, but he always carried it with him.

"What brings you out here this morning?" I asked as I stopped before him. Gordon rarely strayed from the lobby unless he wanted to spy on the employees.

His hair, normally stiffly gelled into uniform rows, drooped in the heat, a lock breaking ranks and falling across his forehead. "That fool, Clarence, called last night to say his wife was in labor and he was taking her to the hospital."

Clarence was our latest staff addition. After attending several organic farming classes, he'd been hired to tend to the ever-growing vegetable and herb gardens, with the understanding that he could take vacation time once his wife had her baby.

I plucked a deep-red tomato off the nearest plant, sure Zennia would find a use for it. "How exciting. I wonder if it's a boy or a girl."

"Makes no difference. He's going to be out for two weeks either way." He grabbed a rotten tomato off the ground and chucked it into a nearby zucchini plant. "I thought women spent hours in labor. I bet he could have finished spraying this morning and still made it to the hospital before that kid pops out."

Gordon, always the sensitive guy. Sometimes I

wondered if he'd been raised by robots. "Maybe he didn't want to risk missing the miracle of life."

"Whatever. Now I'm stuck figuring out what to use to kill the damn worms on these tomato plants."

He pointed to a plant, and I leaned in for a closer look. Nestled on one of the leaves was a plump green worm, three inches in length, with protrusions on his head that resembled horns. As I stared, the worm reared up and waved his body at me.

I drew my head back with a shudder. "Yuck. We definitely need to get rid of those."

"Yeah, but with what? Clarence mixes all his own natural pesticides, and I can't read his labels. I've got half a mind to stop by the hardware store and grab a bottle of bug spray."

"This is an organic farm. You can't use chemicals." If Zennia got wind he'd even suggested such an idea, she'd have to meditate for a week to calm herself down

Gordon grunted, beads of sweat visible on his hairline. "Once wouldn't hurt anything. I don't have time to drive all over town searching for that all-natural nonsense."

"Did you text Clarence about it? I'm sure he could tell you which bottle to use. You know, as long as his wife isn't mid-push or anything." Visions of Clarence in hospital scrubs texting on his smartphone while his wife lay nearby, her mouth open in a scream, filled my head, but I banished the thought and focused on Gordon.

"Texting is for teenagers." He pulled his cell phone from his inside jacket pocket and peered at the screen as if mystified. "But it might be the only way."

"Great. You contact Clarence. I'm off to find Esther." I wound my way through the plants and back onto the path. This time, when I approached the cabins, I spotted the maid's cart in front of the first cabin, the door partly ajar.

I popped my head in and saw Esther running a dust rag over the dresser top, her faded red peasant blouse sticking to her back in places.

"Esther," I said.

She jerked around, a hand flying to her top button. "Mercy me, you scared an extra five years off my life."

"Zennia mentioned that Heather is out today, and I wondered if you needed help with the rooms."

"That would be peachy. Only two cabins have guests right now, but we're expecting a full house after tomorrow's check-in, so I was freshening up the other rooms, too. Why don't you do cabins four and six, where the guests are?" She held up a little American flag on a wooden stick. "I'm also putting these flags you ordered in each cabin to start off the holiday weekend."

"Great, I'll do that, too. Which reminds me, I'm hanging the balloons and banners this afternoon."

"I can always count on you," Esther said. She returned to dusting.

I grabbed the vacuum handle with one hand and the pass key dangling off the cart with the other and rolled down to cabin six. A DO NOT DISTURB sign hung from the knob. I moved down two doors, where the knob was empty, and knocked. No answer, so I used the key to let myself in, steeling myself.

Two months earlier, I'd been in this exact situation when I'd entered a cabin and found a dead body. I'd cleaned the rooms several times since then, but I always got a little shiver when I first walked in.

The cabin was dark, the blackout curtains drawn. I pulled the cord, and sunlight poured into the room, making me squint. Several papers lay on the floor, and

I gathered them up into a stack. I glanced at the top sheet. Baseball teams and odds ran down the page. Maybe this guest liked to bet on the games. I set the pages on the coffee table, near a stack of magazines.

Other than the papers on the floor, whoever was staying here was relatively neat. This person had remade the bed, smoothing out the tan spread with its embroidered leaves. No trash littered the floor, no clothes hung off the chairs. The only other signs of occupancy were a rolling suitcase in the corner, a partly open closet door, and the magazines.

The bright color of the clothing in the closet drew my attention, and I took a peek. A padded jumpsuit, like race-car drivers wore, hung from the rod. Pictures of flames and rocks covered the thick material. A matching helmet with flames sat on the closet floor. I returned to the magazines, wondering what they had to do with the clothes and helmet in the closet. The top one showed an off-road vehicle leaping over a dirt hill. I poked through the rest of the stack. All three magazines focused on off-roading or racing.

Ashlee's comments came back to me. Was this person somehow involved in the big monster truck tournament this weekend? What other reason could they have for that outfit in the closet? I picked up a magazine and flipped through it, seeing page after page of dirt tracks and mud-covered trucks.

"Find something to your liking?" a voice boomed behind me.

With a squeal, I dropped the magazine on the floor and whirled around. The guy from the pool stood in the doorway, water from his slicked-back blond hair running in rivulets down the side of his head and over his bare chest. His hair was a smidge too long, his arms a little soft. I could see the hint of a six-pack outline under the layer of flab covering his belly, making me wonder if he'd been sipping a can from a different kind of six-pack lately.

"I'm so sorry, sir. That magazine caught my eye while I was vacuuming your room."

He gestured at the vacuum sitting in the corner. "It works better if you turn it on." He gave me a slow smile.

I felt my face heat up. This guy probably wasn't even as old as me, and yet I felt as guilty and embarrassed as the time the principal caught me skipping school.

"I'll come back later. I don't want to get in your way."

He rubbed his belly, whether to scratch an itch or draw attention to what he clearly thought was a spectacular body, I wasn't sure.

"Don't worry about it. I'm here for a towel, then I'm back to the pool." He nodded toward the magazine on the floor, and I hastily snatched it up and laid it back on the pile. "If you like monster trucks, you should come to the big rally tomorrow night. I'll be competing. I'm known as Crusher."

I stifled a giggle. The name sounded like something a cheesy WWE wrestler would use. But I wondered how many other drivers were on the monster truck circuit. Was it small enough that he and Bobby Joe would have known each other?

"I might have to stop by. I don't think we've ever had a monster truck driver stay here at the spa."

"All the motels in town were booked, but I'm glad I ended up here. The quiet is helping me focus my thoughts and get ready for tomorrow's competition."

I felt my gaze wander to his bare chest and willed myself to keep my focus on his face. I didn't want to give him the wrong idea. "Have you been competing long?" If he had, he must have met Bobby Joe at some point.

"A few years. I'm starting to make a name for myself again. This rally could be my big shot to the majors." He smiled at me and rubbed his chin.

Ashlee had said almost the same thing about Bobby Joe. "My sister's dating a driver. Well, used to date him. Bobby Joe Jones. Do you know him?"

At the mention of Bobby Joe's name, the toothy smile vanished, replaced by a scowl. His sudden change in demeanor made goose bumps prickle my skin.

He crossed his arms and stepped toward me. "Who did you say you were again?"

Suddenly he looked awfully big and the doorway behind him looked awfully small. "I'm Dana. I work here at the spa." I took a step back as Crusher continued to glare. His name didn't sound so funny anymore.

"So you're friends with Bobby Joe, huh? You digging around in my room, hoping to find out about my moves?" He tapped his temple with his index finger. "Well, good luck, 'cause I've got everything right up here."

This monster truck business was more competitive than I'd realized. And from the sounds of it, he hadn't heard about Bobby Joe's murder. "Look, I wasn't going through your things." I gestured toward the coffee table. "I looked through the magazines and saw that baseball sheet with the odds, that's all."

Crusher held up the piece of paper. "So that's what this is about. Do you even work here?"

"Let me get my boss. She can vouch for me." I craned my head to see if Esther would magically appear in the doorway as if by mental summons, but no one was there.

"I want to know who sent you. Was it Vince?"

"Look, let me find my boss. We'll get this straightened out."

I stepped to the side to maneuver around him, but he matched my step with one of his own. With a coffee table on one side and the couch on the other, I had nowhere to go. I was trapped.

6

Crusher moved toward me, and I held up a hand like a traffic cop. "Stop right there. I am an employee of the spa. I am not a spy. And if you don't let me go, I'm calling the police." A total bluff, but maybe my stern tone would make him reconsider whatever he was about to do.

He stepped back and to the side, gesturing for me to walk through with a sweep of his arm. "Whoa, honey. I'm not keeping you here."

I quick-stepped over to the vacuum and grabbed the handle.

"But the next time you clean my room, try not to snoop," he added.

"I wasn't snooping." Well, maybe a little. Head held high, I wheeled the vacuum out the door and down the breezeway, where I stopped and sagged against the wall.

What had happened there? The man had gone from Mr. McFlirty to Mr. McThreaty as soon as I mentioned Bobby Joe's name. And what was with the spy business? And who was Vince? Monster trucks weren't synonymous with espionage. Maybe Ashlee could clue me in.

I left the vacuum by the wall and hurried down the path. As I passed the second cabin, I heard, "Dana!"

I backed up a couple of steps and poked my head in. "Yes, Esther?"

"Did you finish the cabins already?"

"Both were occupied. I'll come back later." I really wanted to call Ashlee, so I didn't offer to help with the vacant cabins. Before Esther suggested the idea herself, I scooted past the door and around the corner.

This time, the pool area was empty, though someone, probably Crusher, had dragged a chaise longue from under the shade of the redwood tree so it sat directly in the sun. A blue jay squawked on a low-hanging branch, and another jay farther away answered.

With Zennia most likely in the kitchen, I slipped into the dining room through the French doors to avoid further conversation, intent on getting my cell phone. The sky-blue walls seemed to take a couple of degrees off the room's already cool temperature. Zennia had filled the slender vases on each table with red dahlias, and they provided a bright pop against the cream tablecloths. The barn-shaped clock and the framed photographs on the wall, which showed the farm and Blossom Valley five decades ago, combined with the crisp linens and gleaming silverware, gave the room a homey yet elegant vibe.

I stepped into the hall and went straight across to the office where my cell phone waited in my purse. I really needed to remember to carry it with me and save myself some walking.

Gordon sat at the computer, and I almost let out a groan. Couldn't I make one little phone call without his listening in? He'd no doubt have some comment about making personal calls on company time.

He still wore his suit, jacket and all, and had recombed his hair to its usual gleaming helmet. "Dana. Just the person I was looking for."

Yippee, my lucky day.

"I placed an ad in the *Herald* earlier this week for a yoga instructor here at the spa and have already received a few résumés. I'll be calling one or two in and thought you could be the first line of defense. Weed out the riffraff. When you find a decent candidate, I'll conduct a more formal interview and make the final selection."

Even though Gordon wanted me to interview the people first so he wouldn't have to waste his own time, I was secretly pleased. Back when I worked in marketing at a computer software company in San Jose, I'd loved first-round interviews. People who looked fantastic on paper would be far less stellar in person, much like online dating. I recalled the woman who arrived for an interview dressed as a clown and made balloon animals while we talked to convince me of her creativity, the woman who brought her yappy terrier because the dog sitter was sick, and the man who was a construction worker until an alien abduction turned him toward marketing. I never quite got that last one. Did the aliens want him to convince the public that aliens were good and ease the way for when their mother ship landed?

"Dana," Gordon snapped. "Are you listening?"

The man who'd brought UFO bookmarks to the interview vanished from my mind's eye. "What? Yes, that sounds great. Let me know when you've set up the interviews."

I bent down, opened the bottom drawer of the desk, careful not to bang Gordon's knee, and slid my phone out of my purse. I sensed Gordon staring at me as I eased the drawer shut and felt compelled to say something.

"Like to keep it handy, what with that family emergency and all." I had no idea why the guy always made me feel like I needed an excuse. Esther's farm wasn't a jail. I was allowed more than one phone call.

Gordon rested his elbows on the desk and steepled his fingers. "That's right, your sister being a murderer. Make sure it doesn't interfere with your work."

I felt the blood rush to my head as a ringing sounded in my ears. "My sister didn't kill anyone," I managed to squeeze out between my compressed lips. I turned on my heel and marched out, reminding myself that Gordon wasn't my boss, even if he was the farm manager. It was a tricky situation that called for just enough obedience that Gordon wouldn't complain to Esther. Still, if I wanted to take an early break to make a personal phone call, that was well within my rights.

Then again, no need to broadcast it. I slipped out the dining room door, crossed the patio area, cut through the bushes by the redwood tree, and landed on the Hen House Trail near the chicken coop. Both the Hen House and Chicken Run trails looped through the wilder parts of the property, cutting swaths through manzanita, oak, and pine trees and offering guests an opportunity to enjoy nature as they walked around the property.

But it was too hot to walk today. I waved to the chickens out in the yard and spotted Berta pecking at the dirt in the corner. As soon as I rounded the first bend of the trail, I whipped out my phone and checked the reception, always spotty in the area. Two bars. Not the best, but maybe enough.

I punched in Ashlee's number and waited through

four rings. As I started to compose a voice mail message in my head, she answered.

"Hello?"

"Ashlee, it's me. I need to talk to you."

"Good timing. We finished an enema on a Great Dane a minute ago. He ate an entire love seat. Leather. Can you imagine?"

I swatted at a horsefly buzzing around my face. "I'd rather not. I wanted to ask you about Bobby Joe and this truck rally. Did he ever talk about a guy named Crusher?"

Ashlee let out a squeal, and I flinched at the sound. "Great name, right? And man, is that guy hot. I almost asked him out right there at the fairgrounds after I found out Bobby Joe was cheating on me. He would have been so jealous. Wish I hadn't chickened out."

Guess she was recovering from Bobby Joe's death already.

"So he and Bobby Joe competed quite a bit?" I wiped away the trail of sweat running from my temple to my jaw and wished I'd made the phone call from inside the house, Gordon's disapproval and eavesdropping be damned.

"Almost every rally. I know Bobby Joe was super worried about this weekend and was trying out that new stuff I told you about that he wouldn't show me, something that would crush the competition." Ashlee giggled. "Get it? Crush the competition, and his big rival's name is Crusher?"

"Yeah, I get it."

"Why are you asking me about Crusher?"

"He's staying here at the spa. I met him a bit ago." I didn't add how our meeting had deteriorated into accusations of spying, but now Crusher's questions made sense. If Bobby Joe was working on new moves, then Crusher probably was too, and he definitely wouldn't want anyone finding out before the contest, especially with scouts in the audience. No wonder he was paranoid.

"Maybe I should visit you at work," Ashlee said. "Last I heard, Crusher didn't have a girlfriend."

Yep, definitely over Bobby Joe.

"Don't you think you should be more worried about this police investigation? You know, the one where your boyfriend was murdered?"

"Ex-boyfriend," Ashlee said. "Do you think Crusher had something to do with it? 'Course, killers aren't usually that good-looking."

Oh, for heaven's sake. "Haven't you heard of the Preppy Killer? Ted Bundy?" Or was I the only one who watched TruTV? I swatted at another fly. "Never mind that. I have no idea if Crusher was involved in Bobby Joe's murder, but it's a place to start. Now I have to get back to work."

"Me, too. A cat needs to be neutered."

On that note, I hung up. As I stuffed the phone into my back pocket, I heard a rustling sound coming from the direction of the house. Probably a squirrel galloping through the bushes.

I headed back, but stopped when I heard another noise ahead of me, one that didn't sound like a squirrel. Were those footsteps? As I rounded the corner of the trail, I heard louder crackling, followed by a giant splash. I picked up my pace, looped around the redwood tree, and came out on the patio.

Crusher was back in the pool, water marks on the

cement indicating the splash I'd heard. Practicing his cannonballs? Or running back and jumping into the pool so I wouldn't know he'd been listening to my end of the phone call?

I watched Crusher touch the far wall, flip around, and cut through the water for another lap. A monster truck deal that involved sponsors, fame, and a large paycheck might be important enough to kill for. Maybe Crusher had decided to eliminate the competition to guarantee his success.

Definitely worth looking into.

I just hoped my theories weren't all wet.

7

I hurried past Crusher in the pool and went around the corner. Esther was working in the second-to-last vacant cabin, so I grabbed some cleaning bottles and rags from the maid's cart and made short work of Crusher's bed and bath, followed by a quick vacuum. At the last second, I grabbed one of the flags from a stack on the cart and laid it across a pillow.

The Do Not Disturb sign no longer hung from the other cabin door, so after a knock and a pause, I entered. The cover on one side of the bed was smooth, while the other side was rumpled. A pillow rested at one end of the couch, the imprint of a head still obvious. I knew the room belonged to a married couple, and I'd taken to calling them the Bickersons, though the name didn't really fit. You had to actually talk to each other if you wanted to bicker.

I finished cleaning their room, added a flag to the bed and one to the couch, and pushed the vacuum back out the door. Esther was draping her dust rag over the side of the cart outside.

"I can take the cleaning supplies back to the house," I said.

Esther mopped her face with a fresh towel, then added it to the bag of dirty linens. "Thanks. That'll give me a chance to see those giant green worms Gordon was complaining about. I can't imagine they're as awful as he says."

A shudder ran through my shoulders as I remembered the plump, horned worm. "They're pretty bad. One look was enough for me."

Esther patted my arm. "You lived in the city too long. You'll get used to all these creepy crawlies now that you're outside so much of the day."

"No, thanks. If you need me, I'll be in the nice, air-conditioned house."

I attached the vacuum to the front of the cart and pushed the whole thing down the path as Crusher came around the corner.

My heart did a double-beat. Did he know I'd returned to his room to finish cleaning? Would he accuse me of snooping again? But rather than grill me like a hot dog, he scrubbed at his hair with the towel as he walked by, pretending not to see me. Either he was embarrassed by his earlier behavior or he felt guilty about eavesdropping on my phone call to Ashlee. I really wanted to know which one it was.

I wheeled the cart past the pool and patio, the picnic tables still empty, and entered the kitchen. I nodded at Zennia as she hovered over a large plastic bowl at the counter, then pushed the cart down the hall and wedged it in a corner of the laundry room.

Back in the kitchen, I peeked in the bowl and saw that Zennia was cleaning an octopus. I didn't even want to know where she'd found such a thing to feed the poor guests. After more than two months of helping prep and serve meals, my stomach still shrank when I saw most of Zennia's cooking. Why couldn't she use normal ingredients, like something without so many legs? But I knew Zennia prided herself on opening people's minds to unusual foods.

She thrust her knife into the octopus body, creating a squishy tearing sound that made my stomach roil.

"Need any help with lunch?" Please say no, please say no, please say no.

"I'm sure I can find you something to do." She set the knife down and wiped the back of her hand across her forehead. "This octopus has almost gotten the best of me. I've hacked it up so much that I'm worried I won't have enough for the guests. So unfortunate. I really wanted you to try this recipe."

My spirits lifted as the threat of octopus for lunch vanished, but I managed not to smile. "Maybe next time." Guess I'd have to stop in town for some yummy, fat-filled fast food.

"Good thing I saved that natto from yesterday," Zennia said.

Oh, right, that. "Good thing," I muttered. I scanned the kitchen, wanting to change the subject before she suggested I try the natto right now. "How about I whip up a salad for everyone?"

"Great idea. I picked the tomatoes and cucumbers this morning." She placed the octopus parts in a large pot boiling on the stove.

I grabbed a head of lettuce out of the crisper drawer and a chef's knife from the wood block. "Where do you buy octopus anyway? I used to see it all the time at the grocery stores in the Bay Area, but never up here."

"I buy all my seafood from Eduardo. He catches

everything fresh, then drives his truck over the hill and sells it at the junction."

The knife almost sliced my thumb, rather than the lettuce, as I thought about what she had said. "You buy your fish from the back of a truck? In this heat?"

Zennia laughed as she placed a new bowl on the counter and poured olive oil in it. "You make it sound so seedy. Eduardo is licensed, and I like buying local food to help the local economy. Plus, I don't have to feel guilty about buying from large companies who are depleting our ocean's fish supply."

No, instead she could feel guilty when she accidentally poisoned a guest with overheated, tentacled sea life.

"If you say so. Do we still have just the three guests?"

Zennia added a splash of red-wine vinegar to the bowl. "For now, but every cabin is reserved this weekend."

I opened the cabinet door over the counter and removed three salad bowls. After some slicing and dicing, I assembled the salads and set them on the kitchen table to await delivery to the dining room. Guests knew that lunch was served anytime after twelve, and people generally showed up right on time, probably to get the meal out of the way so they could enjoy their afternoon.

The rooster clock on the wall showed one minute to twelve, so I stepped into the hall and poked my head into the dining room. Sure enough, Crusher sat at one table while the Bickersons occupied another. As usual, the two sat in silence, each staring at the wall over the other's shoulder. I wondered which one had slept on the couch. I sure hoped they weren't here to reconcile their marriage. If so, the plan had failed.

I pulled my head back and returned to the kitchen,

where I drizzled Zennia's tofu-based ranch dressing on each salad before taking two bowls to the Bickersons. They nodded their thanks while managing to not look at each other, and I slipped out to grab the last salad bowl.

As I approached Crusher's table, I tried to think of some way to talk to him after the incident in his cabin, but he saved me the trouble.

"Hey, there, gorgeous," he said, a slow smile spreading across his face.

I almost checked behind me to see if a supermodel had shown up, but apparently he was talking to me. Guess he'd forgotten I was a potential spy.

He leaned back in his chair, crossed his arms over his Grave Digger T-shirt, and lifted one boot-clad foot onto the neighboring chair. "Hope I didn't scare you back in my cabin. In my kind of business, you can't be too careful. Everyone knows I'm making a name for myself, and they want to know how I'm doing it."

I set the salad bowl on the table and wiped my hands on my shorts, my palms suddenly clammy as I saw an opportunity to question him. "And how are you doing it?" By killing off the competition?

"Hard work and talent."

"Did Bobby Joe have a lot of talent?" I asked, tensing. Would he freak out again at the name?

But if he was angered by my question, he hid it well. "I guess," was all he said. He slid his foot off the chair and stabbed a piece of lettuce with his fork. "Now, I gotta eat. I've got practice later." He thrust the greenery into his mouth and stared at the dish while he chewed.

The couple at the other table was intent on their own

salads, but I lowered my voice anyway. "I heard you and Bobby Joe were big rivals."

Crusher smacked his lips. "This dressing's great. Homemade?"

Guess that was his not-so-subtle way of telling me he wouldn't be talking about Bobby Joe. "Specialty of the kitchen. I'll let the chef know you like it."

I retreated from the room. In the kitchen, Zennia was slicing the octopus into bite-size pieces.

"Dana, thanks for dropping off those salads. I can handle the entrée if you want your lunch now." She glanced at the fridge, where the natto waited. I still hadn't quite worked myself up to trying the fermented soybeans with probiotics, whatever the heck those were.

"Gee, um, I really need to run an errand first." I stared at the tentacle hanging off the cutting board as I tried to think of a believable errand. I rarely had dry-cleaning. I still had plenty of cash from my last trip to the bank. The bills were in the mail. My gas tank was half full.

Well, half full wasn't completely full, now was it?

"Gas, I need gas. You know how busy it gets in the evenings, especially during the summer." And if I happened to grab a burger while I was in town, who could blame me?

Zennia gave me a funny look, knowing full well the local gas stations were never busy, but didn't challenge my claim. "Don't worry, it'll be waiting for you when you get back."

Yes, of course it would.

I stopped by the office for my purse, then climbed into my car, turning on the air conditioner before I tuned in to the radio. I roared out of the parking lot and down the lane.

I'd told Zennia I was buying gas, and that was exactly what I was going to do. And what better place than Running on Fumes, the place Bobby Joe worked right up until he was killed?

8

Running on Fumes was located on the opposite side of town. I hopped onto the freeway and bypassed Blossom Valley altogether, much like the tourists hurrying to reach Mendocino and its adorable bed-and-breakfasts, boutique shops, and upscale eateries.

The gas station, painted a shiny white with dark blue trim and red lettering, was located off the last exit before the highway vanished among the redwood trees. According to Mom, the owner, Donald something or other, had opened the place back in the eighties when I was still in diapers. The property included a two-story house behind the station, where I assumed Donald lived.

During the lean times, he'd managed to keep the business afloat by operating a souvenir shop attached to the main mini-mart. I still had the clamshell keepsake box I'd bought with my allowance back when I was ten, tucked away on a bookshelf gathering dust.

I exited the freeway, swung a left onto the side road, and pulled into the driveway. A guy in his mid-twenties came out of the store and approached a beat-up Pontiac, the only car in the lot.

As I eased into a parking space, I noticed the guy had an object clutched in his hand. It was a seashell, painted fluorescent pink and yellow with green polka dots. Man, I hoped that wasn't for a girlfriend. She might burst into tears when she saw such a hideous shell.

The guy backed his car out as I headed to the store. I smiled at my good fortune. Donald would be much more likely to talk about Bobby Joe without prying ears and curious stares.

I pushed open the glass door, a bell tinkling overhead. The hum of the nearby waist-high freezer, holding an assortment of ice cream treats, reached my ears as I stepped into the mart. The low-wattage overhead bulbs offered feeble light. Several rows of shelves held the usual assortment of chips, candy, and cheap wine. A refrigerated row in the back stocked milk, energy drinks, and beer.

To my right, an open doorway led to the knickknack shop. I could see a display case with arrowheads, wine-bottle stoppers, and necklaces with charms made of abalone shell. On top of the display case, a row of tiny trees in dirt-filled plastic cups sat before a sign that read, GROW YOUR OWN REDWOOD.

Behind the counter, I spotted the ugly shells, marked for three dollars and ninety-nine cents. Even that low price seemed too high. I could see a little magnet on the back, but no one would stick that on their fridge.

"Can I help you, little lady?" a gruff voice called from the back of the store. I squinted into the gloom and saw a man stocking Twinkies at the end of a row. I gasped at what I thought was a dead squirrel on his head but realized the fuzzy pile was his toupee. He was

in his late fifties, and as he rose to standing, his knees
popped, the sound echoing off the linoleum. His beer
gut jiggled under his striped dress shirt.

Better to question him outright, or take the round-
about approach? "I'm picking up a few snacks," I said. I
grabbed two Snickers bars, a bag of M&Ms, and a pack
of gum from the closest shelf. As I neared the counter
with my treasures, I snatched a bag of Funyuns off the
display rack on the end for good measure. I hadn't had
a bag of those salty, onion-flavored rings in years, and I
had a sudden craving.

Of course, I'd have to hide everything in my car. If
Mom caught sight of all this sugar and saturated fat,
she'd toss everything in the trash without a second
thought.

I dumped my stash on the smooth beige surface, and
the man squeezed into the narrow opening at the end
of the counter to stand before the cash register. He
shuffled the snacks around.

"Guess you're not watching your figure like most of
the ladies I know."

I snapped my mouth shut before I could reply. I
wanted information from this guy, and smarting off
wouldn't help.

"You the owner here?" I asked instead, trying for a
casual tone. He looked like a rounder version of the guy
who used to run the place, but it had been a lot of years,
and I didn't remember the guy wearing an ugly toupee
back then.

"Donald Popielak. This here's my store. Owned and
operated it for thirty years."

So it was him. I looked around, nodding my ap-
proval. "That's impressive, especially now with the
economy so slow."

"I'm great with money, got a real head for business. Plus I'm careful about who I hire. I want customers to have a good experience when they shop here. That way they'll come back."

Just the opening I wanted. I bowed my head and shook it, going for commiserating. "Sure is a shame what happened to Bobby Joe. I heard he was your best worker." Then again, this last bit of information was provided by Bobby Joe himself, so it might have been an exaggeration.

"That fool got his head bashed in, from what I heard. Guess he didn't know jujitsu, like I do. He could have defended himself." He grabbed my candy bars and ran them over the scanner. "'Course, I don't know where you heard he was my best employee. My best employee is me." Donald let out a hearty laugh as he shook out a plastic bag and dropped my purchases inside.

"Still, now you'll have to replace him. What a hassle." This wasn't getting me any closer to finding out about Bobby Joe, but I wanted to keep Donald talking.

Donald let out a growl so deep that for a moment I wondered if he was hiding a pet Rottweiler behind the counter. "Any fool can pump gas. I'll have a replacement by tomorrow. And any new employee is bound to show up on time more than Bobby Joe ever did."

Not exactly singing Bobby Joe's accolades, was he?

I rested my arms on the counter and leaned forward. "Were you having problems with him?"

Donald cocked his head, making the dead squirrel slip down a notch. I kept my gaze fixed firmly on his face.

"Say now, who are you again?"

Oops, too direct. "Um, a friend of Bobby Joe. I'm trying to figure out what happened. Do you know of anyone who would want to kill him?"

Donald pointed to my total on the register, and I scrambled to pull my wallet out of my purse.

"Can't think of anyone right off, but that doesn't mean people weren't gunning for him, especially considering the way he behaved here at work."

I handed over two fives. "What do you mean?"

Donald held each bill up to the light. Guess his station got a lot of counterfeit five-dollar bills. "Look here, missy, I won't speak ill of the dead. But I built this business on honesty and integrity, and I expect the same from my employees. Now here's your change." He shoved the ones and loose coins into my hand, squeezed out from behind the counter, and crossed to the back of the store, disappearing behind a swinging door marked EMPLOYEES ONLY.

What exactly had Bobby Joe done to bring such wrath from Donald? And why hadn't Donald fired him?

I grabbed my plastic bag and left the store, listening to the tinkle of the bell as I went. Out front, a woman not much older than my twenty-eight years smoked a cigarette at the corner of the building, glancing at the door every few seconds. My car was still the only one in the lot, and the spaces in front of the gas pumps were empty, so unless she'd walked here from town, she must work here. Maybe she was Bobby Joe's replacement.

She watched me approach. She wore a too-tight, tiger-striped halter top that accentuated her ample chest and defined biceps. As I got closer, she tugged up the top at the corners.

"You work here?" I asked.

She held her cigarette down near her thigh and waved at me. "Get over here. Don't let him see you."

I glanced to my left at the last pane of the storefront window, but I saw only myself in the reflection cast by the noonday sun. I shuffled forward another two feet until I reached the cement wall.

"Donald will tan my hide if he catches me out here smoking again. Says it's bad for business."

"Well, it is a gas station. All those flammable fumes and everything."

The woman scowled at me. "I haven't blown anything up yet."

Let's hope today wasn't the day she broke her winning streak. "Are you Bobby Joe's replacement?"

The woman laughed and exhaled a stream of smoke. "Donald would never let me work. Says he's the breadwinner, and no wife of his is gonna get her hands dirty with a job. I'm stuck in that house all day." She jerked her cigarette toward the house behind the station.

I almost dropped my bag when she said the word "wife," considering she was young enough to be his daughter. How had Donald landed such a young hottie? I tightened my hold on the plastic bag, crushing a Funyun in the process. "You probably knew Bobby Joe, am I right?"

The woman flicked at something on her fingernail. "Bobby Joe was a sweetie. I was real sorry to hear someone killed him."

"Me, too." Especially since some people thought my sister did it. "How long did he work here?"

"Lemme think." She held her cigarette aloft and tapped her toe. "Seems like Donald hired him right before the Christmas season. We get a lot more business that time of year with people passing by on the highway, off to visit folks for the holidays."

She sounded momentarily wistful, her tone making me imagine a family gathered around a Christmas tree, drinking hot chocolate. I felt a tug at my own heart as I thought of last Christmas, the first year without my dad.

"And did Donald like him?" I asked to drag myself from my memories.

The woman didn't seem at all curious as to why I was asking these questions, but maybe she got lonely, stuck out here.

"At first. But Bobby Joe was friendly. Maybe a little too friendly, if you know what I mean. Donald didn't like him flirting with me. And lately he was grumbling about his work, saying he was getting ready to fire Bobby Joe if only he could find the proof."

I crushed another Funyun as I gripped my snack bag tighter and edged toward her. "Proof about what?"

Behind me, I heard the tinkle of the bell that signaled someone was opening the door. The woman immediately dropped her cigarette on the pavement and ground it out with her wedge heel.

"Tara," Donald's voice roared behind me. "How many times have I told you not to smoke around these pumps? Get your ass back in here. Now."

Tara ducked her head and scurried past me. I turned around and watched as she darted past her husband and inside the store. Donald stared at me for a moment, anger clearly showing on his face. He stepped inside and pulled the door shut behind him.

Well, great. Donald obviously controlled the relationship. How was I supposed to ask Tara what she'd been about to say without Donald interfering? I debated for a moment whether I should march back inside and talk to Tara, Donald or no Donald. But his face was closed tighter than that door. No way would Tara be allowed to speak to me.

Instead, I got in my car, threw the junk food in the backseat, and started the engine, flinching at the clock on the dash. I tried to keep consistent and brief lunch times, and I'd already been gone more than an hour. Of course, my sister was caught up in a murder investigation, so maybe I could make an exception today.

Still, I hovered over the speed limit as I zipped to work, maneuvering around the lumber trucks and slow-moving RVs. I briefly wondered what Jason was up to. He usually called once a day to say hi, but he must be swamped with work since he was covering Bobby Joe's death. I'd touch base with him later.

At the spa, the parking lot held two more cars than when I'd left on my errand. The weekend guests must be arriving.

I parked in my usual spot on the side of the lot but decided to enter through the main door in case the new guests needed anything. On my way by the duck pond, I spotted a yellow head bobbing among the nearby grass, well outside the fenced area. I scooped up the wandering duckling and placed it by the edge of the water before entering the lobby.

I found four people inside, two at the counter talking to Gordon and the other two sitting on the love seat, bags at their feet. Gordon strained so hard to smile when he saw me that I worried a jaw muscle would snap.

"Here's my assistant. Finally."

Inside, I seethed at the word "assistant," but I wouldn't make a scene in front of the guests. "Did you need some help, Gordon?" I asked in an overly perky voice.

Gordon pointed his ballpoint pen at the couple on

the love seat. "The Steddelbeckers have checked in. Could you please show them to their room?"

"I'd be delighted." I grabbed the key from under the counter. "Would you follow me, please?" I said to the couple.

They stood. Mr. Steddelbecker was tall and lanky, his bony knees peeking out from beneath his Bermuda shorts, his ankles hidden under white socks and sandals. An honest-to-goodness non-digital camera, something I hadn't seen in ages, hung on a strap around his neck. Mrs. Steddelbecker was even thinner than her husband but a good foot shorter. She leaned heavily on an oak cane as she shambled toward me, making me wonder if she was older than the sixty or so that she otherwise appeared to be.

I reached for the duffel bag that rested by the love seat, but Mr. Steddelbecker waved me away. "I can carry my own luggage. Otherwise you'll be wanting a tip."

"Good thinking, Horace," Mrs. Steddelbecker said.

I felt my cheeks heat up. "No tip required, sir."

"That's what all these hotel people say, but they always expect one anyway."

Whatever. If he wanted to carry his own bags, I wasn't going to argue.

"As you wish." I led them down the hall and hung a right into the empty dining room. "Breakfast is from seven to nine, lunch from noon to two, and dinner from five to seven."

"You hear that, Darlene?" Horace said. "We have to wait until seven for breakfast."

Darlene thunked her cane on the nearest tabletop, and I jumped as the silverware rattled. Yikes. Guess she wasn't a feeble old lady after all. I'd been fooled by her petite size and need for a cane.

"You all don't serve none of that new-agey tofu nonsense, do you? I'm a meat and potatoes gal."

Uh-oh. "All the food is healthy, organic, and absolutely delicious," I said. I'd better make sure I was nowhere near the dining room when the Steddelbeckers were eating. Darlene might hit me with her cane.

"Let me show you the patio area and pool." I held one of the French doors open for them.

"I don't swim, and the missus has got a bad knee," Horace said, struggling with his grip on the two duffel bags.

I led them across the patio. "What brings you to the O'Connell Organic Farm and Spa?" I asked. It surely wasn't the healthy cuisine or acres of hiking trails.

Darlene smacked a chaise longue with her cane. "My damn fool daughter-in-law set all this up. She hates us."

"If she hates you, why is she sending you on vacation?" I was pretty sure I already knew the answer.

"To get us out of her hair, for starters," Darlene said.

Exactly what I was thinking.

"Plus we heard someone died here a couple months back," Horace added. "I bet Susan is hoping we're next."

He might be on to something there. "The killer's in jail. The spa is perfectly safe." I didn't mention that Bobby Joe had been murdered the previous night. He hadn't died at the spa, so it didn't count for the purposes of this conversation.

I unlocked the door to cabin five and handed the key to Darlene. She stepped inside the room and sniffed.

"Needs airing out." She whacked her cane on the bed. "No dust, that's good."

Thank goodness Esther had freshened all the rooms in anticipation of the guests. "Did you consider giving your vacation to one of your friends?" If they had any friends.

Darlene snorted. "We had no choice but to come

here. If Susan found out we didn't use her gift, she'd never let us see those grandkids again."

"Well, I'm sure you'll have a lovely time. Please let me know if you need anything."

"You can bet we'll need extra soap and shampoo. The missus and I pride ourselves on cleanliness," Horace said.

I knew they really wanted a stash of the boxes and bottles to take home, but an extra shampoo or two wouldn't push Esther into bankruptcy. "I'll bring more in a bit."

I backed out before they could ask for extra towels and robes because they prided themselves on staying dry and went to retrieve the shampoo.

The rest of the afternoon flew by in a whirl of check-ins and odd jobs. With the helium tank I'd rented, I blew up the red, white, and blue balloons and tied them to the patio beams, some bushes near the front door, and all along the fence railings for the pigsty and chicken coop. That done, I hung up the HAPPY FOURTH OF JULY banners and stuck extra flags in the dirt around the cabins and vegetable garden.

I'd forgotten to grab lunch on the way back from the gas station and, after all that work, broke down and tried Zennia's natto. It wasn't half bad if you held your nose while you chewed and washed it down with plenty of water.

When five o'clock rolled around, I stopped long enough to update my time sheet before hopping in my car. The drive home was busier than usual, as week-enders made their way to the Pacific. I got trapped behind a pickup hauling a boat until I could make my escape from the freeway.

As I swung a U and pulled up to the curb in front of the house, I took a moment to lean back in my seat, savoring the momentary silence.

My peripheral vision picked up movement, and I glanced through the passenger window.

Ashlee came barreling down the front steps, her black tank top and yellow shorts making her look like an angry bee. She flew across the lawn and around the car, wrenching my driver's-side door open.

"Dana, I need your help," she buzzed in my ear.

What had happened now?

9

I made a shooing motion for Ashlee to back up, climbed out of the car, and slammed the door shut. "What do you need my help with?" I tried to keep my voice patient, but I'd spent several hours investigating Bobby Joe's murder when I should have been working my regular job, and I wasn't sure I could deal with any more of Ashlee's drama tonight.

"My iPod."

"I don't know anything about programming your iPod."

She waved her arm, almost smacking me in her fervor. "I know that. I need it back."

A missing iPod was not exactly a reason to panic. "What are you telling me for? I don't have it."

Ashlee rolled her eyes. "I know you don't."

At least I wasn't being blamed for anything. "Where do I fit in?" Hopefully nowhere, but I knew better.

Ashlee glanced around at the neighboring houses, then grabbed my hand. I let her drag me up the driveway, curious as to how a missing gadget could cause such theatrics.

When we reached the porch, she dropped my hand. "I need you to get it. I left it at Bobby Joe's place."

That was the big emergency? Retrieving her iPod from Bobby Joe's apartment? "Go over there yourself."

"Are you crazy?" she shrieked, apparently forgetting about any eavesdropping neighbors. "What if the police find out? They'll think I'm taking stuff away, hiding evidence."

I almost snapped at her to stop being such a drama queen, but then I had to wonder. Were the police watching Bobby Joe's apartment? Would they consider it tampering with evidence if they caught Ashlee picking up her iPod? Of course, the police would be just as suspicious if they caught me in that apartment as they would be if it were Ashlee.

"The police aren't going to be happy if either one of us stops by Bobby Joe's place. I think you need to say good-bye to your iPod."

I skirted past her and went into the living room. The room was dark, and the TV was off, giving the illusion of a cool sanctuary. I sank into the balding corduroy recliner that had been my dad's favorite chair and pulled up the footrest, kicking off my sandals.

Ashlee followed me in, standing right by the chair. "Dana, I really need that iPod back."

"What for? You have an iPhone. Doesn't that do all the same things?"

"You don't get it. I need the iPod back because of what's on it."

I saw that Ashlee's cheeks were flaming. What could cause her so much embarrassment?

"Oh my God, tell me you didn't take naked pictures of yourself."

Ashlee's head jerked up. "I'm not a slut." Then her

eyes dropped. "I'm wearing stuff in the photos, only not much."

"Ashlee, what were you thinking?" I'd always thought She was way too confident and streetwise to put herself in such a position.

"The pictures were supposed to be artistic. I'm covered up with flowers and leaves, like some sort of wild nature thing. I did it for Bobby Joe's birthday, but I hadn't worked up the nerve to actually send them to him yet. That's why you need to get my iPod back."

Ashlee was using her best begging face, the one that made men crumble at any hint of a tear, but I wasn't getting stuck doing her errands. I was spending enough time trying to clear her from a murder charge.

I grabbed the TV remote and pushed the POWER button. "You'll need to go yourself. You can dress all in black and linger in the shadows until no one is around. You could even paint those black streaks under your eyes, like in the movies." I was only teasing, but I could see Ashlee's temper getting ready to strike.

She slapped the arm of the recliner. "Don't be stupid. Besides, I don't have a key, and Bobby Joe's roommate would have to let me in. He might tell some of his stupid friends, and then everyone in town would know I was there."

I hit the lever and folded the footstool back down. "Bobby Joe has a roommate?" Maybe a little trip over to his place wasn't such a bad idea. He might be my best shot at getting good intel on Bobby Joe, since Ashlee wasn't much help. And surely the police wouldn't object to Ashlee retrieving her own property. It wasn't connected to Bobby Joe's murder.

"Stump's a total loser," she said.

"Bobby Joe's roommate is named Stump?"

Ashlee nodded. "Totally fits him, too. He doesn't have a job and just sits and smokes weed all day."

Well, good. If he was home all day, he and Bobby Joe probably spent a lot of time together. Maybe he could tell me what had gotten Donald so upset at Running on Fumes.

"What else can you tell me about him? Any chance he and Bobby Joe didn't get along?"

Ashlee studied her hair for split ends. "I only saw him the few times Bobby Joe stopped by his apartment for stuff. We never hung around the apartment because of the smell. But I do know they didn't really get along."

Fantastic. Stump might tell me all sorts of things about his dead roommate.

"Tell you what. I'll go to the apartment and get your precious iPod."

Ashlee immediately jumped up and down and clapped her hands. Was she five or twenty-five? Sometimes it was hard to tell.

"But you have to ride along with me," I added. I didn't even know exactly where Bobby Joe lived. Besides, if I had to go out again in this heat, so did she.

Ashlee stopped clapping. And jumping. "What am I supposed to do while you're inside?"

I stood and slipped on my sandals. "Bring your phone. You can surf the Web."

"But it's hot outside."

"Roll down a window."

"What if someone sees me?"

I reached down to adjust one strap that had hooked on a toe. "For heaven's sake, people have more interesting things to do than look inside parked cars all day. No one will even notice you."

Ashlee crossed her arms. "Fine. Let's go."

I listened to the clink of glasses and clatter of pots coming from the direction of the kitchen. "We'll go after dinner. I missed lunch."

"Think of all the calories you saved," Ashlee said. "It's the start of bikini season, you know."

"I'm not missing any more meals. You'll have to wait."

Grumbling under her breath, Ashlee snatched the remote from my hand and flopped back onto the couch. I wandered into the kitchen where Mom was unwrapping a package of boneless skinless chicken breasts. Ugh. As much as I liked chicken, four times a week was a bit much.

"Chicken again, huh?"

Mom stuffed the Styrofoam tray and plastic wrap in the trash can under the sink. "I figured you girls wouldn't want salmon, since we had that last night. Besides, I'm trying a new recipe where you poach the chicken in red wine."

I had a sneaking suspicion it'd still taste like chicken. I studied Mom, noting how she'd put on a little weight during the last few weeks. Her cheeks held more color, and today she wore lipstick, something she'd stopped doing completely after my father had died.

"Go anywhere fun today?" I asked as I pulled a bar stool out from under the counter and perched atop it. I grabbed the *Herald* off the kitchen table and flipped it open.

"My bunco meeting. We have some new members."

"That's nice," I said absentmindedly as I scanned the want ads to see if the spa's listing for a yoga instructor was there. "Do they seem friendly?"

"Yes, very."

Hesitancy in her voice made me look up to find her blushing. Odd. Bunco didn't usually have that effect.

"Now let me finish dinner," she said, and hustled over to retrieve the salt and pepper shakers.

"Need any help with the side dishes?"

"No, I'm zapping one of those rice pouches in the microwave. The sodium's too high, but it's so easy to prepare."

"You know, Mom, Ashlee and I can make dinner some nights. Give you a break." And you could bet I wouldn't be making fish or chicken. Maybe tacos. Beef. With extra sour cream.

"Nonsense. You girls work hard all day. I can make dinner." She laid the chicken breasts in a pan and poured red wine over them. I recognized the bottle as one a neighbor had given us for Christmas. She placed a lid on the pan and turned from the stove. "Now," she said, her voice low, "your sister tells me you're helping with Bobby Joe's murder investigation. What have you found out?"

I folded up the paper and tossed it on the table. "Not much. I know Bobby Joe's boss was mad at him but wouldn't fire him until he had more proof. Unfortunately, I don't know what proof he was looking for. Right when his wife was about to tell me, we got interrupted."

"Sounds like you need to visit that gas station again," Mom said.

My thoughts exactly. "Donald, the boss, isn't likely to tell me anything. I really need to talk to his wife, but she spends all her time at the station, too. With their house right there on the property, who knows if she ever leaves the place."

"Didn't he marry that young waitress from the

Central Valley? Well, she must go into town sometimes. I'm sure I've seen her at the grocery store."

"Probably. But I can't exactly stake out the station until she runs an errand. I have to work." I shifted my weight on the seat. "Speaking of work, one of Bobby Joe's monster truck rivals is staying at the spa, so I'm hoping to glean some info from him."

Mom opened the pantry door and pulled out a pouch of rice. "Great. Keep at it. But be careful. Make sure you only talk to people when someone else is around. Don't do anything dangerous."

"I won't."

"Good. We have to clear your sister's name."

We? I felt a swirl of irritation in my throat. "I'll help if I can, but the police are the ones who should be proving Ashlee's innocent. In fact, I'm sure they already know she didn't do it." But what if they didn't?

Mom placed the rice in the microwave. "I'm not taking any chances waiting for the police to solve this. Half the town is already wagging their tongues." She slammed the microwave door shut. "Have you talked to Jason? Doesn't he know a lot of cops around here? He might know something we haven't heard."

"I'll check with him, although he can't always tell me everything he knows. If he did, the police would never confide in him again."

"Still, you might try." She punched buttons on the microwave's control panel, and it hummed to life. "How I wish your father was still alive. He'd know exactly what to do."

My eyes burned as tears formed in the corners. I pinched the bridge of my nose. "I know. He was always so levelheaded, no matter what. Remember that time

Ashlee's baby guinea pigs escaped after she left the cage door open?"

"And your father managed to scoop them up in my purse, while you two girls ran around and almost stepped on them, and I sat on the counter and screamed. I never did get that purse clean."

Mom and I were still laughing at the memory when Ashlee walked into the room.

"What's so funny?" she asked.

"Dana and I were reminiscing about when your father saved us from those runaway guinea pigs."

Ashlee put her hands on her hips. "I swear I didn't leave that cage open."

"I'm sure you didn't," Mom said as she pulled the rice from the microwave. "Now, who wants to set the table?"

We spent dinner chatting about what we'd done all day. When I mentioned visiting the gas station where Bobby Joe had worked, Mom shot me a look that said we wouldn't be discussing murder over our poached chicken. After clearing the table and washing the dishes, I grabbed my car keys and my purse.

Ashlee ran into the bathroom for a few minutes and emerged with brushed hair, a touch of blush, and a new layer of lipstick. Was I supposed to get dolled-up, too? I frowned at my reflection in the hall mirror and ran my fingers through my blond hair, wincing as I hit a few snarls. I was stopping by a dead guy's apartment to pick up an iPod and quiz his roommate. I didn't need to dress up.

I walked out to my car and settled into the driver's seat, while Ashlee got in the other side. "Think we should call first?" I asked as she buckled her seat belt. "Let him know we're dropping by?"

"Seriously, Dana, he's a guy. He doesn't care about those things."

"If you say so." I started the car and backed out of the driveway.

I knew from comments that Ashlee had made that Bobby Joe lived across town in a complex by the train tracks. I drove down the main strip, noting that the Get the Scoop ice cream parlor was doing a brisk trade on this sweltering summer evening.

In the passenger seat, Ashlee looked out the window and sighed. "Bobby Joe and I used to always have ice cream after we saw a movie. We'd share a banana split sundae."

I swore I saw a legitimate tear in her eye. "I don't know if I've said it, but I'm really sorry he'd dead," I told her.

"Thanks. This weekend's rally would have been huge for him. We'd be at the fan appreciation night right now."

We were both silent as we passed the row of new businesses that had opened two weeks earlier, signs of life on what had been a dying block. Blossom Valley was starting to drag itself out of the recession, one business at a time.

I turned off Main Street and drove down Jasmine Road, past a long row of small, worn-down tract houses. This was the old part of town, where the cracks in the sidewalks and potholes in the street were extra deep.

"Where did Bobby Joe live again?" I asked as we got farther away from the main drag.

"The Palm Villa Apartments. Sounds way more posh than it is." Ashlee gestured toward my side of the car. "It's up here on the left."

I drove a couple more blocks, pulled into the apartment lot, and parked in a visitor space. Behind the cluster of apartment buildings, I spotted a lone palm leaning to one side, only three fronds left on the thin trunk.

Shutting off the engine, I handed the keys to Ashlee. "In case you want to listen to the radio."

"How long are you planning to stay in there? You're only here for my iPod."

"That and to talk to Bobby Joe's roommate, if he's around. He might be able to give me a lead on who hated Bobby Joe enough to kill him."

Ashlee waved her hand. "Good luck. Half the time, that guy's too stoned to make a sentence."

"Great, I can't wait to talk to him." I stepped out of the car, then leaned back in. "Guess it'd help if I knew which apartment."

"Follow the stink of ganja."

"Ashlee."

"Twenty-seven. It's the second building back."

I slammed the door shut and stepped onto the walk-way, following it along the side of the closest building. The complex had eight or ten buildings, as far as I could tell, each two stories tall with four apartments per building. Once I got around to the back of the first building, I could see that each apartment had a small patio or balcony. Someone had draped a large beach towel over the nearest railing. Below it, planters hung above a patio.

I moved to the next building and checked the numbers on the side. Number twenty-seven was the ground-floor apartment on the right. A hibachi grill was visible through the fence slats, along with a couple of cheap lawn chairs. I went up the walk and under the stairs, where I stopped and stared at the door. Was I an idiot for going into the apartment alone? Did Stump kill Bobby Joe?

Even if he did, surely he wouldn't kill me with the sun still shining and neighbors so close. I knocked on the door.

Music pulsed through the thin wood. As I raised my hand to knock louder, the door flew open. The smell of pot hit me full force, and I staggered back, coughing.

"Hey, man, how's it going?" the guy who opened the door asked. I could only assume this was Bobby Joe's half-baked roommate. He wore denim shorts and a T-shirt that had a picture of a lawn on it and said, "I Love Grass." His feet were bare, but I just knew he had a pair of flip-flops lurking nearby. His brown hair hung well past his collar, a scruffy beard covered his chin, and as he spoke, I could see bits of food in his teeth.

As I fanned the air in front of my face, another guy slipped around the first. He glanced at me on his way by, his intense gray eyes the color of thick ice, and I was momentarily mesmerized.

"Later, dude," he called over his shoulder as he headed down the walk.

I cleared my throat a couple of times, trying to rid myself of smoke. "I'm Ashlee's sister," I said to the guy who had answered the door. "I stopped by for some stuff she left here."

"Right on, dude. I'm Stump. Come on in."

And here I'd thought Ashlee might be lying about his name.

He stepped back to allow me to enter, but I paused. What if Detective Palmer stopped by for some of Bobby Joe's personal effects? Would I end up in jail for being in an apartment where someone was smoking pot, even if I wasn't?

Stump seemed to understand my hesitation. "Don't sweat it. I've got a medical marijuana card. It's all good."

Well, in that case. I moved past him into the apartment, taking shallow breaths to limit how much pot I inhaled. I wasn't sure if someone could get high from secondhand smoke, but I had a feeling I was about to find out.

Stump closed the door, crossed the tiny living room, and twisted a knob on the stereo. The volume of the music dropped a few decibels. He settled on a threadbare plaid couch he'd probably retrieved from a Dumpster and stared at the giant-screen TV eight feet from his face.

I waited for a moment, but he didn't move.

"So, um, any idea where Ashlee's stuff might be?" I asked.

Stump blinked a couple of times. "What? Oh, right. Probably Bobby Joe's room, if the fuzz didn't take everything already." He gestured vaguely to a short hallway on the other side of the living room, where I could see three doors.

I tried the closest one and found myself in a bathroom, illuminated by a night light. The shower curtain showed streaks of something, and the toilet bowl looked suspiciously dark. I shut the door before I felt the need to call my doctor for antibiotics.

I tried the next room, flicking on the light. Every wall was covered with posters of monster trucks, each with names like Black Stallion and Eradicator. I stepped inside, shut the door, and allowed myself to breathe a little deeper. The bed was unmade, jeans and T-shirts were strewn across the floor, and a half-eaten slice of pizza was growing mold in an open box.

I felt a wave of sadness as I surveyed the remains of

Bobby Joe's life. No one had bothered to come in and clean up. Did he have any family? Anyone close by? I hadn't even asked Ashlee if a service was planned.

The only other furniture in the room besides the bed was a beat-up desk. I sorted through a handful of papers on the scratched surface. Each was a pencil drawing of a monster truck, some doing wheelies, some upside down, and one doing some corkscrew maneuver that defied gravity. Notes were scribbled at the bottom of each page. Bobby Joe had been quite the artist.

I shoved those papers to the side and uncovered an assortment of receipts, movie-ticket stubs, and loose change. The desk seemed to be his dumping ground when he emptied his pockets at the end of the day. I poked among the papers and found an ATM receipt from two days before Bobby Joe's death. He'd withdrawn a hundred dollars, leaving an account balance of two hundred and seventy-six dollars. Not exactly rolling in dough, unless he had a secret offshore account somewhere. Based on the sparse furnishings, that seemed unlikely. I opened the desk drawers but didn't find anything worth noting. And there was no sign of Ashlee's iPod.

My phone rang, and recognizing Ashlee's ring tone, I pulled it out of my pocket. "What?" I didn't hide my irritation.

"How much longer are you going to be? The car's getting hot."

"Take a walk outside." I kicked at a heap of clothes as I talked, but only the dingy, stained carpet lay underneath.

"Forget it. A nosy neighbor already came out and pretended to water her flowers while she tried to spy on me. That old biddy's always poking around."

Old biddy? Was my sister watching Andy Griffith reruns? "I'll be out in a bit. I still need to talk to Stump."

"Well, hurry up, would ya?" She clicked off without saying good-bye.

Nothing like a little gratitude when you were trying to clear your sister of a murder rap.

The floor of Bobby Joe's closet held three pairs of shoes and a pair of heavy work boots. On one side of the clothing rod, a heavy jumpsuit much like the one in Crusher's cabin hung from a plastic hangar that sagged from the weight. A black helmet with lightning bolts sat on the shelf over the rod.

Stepping to the bed, I hefted the thin mattress and checked underneath, as I'd seen detectives do on TV. Only a box spring with holes in the thin fabric greeted me. I had no idea whether the police had already searched through Bobby Joe's belongings and taken some items. I had to assume they had, though it was impossible to know if the cops had left this mess or if it was Bobby Joe's natural state.

Disappointed that I hadn't found a note with a list of people who hated Bobby Joe or maybe a diary full of blackmail evidence or even Ashlee's iPod, I dropped the mattress back down and left the room, switching off the light on my way out.

As I shut the door, the smell of pot wafted down the hall and tickled my nose. I went back to my shallow-breathing routine. I was definitely going to keep my questions brief.

Stump sat on the couch, staring at a group of meerkats on the TV. The sound was off, and the stereo in the corner still blared rock music. He smiled at the animals and sipped a beer.

"Thanks for letting me look in Bobby Joe's room," I

said, stepping in front of the giant screen so he couldn't miss me.

Stump lowered his beer can and raised his eyebrows. "Hey, when'd you get here?"

I couldn't picture this guy clubbing Bobby Joe over the head. It required too much effort. Too much concentration. "You let me in a few minutes ago, remember?"

He squinched his eyes, apparently in deep concentration, then smiled. "Yeah, dude, right on."

At least Ashlee hadn't hooked up with this guy. Bobby Joe was starting to look like Bachelor of the Year.

I sat on the other corner of the worn couch, the thin cushion flattening even more under my weight. "Were you and Bobby Joe roommates for a long time?"

Stump scratched his beard. "Uh, a year, I think."

"So you must have known all of Bobby Joe's friends. Can you tell me about them?" I suspected Stump could barely remember what he'd had for lunch today, but maybe he'd surprise me.

"Bobby Joe's friends didn't really come here much. He was dating some hot chick for a while, a real nice piece of tail." He squinted at me. "Wait, that's your sister, right?"

"Right." I'd be sure to pass the compliment along. "Did Bobby Joe ever talk about people who might want to harm him? Anyone who held a grudge?"

Stump took a swig of beer and burped. "We didn't talk about anything that deep, man. Mostly sports and stuff. Bobby Joe spent most of his time in his room when he was home. I think it's cause I play my Christian Rock so loud." He gestured with his can at the stereo.

"You like Christian Rock?" Guess he didn't actually listen to the words.

"You bet. I'm way spiritual. Go to church every Sunday."

I sniffed the air and wondered if he kept his nice church clothes in the car so they wouldn't reek.

"So you can't help me with Bobby Joe?" I asked. If Stump couldn't provide anything new, I wanted to go home, breathe some fresh air, and wash my clothes.

"Naw. Everything was going great for him, man. He was real jazzed about this monster truck rally. Thought it'd be his big break."

Exactly what Ashlee had said. Maybe Bobby Joe had more ambition than I'd given him credit for.

"Well, thanks again. I'll let myself out."

He hadn't actually moved, but I figured I'd say that anyway.

I stepped outside, closed the door, and took three deep breaths of muggy air. Heaven. An African American woman on the patio directly in front of me was watering the geraniums in her hanging pots, only she was mostly watering the cement as she tried to surreptitiously watch me and kept missing the plants. Perhaps this was the neighbor Ashlee said was spying on her.

With a little wave, which the woman ignored, I followed the path out to the front and stopped at the curb. I looked to the left, then to the right, then in front of me again.

My car was gone.

And so was Ashlee.

10

I stared at the empty parking space, as if my car might magically materialize, then yanked my cell from my pocket and speed-dialed Ashlee. As I listened to first one ring, then another, a whisper of panic started in my stomach and slithered its way up my throat. I'd left her alone in an iffy neighborhood. What if someone had decided to steal my car and Ashlee along with it?

Ashlee answered on the third ring. "Hey, you finally done?"

Guess she hadn't been kidnapped. I scanned the street, wondering if she had parked out of view, playing a little prank on her older sister.

"Where are you?" I asked. "And where's my car?"

"Don't get all bent out of shape. I told you it was too hot to sit out there, so I drove over to Get the Scoop."

My earlier thread of panic twisted into a knot of anger. "Get back here and pick me up." I could barely get the words out from between my clenched teeth.

"Relax, I'll be right there. I'm almost done with my cone, anyway."

"Forget your stupid ice cream and get over here." But I was talking to myself. She'd already hung up.

I jammed my phone into my pocket, then paced up and down the sidewalk, working myself into a sweat. The nosy neighbor came out front to water her daisies. Those must be the most overwatered flowers in the neighborhood.

I wiped the sweat off my forehead with the back of my hand and walked over.

"Beautiful flowers," I said to the woman. The deep lines in her face and white hair put her age at eighty or so. Her T-shirt said, "Official Antique."

"Thank you, honey. I do love to garden." She plucked a dead leaf off a stem.

"It shows. I'm Dana, by the way."

"Yolanda."

I pretended to admire the blossoms for what I deemed an appropriate amount of time. "Say, I bet you have a good view of everything that goes on around here."

Yolanda sniffed. "Well, I try to stay out of other people's business."

Yeah, right. "I'm sure you do. But it can't hurt to keep an eye on things, make sure the neighborhood's safe."

"So true. I do my part." She glanced around to make sure no one was watching us. "I couldn't help but notice you went into that riffraff's apartment. They're not friends of yours, are they?"

"No, ma'am."

Yolanda gave me the once-over. "I didn't think you were the type."

"What type is that?" Even as I asked the question, I'd swear I caught a whiff of pot floating by.

"Druggies, stoners, potheads."

Wow, Yolanda was pretty hip.

Her enthusiasm increased as she talked, her arms waving more and more, watering can swinging. "These guys traipse through here all hours of the night. They think no one notices how they stop by for five minutes and then come back the next week and do it all over again."

This was certainly a new angle. I swiped at my temples again as I felt sweat trickle down the side of my face. "Are you saying Stump was dealing drugs?"

"Not just Stump, but Bobby Joe, too. And what kind of stupid name is Stump?"

Bobby Joe might have had his faults, like cheating on my sister, but I hadn't pegged him as a drug dealer. "Are you sure?"

Yolanda cackled. "Of course I'm sure Stump is a stupid name. Might as well call himself Log."

"No, I meant are you sure Bobby Joe was involved?"

"Yessum. I happened to be crouched down, pruning the base of my lemon tree one afternoon, and overheard him making a deal right at his apartment door, in front of God and everybody."

I had to take a moment to digest that information. My little sister had been dating a drug dealer? Did she know?

"Sounds like their operation was pretty big with all the people coming and going," I said.

"Big as the great sky." Yolanda said. "'Course, that don't mean they didn't have their differences. They were shouting at each other something fierce a couple of nights ago."

Now that was interesting. "Any idea what they were arguing about?"

Yolanda started to say more, but her voice was drowned out by my own car horn beeping as Ashlee barreled into the parking lot and screeched to a halt in front of Yolanda and me.

Yolanda frowned. "There's one of their customers now. She must have a real problem what with all the times she's been here."

"Um, actually, she was dating Bobby Joe. But I'm sure she didn't know about the drugs."

Ashlee stuck her head out the driver's-side window. "Get a move on, Dana," she shouted. "I don't have all day."

Oh. My. God.

I tried to ignore her. "Yolanda, could you hear what Bobby Joe and Stump were yelling?"

Yolanda tugged on her T-shirt and fanned her face. "Afraid not. I got out here right at the tail end. Bobby Joe said something about how this wasn't over and then got in his truck and drove off."

"Come on, Dana. Let's go," Ashlee shouted behind me.

Man, she could be annoying.

I offered Yolanda a tight smile. "Nice talking to you." I slunk to the car, sure she'd already tucked me away under the riffraff category in her mental filing cabinet, now that she'd seen me with Ashlee.

I yanked open the passenger door and slid into the seat. My gaze immediately fell on the ice cream cone propped in the cup holder, melted vanilla and chocolate swirl oozing down the sides of the cone and dripping onto my car's interior.

Ashlee followed my gaze. "You sounded kind of mad, so I bought you a cone. I've been blasting it with the AC, but you took so long to get in the car, it's starting to melt."

Not wanting my car awash in sticky dairy products, I pulled the cone from the holder and licked the sides.

"See, I knew you'd want it," Ashlee said.

I checked the cone to make sure I'd gotten most of the drips. "Don't ever take my car again."

"It was your own fault," Ashlee retorted. "You left me in the car like a dog."

"That's not true. I'd never leave a dog in the car in this heat." I stared at the rapidly melting ice cream that I hadn't wanted. I could throw it out the window, but I wasn't a fan of littering. I could give it to Ashlee, but she could barely drive with two hands. As I debated, the ice cream continued to melt until I had no choice but to eat it. I didn't want Ashlee to think I was enjoying the ice cream, but man, it was tasty.

"How about my iPod?" Ashlee asked. "Did you at least get that?" She slammed on the brakes after almost running a stop sign.

I jerked forward in my seat as the belt tightened and held me in place. "Watch it," I snapped. She pressed the gas as I braced myself for what I had to tell her. "It wasn't there."

"What?" she shrieked, jerking the car to the right as she turned to face me. "Are you sure you searched everywhere?"

"Positive. The police must have taken it. Maybe they thought it was Bobby Joe's and wanted to see all his contacts or e-mails."

Ashlee shook her head. "The cops would never think it was his. It had a bright pink cover with stickers. You must have missed it."

I felt my body warm up. "I've spent the last two days talking to people, trying to help figure out who killed your stupid boyfriend, and all you can do is whine, complain, and steal my car. Well, I'm done. You want to know who killed Bobby Joe or what happened to your iPod, you can figure it out yourself."

I banged my fist on the dash for good measure, then patted the spot when I remembered this was my car.

Ashlee was silent, and I sneaked a glance in her direction. She faced straight ahead, tears running down her cheeks. I looked out the window at the passing houses, feeling guilty for making her cry, then angry at myself for feeling guilty. I had every reason to be mad. I was busting my butt to help her, spending all my free time talking to people I didn't know, inhaling the stench of pot, while she took my car on an ice cream joyride.

Then again, her boyfriend *had* been murdered. After she'd found out he was cheating. And she'd been interviewed by the cops, even gone to the station for fingerprints. The stress of the last few days was probably making her act even more immature than she usually did.

"Ash . . ." I started to say, right as she said, "Dana."

She held up a hand. "You're right," she said. "I shouldn't have taken your car. And I'm glad you're helping me. My life is usually so awesome. I work, I date, I shop. But I don't know what's going on anymore." She eased up to a red light, not looking at me. "I'm scared."

I'd never heard her use those words. Maybe her life wasn't always the beach party I'd pictured. "I shouldn't have yelled at you," I said. "I'm as worried as you are. If only the police could come up with a suspect, I'd be a lot less stressed."

"You and me both," she said.

The light cycled to green, and she stomped her foot on the accelerator. The force pushed me back against the seat, and I said a Hail Mary that both my car and I would arrive home in one piece.

After a few more turns, including one where I thought she would swerve into oncoming traffic, Ashlee pulled up to the house. I held out my hand, and she dropped the keys in my palm. I gave the warm metal a kiss.

"Sorry you had to go through that," I whispered to the keys.

Ashlee rolled her eyes. "You're so weird." She hopped out the driver's side while I stuck my tongue out at her as she walked away, our sisterly love back where it belonged.

Once inside the house, I stopped by the kitchen for a glass of milk while Ashlee headed to the living room. Mom was already in bed, and after a long day of work and talking to Mr. Pothead, that sounded like a brilliant idea. In my room, I booted up my laptop for long enough to check my e-mail and Facebook, then powered down both the computer and myself, realizing that I'd forgotten to ask Ashlee about whether Bobby Joe was really involved in selling pot. If so, had Ashlee been involved, as unlikely as that seemed?

These thoughts plagued me as I drifted off to sleep, leaving me to wonder what I'd be facing tomorrow.

11

While I drove to work the next morning, I thought
about what my next step should be as I dug into Bobby
Joe's life. I'd met quite a few people, but wasn't sure I'd
learned much. Maria had vanished the second I tried to
talk to her, Crusher had evaded my questions about
Bobby Joe, and Tara had almost told me something,
but her husband had whisked her back inside before
she could. Yolanda had given me some interesting info
about Bobby Joe and Stump being drug dealers, but I
had to wonder if that was merely the imaginings of a
lonely, old woman.

Maybe with a little more digging, I could find out
what Tara had been about to tell me. And if I staked out
the Breaking Bread Diner long enough, Maria might
tell me how serious her relationship with Bobby Joe had
been. A long-term relationship would involve feelings,
possibly even murderous jealousy, if Bobby Joe had
tried to break up with Maria.

I pulled into the spa's almost full lot and parked in
my usual spot. The rest of the weekend guests must
have arrived last night, which meant a full dining room

for Zennia. Once I typed up the day's blog, the kitchen would be my next stop. Of course, first, I needed to think up a topic for the blog, not always the easiest of tasks. After only two months, I felt like I'd covered almost every aspect of the spa and farm.

I entered through the front door, figuring no one would be arriving this early. I didn't feel like chatting with any guests just yet. When I'd lived in San Jose, I'd had a forty-minute commute during which I could drink coffee, listen to talk radio, and generally wake up to the day. My current ten-minute commute wasn't the same.

As I approached the lobby door, I spotted a fuzzy yellow blob waddling across the sidewalk. Another loose duck. Esther really needed to add that bottom board to the fence. I gently picked up the duck and put it with the others, counting to make sure no one else had made a run for it. That finished, I went inside.

Both the lobby and the office were empty, and I settled into the desk chair to think up a topic. The last several blogs had covered this heat wave. The ones before that had covered perks of the spa, including the benefits of regular exercise, soaks in the hot springs, and breathing unpolluted air. Maybe I should write about green cleaning products today. Or the old-fashioned method of making your own. People might find that useful.

I did a little research and found recipes for self-made window cleaners, bleach solutions, and sink scrubbers, then typed up and posted the blog.

Gordon walked in as I brought up my Yahoo e-mail account.

"Working hard, I see," he said. He pushed some papers aside on the desk and picked up his trusty clipboard. The way he carried it around with him all day, I'd assumed he slept with the thing, but apparently not.

He consulted the top sheet. "What are you doing this morning?"

"I unearthed a few more Fourth of July decorations that I wanted to put up, plus I noticed the parking lot was full when I arrived, so I figured Zennia could use my help prepping lunch."

"Zennia's fine. I spoke with her a moment ago. I've got two candidates coming in for the yoga instructor position. You need to interview them."

Could be an interesting way to spend a Saturday morning. It beat catching loose ducks or cooking octopus. "What time are they scheduled?"

"Nine and ten." He pulled a stack of sheets off the clipboard and handed them to me. "Here are their résumés. See if you can base some of your questions on what's in them."

"Got it. What about salary and benefits?"

"I'll handle the salary aspect for anyone who makes it past this first round. Remember, we want someone who shows up on time and knows how to follow instructions."

Well, that's what *Gordon* wanted, at any rate. "And someone who knows yoga, right?"

Gordon straightened and reclipped the remaining pages. "That goes without saying."

"I should have enough time to read over these résumés and do a little yoga research before anyone arrives."

"Then get to it."

I gave Gordon a mock salute, but he'd already walked out. Probably for the best. Gordon wasn't known for his sense of irony.

Travis, the first guy I'd be interviewing, had almost no yoga experience. According to his résumé, he'd earned an associate's degree from Sonoma State and done a summer stint at a yoga studio. Considering Gordon's usually high standards, I wasn't sure why he'd called Travis in, unless he wanted me to interview anyone who submitted an application and weed out all the misfits.

Evan, the ten o'clock appointment, had worked in a yoga studio in San Francisco for three years, plus he had a degree in kinesiology. He definitely had promise.

I had twenty minutes before Travis's scheduled arrival, so I surfed the Web for trick questions I could ask each applicant and brushed up on my yoga knowledge. If nothing else, I'd taken a few yoga classes down in San Jose and could ask the candidates to demonstrate a pose or two. If I wanted to get really tricky, I could ask about alternate poses for people with back injuries or disabilities.

Nine o'clock arrived. I grabbed the résumés, a tablet, and a pen, and hurried to the lobby to greet the first applicant. Gordon stood at the front desk. The love seat and chairs were vacant.

"No Travis?" I asked.

Gordon consulted his watch. "Two minutes late already? You can send him home when he gets here. I won't hire him."

"A bit harsh, don't you think? Maybe he had car trouble, maybe he's ill."

"No, he's lazy. And lazy people have no place at this spa."

Good grief. Gordon should work at West Point, not a vacation resort. "All the same, I'll at least talk to him."

After another minute, a beat-up faded green Pinto

pulled into the lot. Hadn't all those exploded by now? The car squealed to a stop, and the driver's door creaked open. A young man emerged, looking slightly unsure whether he was in the right place. He wore a Nirvana T-shirt and faded jeans with a hole in one knee.

Was this my first interviewee? I couldn't let Gordon see this guy, or he'd kick him out on the spot.

"I think Travis is here. I'll take him around to the dining room for his interview," I said to Gordon, who was bending down and peering into one of the cabinets under the check-in counter. I darted out the front door before he could get a look at the applicant and stop me. Sure, first impressions were important, but sometimes decent people hid behind sloppy exteriors. Of course, Bobby Joe had dressed like a slob and cheated on my sister, so what did I know?

The guy reached the sidewalk as I stepped out the door.

"Are you Travis?" I asked.

He hesitated, then nodded. If he wasn't sure of his own name, this was going to be a short interview.

"I want to be the yoga guy."

"Let's talk about that. I'm Dana, the marketing coordinator." A slight exaggeration, with the small amount of marketing I did these days, but Travis didn't need to know the details. "We'll talk in the dining room."

I led Travis around the hedge that separated the sidewalk from the large, covered patio and entered through the French doors. At this mid-morning hour, the room was deserted, though I could still discern the faint scent of scrambled eggs that Zennia always whipped up for breakfast. I sat down at the closest table, my back to the patio area, and gestured for Travis to sit across from me. He hadn't said a word since our introductions and now stared at his hands resting on the tablecloth. Not a promising start.

"Travis, what made you apply for this job?"

He scratched his knee through the hole in his jeans. "I lost my last job a while back, and this one sounded pretty fun."

Well, I'd give him points for honesty.

"Tell me about the summer you worked at . . ." I glanced at his résumé. "The Yoga Palace."

A chime sounded from Travis's direction, and he reached for his back pocket. He pulled out his phone, chuckled at whatever he read on the screen, and set the phone on the table.

Was he kidding me? This interview was going downhill faster than Lindsey Vonn at the winter Olympics.

Travis caught my glare and blushed.

"Sorry. One of my buddies keeps texting me. What were you asking? Right, the Yoga Palace. Yeah, I worked there about three months."

I expected him to describe his duties, but he stopped talking and leaned back in his chair.

"What did you do there?" I asked.

"Janitorial stuff, mostly. Washed towels, filled water jugs, mopped the floors. I watched a bunch of the classes while I was working. It looked pretty easy."

Hmm . . . so no actual yoga experience.

Travis saw something over my shoulder, and his eyes widened. I turned and spotted Crusher sitting down at one of the picnic tables on the patio, a magazine in his hand.

"I don't believe it," Travis said. "Isn't that Crusher?"

"He's a guest here this weekend."

"I knew he was around for the big rally, but I never

thought I'd see him this close." He jumped from his chair and grabbed his phone. "I'll be right back."

"What about our interview?" I asked, but he was already out the door. Who was I kidding anyway? This interview was over the minute it started. I hated when Gordon was right.

I watched as Travis talked to Crusher. Well, talked at him really. He snapped a few pictures with his phone, shook Crusher's hand, and came back in the dining room as I was preparing to leave.

"Man, I can't believe it," he said.

"Big Crusher fan?" I asked.

Travis squeezed his knees together like he was going to wet his pants. "You bet. I've followed that guy for years."

I stacked the papers together on the table. "Sounds like he's good."

"The best. He hit a rocky patch the last couple of years. Heard he got dropped by his sponsors, but this event tonight could be his big comeback."

Travis noticed for the first time that I was holding the papers and walking to the door. "Hey, is the interview over?"

"Oh, it's over," I said, not bothering to hide the disdain in my voice.

We crossed the patio with Travis waving at Crusher like a six-year-old would wave at Mickey Mouse. Once we stepped past the hedge and reached the sidewalk, Travis seemed to remember the point of his visit.

"Do I start right away? I mean, I have plans later this afternoon, but I could work until then."

How accommodating of him. "Look, Travis, thanks for coming in for the interview, but we need someone with experience." I was going to stop there, but really, someone needed to help the kid out. "And if I could give you a bit of advice, don't answer your cell phone next time you're being interviewed. Or run out to photograph a celebrity. It's not professional."

"You mean I'm not getting the job?" Based on his raised eyebrows and open mouth, the news came as a surprise.

"I'm afraid not."

"Geez, my mom's gonna be pissed. She really wants her scrapbooking room back."

I held out my hand. His face lit up like maybe I had money hidden in my palm and was offering it to him, then realized I was waiting to shake.

"Good luck to you," I said.

He stomped across the sidewalk, yanked open the Pinto door, the hinges screaming in protest, and slammed the door shut. Guess that hadn't gone like he'd expected.

As Travis puttered out of the lot, I reread the papers in my hand, verifying that Evan, the next candidate, had some actual yoga experience. I didn't want a blank stare when I asked about a Sun Salutation or the Triangle Pose.

Car keys jangled behind me, and I turned to find Crusher coming around the hedge from the patio.

"Hey," he said, "I've been meaning to talk to you."

His tone sounded friendly enough, but I worried for a second that he'd complain about Travis drooling all over him. I hadn't exactly stopped the kid.

Instead, Crusher handed me two slender pieces of paper: tickets to the monster truck rally.

"You look like the kind of girl who likes excitement. And since I'm busy tonight, watching me is the next best thing."

If that was a pickup line, he needed more practice. "Thanks. I'll try to make it."

"I gave you two tickets so you can bring one of your girlfriends along. I hate to see a pretty lady sit alone."

"Great." I was thinking about inviting Jason but kept that to myself.

Crusher broadened his smile. That grin could make a grown woman squeal like a teenager, and I was pretty sure he used that to his advantage. But with his ability to turn it on and off like a light, you had to wonder how sincere it was.

Crusher broke into my thoughts. "It's my way of saying sorry for the way I acted yesterday."

Wow, I hadn't expected an apology. "That's okay. I mean, I was reading your magazines instead of cleaning your room." And Crusher had caught me, which was beyond embarrassing.

"I'm not normally like that," he said. "I'm hyped up about this rally. It's a big deal for me."

If Travis was right that Crusher had been in a slump the last few years, I could understand his anxiety.

"A misunderstanding," I said. "Let's forget it happened."

Crusher threw his arms around me in a bear hug, and I automatically returned the embrace. He smelled of motor grease, and I wrinkled my nose.

He released me and stepped back. "See you tonight, then."

Why did the way he said that make it sound like a date?

12

Crusher headed to the tall pickup truck parked at the outer limits of the lot, and I returned to the house. I cut through the lobby, nodding to Gordon, who was talking on the phone, and went into the office to drop off the tickets, checking the clock on the wall on my way in. Two minutes to ten. My next interview could arrive at any time.

As I opened the bottom desk drawer and stuck the tickets in my purse, my cell phone rang from its depths. I rustled around, shoving my wallet and sunglass case to one side, and finally grabbed the phone, cursing all the while. When would I remember to carry this thing in a pocket?

"Hello?"

"Dana? It's Jason."

Instant guilt flooded through me. For one wild moment, I thought he'd seen Crusher hand me the tickets and was calling to stake his claim, but of course that was absurd.

"Dana, hello?"

I sat down and rested one foot on the open desk drawer. "I'm here."

"Are you available for lunch today? We could meet at Eat Your Heart Out cafe, my treat."

"Your treat? What's the occasion?" Did that question imply he was cheap? I needed to work on my flirting skills.

"Lunch with a gorgeous lady is occasion enough."

I twirled some hair around my finger. "Maybe I can sit with you until she shows up."

Jason let out a low chuckle that quickened my pulse. "She'll be so jealous when she sees you that she'll cancel."

"You've convinced me. See you at noon."

I pushed the OFF button, dropped my phone in my purse, and vowed to start carrying it tomorrow. I grabbed the papers and pen I'd set on the desk and hurried back out to the lobby to see if my interviewee was on time.

Gordon stood by the ficus, talking to a man in tan Dockers, a white dress shirt, and a navy blue sports jacket. Already an improvement over Travis.

I joined the two men by the potted plant, glancing quickly at the top sheet to remind myself of the man's name. "Evan?"

He stuck out his hand, giving me a firm and dry shake. "You must be Dana."

"I am. Let's go talk in the dining room."

Evan shook Gordon's hand while Gordon used his left hand to clap him on the back and give me a thumbs-up that Evan couldn't see.

Gordon had been right about the last guy, but I'd wait and talk to Evan before I agreed with his assessment of this one.

Once settled in the dining chairs, Evan and I spoke for a good hour; for most of that time he described his childhood in a Buddhist home and how it'd set the course for his life. He insisted on demonstrating several moves, from Downward-facing Dog to the Boat pose. The Dockers gave the effect that he was a businessman on a lunch break, though his flexibility made it clear he didn't sit behind a desk all day.

After we'd covered his work history and I'd already decided he definitely qualified for Gordon's second-round interview, I capped my pen and stood.

"Thanks for coming in," I said. "You'll be hearing from us, I'm sure."

"Wonderful," Evan said. "Any chance I can see where the classes will be held?"

I stepped outside the French doors and pointed to the smaller patio near the pool. "Right there."

Evan frowned. "In the open like that?"

"Sure. Nothing beats practicing yoga in the fresh air and sunshine, right?"

"I'm worried about the Kama Sutra poses."

I tapped my palm against my ear to see if my hearing was blocked. "What's that now?"

Evan reached an arm behind his back and thrust a hip out. I wasn't exactly sure what that meant.

"My Kama Sutra poses. I pair off the men and women and have them reenact the more yoga-based moves."

Did he really use a sex book to design his yoga teachings? I should have known his polished style and stellar résumé were hiding a giant gotcha. "I don't think that'll work here. The guests wouldn't be comfortable with that idea."

"Not at first, but I give everyone a cup of my kava root tea. It relaxes the mind and lowers inhibitions."

Why did his tea sound suspiciously like a roofie?

Evan was waiting for a comment. "Get out of here, you pervert" ran through my mind, but instead I said, "I'll mention that to Gordon."

"Excellent. I can already tell this place is more open-minded than Yoga for Yuppies. Boy, did they get mad when I held naked yoga week. So did the cops. Apparently you need a permit for that kind of thing."

Okay, time for this guy to go. Now. "Thanks again. The parking lot's over there." I gestured toward the hedge and hurried back inside the dining room before Evan could say more. I glanced once over my shoulder to see him still standing by the doors, a frown on his face. Guess he realized there wouldn't be a follow-up call.

I went into the office to drop off the papers. Gordon sat in the desk chair, talking on the phone. I signaled to him that I'd finished with Evan, but he waved me away and turned his back. No way did I want him calling Evan back before I had a chance to talk to him, so I jotted down a note that Evan didn't pass the first interview and left it on the keyboard. That finished, I joined Zennia in the kitchen.

Following her instructions, I prepped the green salads for lunch, laid out the linen napkins and silverware in the dining room, and placed red, white, and blue carnations in the vase on each table. By that time, I already knew I'd be a few minutes late meeting Jason, so I stopped in the bathroom only long enough to brush my hair and apply lip gloss. That done, I breezed past Gordon in the lobby and trotted to my car. I'd fill

Gordon in on his little yoga instructor pick when I got back.

The parking lot of the Eat Your Heart Out cafe was full, and I parked on the street under the giant shadow cast by the smokestack of the now-defunct lumber mill. By the time I walked across the potholed lot and stepped onto the wooden walkway with the missing planks, sweat trickled down my back and along my hair-line. At least my work shirt was navy blue, which might mean the sweat circles wouldn't show as much.

I opened the door to the cafe, and a wave of air greeted me as the giant fan near the counter rotated in my direction. I held my arms a few inches from my body in hopes the air would dry my shirt a little.

All the booths were occupied, but I saw an arm waving from the back. I recognized Jason and headed over. As I slid onto the cloth-covered bench seat, a wait-ress arrived.

"Iced tea, please."

She noted the soda already in front of Jason and left.

"Most people towel off after a shower," Jason com-mented as I plucked a napkin from the dispenser and dabbed my forehead.

"Ha, ha, very funny." I crumpled up the napkin and dropped it on the table. With only the standing fan near the door and a handful of ceiling fans, the place was just short of stifling. "Maybe we should have met at the ice cream parlor."

The waitress reappeared with my iced tea, and Jason and I ordered, a club sandwich for him and a Cobb salad for me. The burgers here were the best in town, but I wasn't ordering food off the grill in this heat.

I sucked down half my iced tea and felt a hint cooler.

"I haven't been this hot since I took a summer job at the stir-fry place."

Jason winked at me, drawing attention to his green eyes. "Oh, I don't know. You're pretty hot most of the time."

Well. That little comment didn't help my already overheated face. I pulled the plastic drinks menu from behind the salt and pepper shakers and fanned myself.

"Anyway," I said after I'd cooled down, "what have you been up to these days? Focusing on Bobby Joe's murder?" I tucked the menu back behind the shakers.

Jason pulled a napkin from the dispenser and placed it in his lap. "Writing about the murder has definitely been taking all my time. And this morning, my boss handed down a list of other stories I need to cover. It'll take me all night to get them done."

I felt a flicker of discontent in my belly. "Too bad. I have tickets to tonight's monster truck rally. I was wondering if you wanted to go."

"I didn't know you were a fan."

"I'm not. One of the guests is performing tonight. He gave me the tickets."

Jason offered a half-smile. "Should I be jealous?"

"You should always be jealous, what with my being so hot and all."

The waitress appeared with our orders and set the Cobb salad in front of me before moving to Jason's side to hand him his sandwich. I'd swear she brushed her boob against his upper arm, and a jolt of irritation lodged in my throat. Who was the jealous one now?

I speared an avocado chunk with my fork. "Guess I'll see if Ashlee wants the tickets."

"How's she doing?" Jason took a bite of his sandwich,

a glob of mayo sticking to the corner of his mouth. I resisted the urge to lick it off.

"She's mostly her perky self. But I wanted to ask what you know about Detective Palmer. I'm assuming he's in charge of the case since he interviewed Ashlee."

Jason wiped the mayo off his lip. "He moved up here a few years ago from somewhere down near L.A. Wanted to work in a smaller community where he could get to know the people."

"If you're looking to move to a small town, Blossom Valley definitely meets the requirement. Is it true he's Detective Caffrey's cousin?"

"Yep. Loved it here so much that he convinced Caffrey to move up, too. I heard they grew up down the street from each other, so they're real close."

I groaned. "So it's possible that Detective Caffrey might complain to his cousin about my snooping around in the last murder?"

Jason tried to suppress his smile and failed. "Almost definitely. That was his first homicide, after all, and you stomped all over it. I'm sure he let Palmer know about it, especially if he's heard your sister is involved this time."

"Speaking of which, have the police made any progress in Bobby Joe's murder?" I briefly wondered if the cops had looked at the pictures of Ashlee on her iPod, but I wouldn't be asking Jason about that.

"No. They're still tracking down alibis for that window of time between eleven and one."

I poked at a slice of hard-boiled egg. "Ashlee said she and Bobby Joe got out of the movies around nine. After that, they stopped for gas and then got in a big fight and she was home before I got back at ten. Any idea what Bobby Joe did after that?"

"According to the group he hooked up with, he moped around and tried to get sympathy over being dumped. When that didn't work, he decided to go practice for the rally. Everyone else went home or hung around in the parking lot. No one saw him after that."

I set my fork down so fast it clanked against the plate. "If they were in the parking lot, then Ashlee couldn't have come back without being seen. Surely the police must realize that, right?"

"There's more than one entrance to the fairgrounds. The detective mentioned that Ashlee could have snuck in another gate."

The glistening bacon crumbles in my salad looked like fat, greasy worms. "Ashlee didn't go back out. She was home with me."

"I know. But they don't have a better theory right now."

"What about his employer being mad at him?" I filled Jason in on my conversations with Donald and Tara. "And a neighbor swears Bobby Joe and Stump were both dealing drugs. Maybe they had a fight about business. And Crusher could have wanted his biggest competitor out of the way before the rally tonight."

Jason smirked. "Crusher?"

"Probably not his given name. Unless his parents had a weird sense of humor. He's the guy at the spa who gave me tickets for tonight. He's one of Bobby Joe's rivals." I sipped my iced tea. "That leads me back to my point that there are lots of suspects the police should be focusing on. Have you found out anything about Maria? Maybe she had a reason to kill Bobby Joe."

"I'm looking into it. Same with her husband."

I swallowed a slice of hard-boiled egg. "I saw her wedding ring, but I thought they might be separated."

"Nope, in fact they've only been married a few

months. And the word on the street is that Todd Runyon is the jealous type."

Jealous types often had violent tempers. I needed to find out more about Maria's husband and their relationship. But how?

13

I leaned toward Jason so far, my hair dipped into my salad dressing. I grabbed a napkin and wiped off the strands. "How awesome would that be if Maria's husband found out about the affair and killed Bobby Joe?"

Jason raised an eyebrow at me, and I felt instantly chastened.

"Don't get me wrong. It's tragic that Bobby Joe was murdered, but it'd sure be nice if the police could prove the betrayed husband did it and stop considering Ashlee a suspect."

"There's no evidence that the husband is guilty," Jason said. "He claims he didn't even know about the affair."

I wadded up the napkin and set it on the table. "Exactly what I would say if my wife's boyfriend was murdered."

"Sure, but the police are thinking that if this guy's lying, who's to say Ashlee isn't lying, too?"

I shoved my salad away, my appetite gone. "I'm saying she's not."

Jason reached across the table and squeezed my hand, but I pulled out of his grasp.

"Ashlee didn't kill Bobby Joe," I said.

"I know. I'm looking at it from the point of view of the cops."

I leaned back in the booth and crossed my arms. "How about looking at it from my point of view?"

Jason fidgeted with his knife and fork until he'd lined them up. "Look, I'm only pointing out that the cops think Ashlee had plenty of time to go back and kill Bobby Joe."

"But she didn't."

Jason tried again to grab my hand, but I was too far away. "Dana, I know Ashlee is innocent. We're on the same side here."

"Not really. You're a journalist. You're only after the story. Whatever sells." I knew I was being silly and defensive, but I couldn't stop myself. Would it have killed him to not mention Ashlee as a possible suspect when talking to me?

Jason lowered his voice with a tone that bordered on condescending. "That's my job. But I'm always fair."

"Good to know."

We broke into an awkward silence. I pulled my phone of my purse and glanced at the time. "Guess I'd better get back to work." I retrieved some bills from my wallet and threw them on the table.

"Lunch was my treat, remember?" Jason said.

"I'd rather pay for mine, thanks." I stood and hoisted my purse strap onto my shoulder.

Jason half-rose, but I waved him back down.

By the time I'd crossed the parking lot and gotten in my car, I was over my fit of anger and had moved to bewilderment. The sweltering air felt heavy as it settled in my lungs, threatening to suffocate me. Maybe I should go back in and apologize. Or maybe Jason should have been more supportive. Or maybe we both needed a cooling-off period.

I was glad Jason was busy tonight. I didn't want to take him to the monster truck rally anyway. At least that's what I'd tell myself.

I started the car and drove back to work.

In the lobby, Gordon scribbled on his clipboard at the counter. His unnaturally dark hair gleamed under the overhead lights as he bent forward. As soon as he noticed me, he set his pen down, automatically adjusting the knot in his tie.

"Didn't realize you were taking a lunch break today."

"Yep, decided to grab a bite in town." My voice held a note of challenge. After my spat with Jason, I wasn't taking any of Gordon's guff.

"I wanted to know why you left me that note saying I shouldn't hire Evan."

I gave Gordon a thumbs down. "Evan's out. We'll need to interview more candidates."

"I don't understand. He was on time. He wore a jacket. He's perfect."

If only Gordon had heard the Kama Sutra comments, but the idea of repeating them made me want to gag. "A perfect pervert. Trust me. He's not a good fit."

Gordon opened his mouth, no doubt to argue more, but he must have seen I wasn't in the mood. "I'll arrange for more interviews. We've had a few more résumés come in."

"Good."

I stalked to the office, where I thumped down on the

office chair and dropped my purse in the drawer. I spent the next couple of hours pretending to work on marketing brochures while pouting about my lunch with Jason. My sulk fest was temporarily interrupted when the Steddelbeckers requested more towels. Considering how many I'd already taken them, they must be furnishing a spare bathroom or two at home.

That task completed, I helped Zennia prep for dinner, checked on Wilbur and his pig friends, and counted the ducks. Twice. By that time, I'd run out of ways to pretend I was working and decided to call it a day.

Nothing wrong with that. I set my own hours, per my agreement with Esther. Still, I left through the French doors in case Gordon was staking out his usual spot at the computer. I didn't need his critical gaze on me. By the time I reached home, I had all but decided to skip the rally tonight.

Ashlee's Camaro occupied the driveway, and I parked on the street. I half expected her to come running out the front door, screeching, like she had yesterday, but the door remained closed, the yard quiet. The African daisies in the planter drooped, a reflection of my mood, while yellow jackets hovered over the brown-tinged grass.

Inside the house, the air conditioner hummed quietly. Ashlee sat in the recliner in a tube top and short shorts, her gaze riveted on the TV. I dropped my purse on the coffee table, sank onto the couch, and kicked off my sandals.

When a commercial advertising male-enhancement drugs appeared, Ashlee dragged her gaze from the screen. "Dana, I didn't see you come in."

Heaven help us if the house ever caught fire. She'd never notice.

"I got home a minute ago. Where's Mom?"

"She went to Martha's house for an early dinner, and then they're catching some old-lady movie down at the theater."

I didn't bother asking if the movie starred a bunch of old ladies or appealed to old ladies. Probably neither. For Ashlee, anyone over forty was old. I was just happy Mom was socializing more these days, rather than staying home and grieving over Dad.

"You got plans tonight?" Ashlee asked.

"Not anymore." Maybe never again with the way things had ended with Jason. "You?"

"Nobody asked me out this week." She stuck out her bottom lip. "Do you think it's because of Bobby Joe? That guys think I'm a murderer?"

If I was a guy, I wouldn't date someone whose last boyfriend was murdered, especially since the police hadn't caught the killer, but the type of guys Ashlee attracted might not be as choosy. "They probably figure you're in mourning," I offered.

Ashlee put her lip back where it belonged. "You're right. Guys can be so sweet that way."

Or maybe they figured they wouldn't get lucky if she was too distraught over Bobby Joe's death.

She picked at her fingernail polish. "I hate being home on a Saturday night. I feel like such a loser."

I stifled the urge to roll my eyes. "Staying home on a Saturday night does not make you a loser. I do it all the time."

Ashlee raised her eyebrows and tilted her head as if I was merely proving her point. Gah, she was so frustrating.

I rubbed my forehead. "Tell you what. Crusher gave

me a couple tickets to tonight's rally if you want them. You can take one of your friends."

"All my friends have dates on Saturday night. They're not losers."

One more loser comment and she wouldn't live to see next Saturday night. "Find yourself a date. Ask a guy out."

Ashlee's mouth dropped open, and I had the urge to throw a penny in it, like the clown's mouth at the carousel.

"Are you kidding? That would be social suicide, taking another man to a place where Bobby Joe was supposed to perform tonight. Can you imagine what people would say?"

She actually had a point, for once. Even I would be gossiping about that one.

"Well, you can always go by yourself. Or not go at all. It was only a suggestion."

"Or . . ." Ashlee didn't finish the sentence, just smiled at me.

"No, forget it."

"Please come with me," she said, clasping her hands under her chin like a beggar. "You need to get out more, meet some guys."

I lifted one foot onto the coffee table and studied my toes to avoid her gaze. "I have Jason." At least I did until our little tiff at lunch.

"You guys aren't married. You need to live a little. Crusher obviously thinks so if he gave you those tickets. He was probably flirting with you."

I felt my resolve weakening like a dieter at an all-you-can-eat buffet. Why stay home because I was mad at Jason? No need to sequester myself from the rest of life.

And I'd never been to a truck rally before. Maybe some of Bobby Joe's buddies would be there. Or some of his enemies. I still needed to find out more about my sister's boyfriend.

"Fine, I'll go."

Ashlee squealed and ran off to her room, no doubt to start the primping process.

I heard the grinding hum of the garage door. A moment later, Mom stepped into the house carrying a hanger, her purchase hidden in a long plastic bag.

I rose from the couch. "Ashlee said you and Martha were going to dinner and a movie tonight. Did something happen?"

"Martha got one of her migraines, so I decided to do some shopping. Going Back for Seconds was having their annual Fourth of July sale." She held the hanger higher. "I picked up this beautiful dress with a matching brocade jacket for half off."

"Maybe I should go down there before the sale ends." Although the idea of wearing a skirt or dress made me tired. The pantyhose, the slip, the heels. So much work. And then you had to find matching jewelry. Thank God I worked at a farm and spa, where the animals couldn't care less what I wore.

Mom glanced at the clock on the mantel, and I automatically looked as well, my gaze pausing on Dad's nearby picture before moving on to the time. Half past five.

"You girls have anything fun planned tonight?"

"We're going to the monster truck rally." As usual, I felt guilty at the idea of leaving Mom alone in the house at night. Too bad Martha was sick. "Say, Mom, why don't you come? It's bound to be fun." And surely tickets were still available.

Mom scrunched up her nose. "I'm not much of a monster truck gal. Now that my plans with Martha have fallen through, I might attend the seniors' dance down at the community center. Some of the girls are supposed to be there."

I knew from past references that the girls in question all belonged to Mom's salsa class. Guess my image of Mom as a lonely, sad widow needed an update.

"Speaking of which," Mom said, "let me get ready. I'm wearing my new dress."

"I should change, too. My spa shirt isn't the cleanest thing." I followed Mom down the hall and made a detour into my room. I stood before my open closet and stared at my clothes. Let's see, a bunch of guys would be driving giant trucks around a dirt track. I could probably get away with casual wear. I grabbed a sleeveless cotton top off a hanger, pulled a pair of jeans from the dresser, and changed. That done, I brushed my hair and teeth and touched up my lip gloss. What the heck, it was Saturday night; I added a coat of mascara and smidge of eyeliner for good measure. Then I went back to the living room to wait for Ashlee.

After twenty minutes, the fastest she'd ever gotten ready, I heard her emerge from her room. She stopped before the recliner and held her arms out.

"Ta-da. What do you think?"

She wore a denim miniskirt with a button-up, short-sleeved black blouse and strappy heels. She'd pulled her hair back into a bun, and her makeup was barely discernible.

"Um, you look good?" My comment came out as a question. I wasn't sure what she expected me to say.

"My top half says I'm sorry Bobby Joe is dead. My bottom half says, 'Hey, I'm not dead. Don't forget about me.'"

If scientists ever figured out a way to observe someone's thought processes, I was volunteering Ashlee. "I think you nailed it."

"Thanks." She squinted at my face. "Hey, you're wearing eyeliner. Good to see you putting in an effort for a change."

If I smacked her hard enough, maybe I could knock her out and go to the rally without her. Or better yet, stay home.

"Shall we go?" I asked, rising from the chair.

I decided not to lug my purse with me and instead put my ID, a couple of twenties, the tickets, my phone, and my keys in my pocket. God only knew why I was bothering to take my phone. Jason wouldn't be calling.

With Ashlee strapped into the passenger seat, I drove through town past a smattering of fast-food restaurants and gas stations. Beyond the Taco Bell, I hung a right into the fairgrounds lot.

I'd last been to the fairgrounds back in May, when I'd helped set up and assist at the annual cricket-chirping contest. The contest had been a success as far as cricket chirping went, but the twenty or so attendants seemed paltry in comparison to the hundreds of people weaving their way between parked cars on their way to the track.

As I slowed to a crawl to avoid running over any spectators, I thought about how the cricket-chirping contest was where Ashlee and Bobby Joe had met. I suddenly wished Ashlee had never gone with me to that contest. Then she never would have met Bobby Joe, and she wouldn't be in this mess.

The paved main lot was full, and an attendant in an orange vest waved us around back to the dirt overflow lot. My car was old, and I didn't mind driving through the rutted dirt, but Ashlee was gonna have a hell of a time in those heels.

Sure enough, as soon as she stepped out of the car, I heard all about it.

"My shoes! They're filthy! Do you have any idea how much these cost?"

I held up one foot, my white Keds showing the strain of working at a farm. "More than mine?"

Ashlee slapped a hand to her chest. "God, I don't know why I talk to you about fashion."

"You can stop any time."

She growled at me like an angry kitty, and I smiled back.

We made our way across the dirt expanse, dodging the steady stream of cars pulling into the lot. Had the whole town turned out for the truck rally? I felt my pocket to make sure the tickets were still there as I bypassed the ticket booth and headed for the main entrance.

I handed the tickets to the beefy security guy, who tore off the stubs and handed them back. Then I tossed my keys into a little plastic bowl and waited while he passed a wand over my body. When it didn't shriek, he waved me through and repeated the process on Ashlee.

When he nodded at her, I took a few steps forward to get out of the way of people behind me, then paused to assess. I was expecting a small crowd with easy access to the drivers, allowing me to talk to anyone who might have known Bobby Joe. But we'd be sitting in the stands, completely separated from the participants. I might not be able to interview the other drivers at all.

"Let's get our food first, then sit down," I told Ashlee as I listened to the murmur of the crowd inside. "Who knows if our seats will be boxed in." Plus it would save Ashlee an extra trip up and down the stairs in those shoes.

"Sounds good. I'm starved. Wonder what they have here."

"Probably the usual mix of hot dogs, hamburgers, and fries."

Ashlee tugged at her waistline. "This skirt barely fits as it is. Maybe I'll just have a Coke. Diet."

I wasn't wasting this chance to eat something deep fried, but Ashlee was more calorie-conscious than I was. "Suit yourself."

We went inside the stadium, where the noise increased significantly. People milled about in the aisle, drinking beer out of plastic cups and high-fiving each other for no obvious reason. Most of the girls wore tank tops and short skirts, while the guys wore T-shirts and ratty jeans. The air practically crackled with energy.

I got in the concession line, already picturing a corn dog.

"Grab my Diet Coke, will you?" Ashlee said. "I need to use the little girl's room."

I nodded and faced forward again, watching as a heavyset guy with pork-chop sideburns tried to carry four beers in his meaty hands. With each step he took, beer sloshed over the sides, followed by cursing that would make Chris Rock blush.

I felt a tap on my shoulder and turned around, wishing I hadn't when I saw who stood behind me.

"Dana! It's so lovely to see you again."

Kimmie Wheeler, former classmate and current snob, leaned toward me. She'd darkened her long straight hair since the last time I'd seen her, but she still wore shrink-wrap clothes and blindingly bright jewelry.

"Kimmie, it's you," was all I could muster.

"How have you been?" She lowered her voice. "Are you still working at that spa?"

"Yep, it's going great."

Kimmie tilted her head and gave me a sympathetic frown. "Still can't find anything else, huh?"

I straightened my posture so I could look down on her. "I like working at the spa, thanks."

"Good for you. The world always needs helpers."

Ugh. I checked the front of the line, but it had barely moved. I was stuck with Kimmie for a while.

"What brings you to a truck rally?" I asked. I knew operas and symphonies were more her style.

"One of our customers had tickets and asked us to join him. Normally my hubby and I wouldn't bother, what with how busy we are running the most popular restaurant in Mendocino, but he donates a considerable amount to our fund-raisers, so we couldn't say no."

"Sounds like business is going great for you."

"We're booked through September. Everyone wants to eat there and tell their friends they got a table." Kimmie petted the chunk of black hair that lay over one shoulder, smoothing it down. "I'd try to squeeze you in, but I can't even fit in my friends these days."

"No worries. I don't get to Mendocino much anyway." And when I did, I certainly wouldn't give my money to Kimmie by eating at her restaurant.

"Right, you do have to work and all."

The line moved forward, and I felt a spark of hope. My escape was only three people away.

Kimmie lowered her voice again and leaned in closer, placing her hand on my arm. With the buzz of the crowd, I could barely make out the words.

"I heard about your sister killing her boyfriend. How are you holding up?"

I stepped back, jerking my arm away. "She didn't kill him." I might have spoken too loudly since the guy behind Kimmie stared at me and shuffled backward.

Kimmie reached for me again, but I shifted away. "I didn't mean to upset you," she said. "I totally understand why she killed him. If my husband cheated on me, I'd kill him too. Not that he ever would. He adores me."

"I'm not kidding. Ashlee did not kill Bobby Joe."

"Of course, of course, don't get upset." Her gaze flickered from one side to the other, her face tight with faint panic. Looking for security? Worried that killing was a genetic trait in my family?

Disgusted, I faced the counter, intent on ignoring Kimmie, but then I thought about her remark and turned back.

"How did you know Bobby Joe cheated on her?" I was pretty sure Kimmie hadn't been loitering around the fairgrounds two nights ago, and I didn't know how in tune she was with Blossom Valley gossip. She only dragged herself here from Mendocino to visit her aging mother or pander to a donor.

She stepped closer once more. Apparently her desire to gossip beat out her fear that I might kill her. "Everyone knows. Of course, I knew first, but then I have an inside connection."

"What do you mean?"

"You know Maria, the one Bobby Joe cheated with? Her mother works for me, although I'm considering firing her. I mean, if you can't clean a toilet properly, you shouldn't be in the maid business."

I tried not to think about Kimmie's toilets. They probably had solid-gold seats and diamond-studded flush handles. "And Maria's mom knew about the affair?"

"What's with the questions?" She poked me in the shoulder. "You little devil. You're trying to solve Bobby Joe's murder. That's so cute."

"My sister is in the middle of this. Nothing cute about that. Now tell me whether her mom knew about Maria and Bobby Joe."

"She did. In fact, Rosa was so upset that she forgot to dust the top of my refrigerator." Kimmie wrinkled her nose. "Sloppy, sloppy. But she couldn't believe her daughter would step out like that. Of course, I wasn't surprised in the least, with how Maria's husband treats her."

"How's that?"

"He beats her. I don't know why she doesn't pack up and leave."

The guy in front of me stepped to the side, and I reached the front of the line, but now I wasn't so eager to leave. I mulled over the information as I absentmindedly placed my order.

If Maria's husband smacked her around, then he had a temper, just as Jason had said. What would he do if he found out Bobby Joe was sleeping with his wife? Kill him?

Kimmie had confirmed that Todd was a solid suspect. Now I just had to figure out what to do with the information.

14

I stepped over to the condiment stand and grabbed a handful of napkins while I waited for my order, all the while thinking about Maria and her abusive husband. What I'd taken to be under-eye circles the one time I'd seen her at the Breaking Bread Diner could in fact have been black eyes. I'd even thought those circles looked like bruises. Had he hit her after finding out about Bobby Joe, then hunted down Bobby Joe and finished the job?

As Kimmie joined me to wait for her food, Ashlee headed over from the direction of the bathrooms. Kimmie spotted Ashlee and rushed to her, throwing her arms around her. Trapped in the embrace, Ashlee raised her eyebrows at me, and I offered a little wave. Kimmie let go and stepped back, giving Ashlee a chance to escape to my side.

"Who the hell is that?" she whispered out the side of her mouth.

"She and I were friends in high school, but I guess you don't remember her. She heard about Bobby Joe."

Kimmie's gaze started at Ashlee's styled hair and

ended at her sandals. "You look wonderful after all that's happened. It's so nice of the police not to arrest you yet."

"Why would they arrest me?"

Kimmie smiled at Ashlee like they shared a big secret. "You know why."

Ashlee stepped up to Kimmie so they were toe to toe. "No, I don't. You're going to need to spell it out for me."

Kimmie's eyes narrowed, but her smile never faltered. "Fine. Everyone knows you're a killer."

I gaped at Kimmie. Did she really just say that?

Ashlee stood a little taller, seemingly unfazed. "Did one of your customers tell you that? Maybe you should worry less about me and more about your food. I hear you serve frozen scallops at that restaurant of yours."

Kimmie gasped. "I do not!"

"Order up!"

Thank God.

I snatched the cardboard containers from the take-out window and shoved Ashlee toward the stairs. "'Bye, Kimmie. Gotta go see the rally."

I hustled Ashlee in front of me, but she managed to crane her head around for one last comment. "By the way, your roots are showing."

I glanced back in time to see Kimmie slap a hand on top of her head, then concentrated on fighting my way through the crowd.

When I reached the bottom of the stairs, I inspected the food in my hands. Three burgers peeked out at me from beneath yellow paper.

"Where's my Diet Coke?" Ashlee asked.

And where was my corn dog? I'd been so caught up

in what Kimmie had said that I'd flubbed the entire order.

"I'll grab your soda in a bit. Have a burger."

She stared at the open cardboard boxes in my outstretched hands, shrugged, and grabbed one. Guess her jean skirt had a little give after all.

I balanced the remaining two boxes in one hand and pulled out the tickets, searching for the seat numbers. Crusher had hooked us up with seats only three rows back and on the end of the aisle so we wouldn't have to climb over anyone to get to the bathroom or food stands. Nice.

We sat down, and I surveyed the crowd. Everyone was chowing down on burgers and hot dogs, chugging beer, and chatting up their seat mates. I finished the last bite of my second burger, my stomach grumbling in protest, and crumpled up the wrapper.

Below us, shells of Volkswagen beetles and compacts, painted green, purple, or yellow, windows and all, sat wedged between mounds of dirt in the center of the arena. A stoplight-type contraption hung against a pole to the side. American flags hung from the light posts. Several more had been stretched along the boards that lined the track.

A roar rose from the crowd, competing with the sound of an engine as a monster truck rolled onto the course, kicking up dust. The sides were painted in a tiger-stripe pattern; giant flaming eyes stared from the hood and long fangs protruded from the grill. The oversize tires looked cartoonishly inflated, as though Bugs Bunny might suddenly show up and pop one with a giant needle. The driver sat square in the middle of the cab and waved through the grimy windshield.

The crowd's yelling grew to a feverish pitch as a

second truck, this one painted like a ghost, zoomed out.
I clapped my hands over my ears. Whose idea was this
again?

The trucks drove around until they were at opposite
points on the circular track, then the stoplight turned
green. Each truck scrambled forward, accompanied by
more cheering as they raced around the track, leaping
over the outermost dirt piles.

I leaned toward Ashlee, who was busily texting. "Why
did they start so far apart? How can they race like that?"

She glanced toward the track, then down at her
phone, her fingers never slowing. "It's based on time,
not actual racing. Whoever drives the fastest moves on
to the next round."

"You mean there are more than these two trucks?"

Ashlee snorted in response.

Then again, two trucks would make for a very short
rally. Plus, I hadn't seen Crusher yet, and I knew he was
competing tonight.

The two trucks stopped racing, and the guy in the
ghost truck pumped his fist in the air while the announcer on the loudspeaker rattled off a time. The first
strains of "Stars and Stripes" blared from the same loudspeaker as the trucks cleared the track. I used the break
to study the crowd.

To my right and a few rows up, a flash of cheetah
print caught my eye. Who did that remind me of? The
woman turned in my direction. Tara, Donald's wife. As
I watched, she squeezed past the other people in the
aisle and headed toward the concession stand.

I whipped around to Ashlee. "I'll get your Coke now."

"Diet," Ashlee said, as if I needed yet another reminder.

Jumping from my seat, I trotted after Tara, following

her progress as she climbed the stairs and headed away from me. I thought she'd stop at the closest food stand, but she passed it without slowing. Heading to the bathroom maybe? Nope, she walked right by the entrance. I followed her across the concrete expanse, down a flight of steps, and over to a large patio area.

A cluster of people stood in the fenced-in space, all puffing on cigarettes. Aha. Now it made sense.

Tara joined the group, a cigarette and lighter already in her grasp, like a sleight-of-hand magic trick you wouldn't want your kids to see. She caught sight of me as I struggled to think up an excuse for my presence.

"Hey, didn't I see you yesterday?" she asked. She flicked the lighter, touched her cigarette to the flame, and inhaled.

Busted. "Tara, right? I'm Dana. We spoke outside your gas station." Technically her husband's station, but that sounded rude.

"Yeah, I remember now." She noticed my empty hands. "Do you smoke?"

"Uh, no, I mean, um, I used to?" She remained silent as she tapped ash off the tip of her cigarette, and I plunged ahead. "I quit a while back, but I miss this." I gestured with my arm at the other smokers, some coughing, others checking their phones or fidgeting with their lighters.

Tara immediately nodded. "I know, right? People don't understand how smoking brings everyone together. They keep banning it everywhere, thinking people will feel all lonely and give it up. But the fewer places there are to smoke, the more people will have to hang around the same places. It's like our own private club."

Huh, I'd never thought of it that way before. Maybe

I should send an e-mail to the anti-smoking lobbyists with this bit of insight.

"The only thing is I have to make sure Donald doesn't catch me. Lucky for me, he's sponsoring one of the trucks and wanted to talk to the driver about where to place the sticker for the station."

Lucky for me, too, since it gave me a chance to talk to Tara alone.

"We never finished our conversation from yesterday," I said, "and I was really interested in what you had to say."

Tara flicked more ash. "Oh yeah? Why's that?"

Because my sister's boyfriend was murdered? Because the police had their eye on Ashlee, and I needed another suspect? Sure, Maria's husband was at the top of my list, but it never hurt to have a backup.

I opted for a vague version of the truth. "My sister was dating Bobby Joe, and I'm trying to find out who would want to kill him."

"So you want to know if Donald did it."

"No, of course not." Okay, yes, I'd love to know that, but I couldn't very well admit it. "If I can find out why Donald was upset with Bobby Joe, it might point me in another direction."

Tara puffed on her cigarette while she studied me with an intensity that made my insides quiver. She was proving to be shrewder than I'd originally guessed.

"I don't believe that for a minute," she said. "But I don't want you bothering Donald about Bobby Joe anymore. The cops are already pestering us enough. So I'll tell you, and then you leave us alone. You got it?"

"Got it." What else could I say? Whether I meant it was another story.

"Donald thought Bobby Joe was skimming off the till."

First a womanizer, then a possible drug dealer, and now a thief. What the hell kind of guy was Ashlee dating?

"So when Donald said he wouldn't fire Bobby Joe without proof, he meant that he only suspected Bobby Joe of stealing but didn't know for sure?"

Tara nodded. "The money kept disappearing during Bobby Joe's shifts, or at least that's when Donald would notice. He was gonna install a camera right over the cash register to catch him in the act, but now I guess he doesn't need to."

"Did you think Bobby Joe was stealing?"

"Heck no. Bobby Joe was a sweetheart. I told Donald it's that girl, the new one, but she bats her eyelashes at him and sticks her chest out every time he walks by, so he doesn't listen to me. And here I'm supposed to be his wife."

She dropped her cigarette and ground it into the dirt with her strappy heel. She and Ashlee had the same taste in footwear. "Look, I need to get back." She poked her finger against my breastbone. "Stay away from Donald."

I batted her finger away. Why was she so afraid of me talking to Donald? "I will if you answer one more question. Where were you and Donald on Thursday night?"

Tara looked like she wanted to poke me again, but she didn't. "At the gas station, like I always am. Donald was running the store, and I was in the house watching TV. Now, excuse me." She hurried off.

I watched her go, disappointed. I'd been counting on Tara to reveal a secret worth killing over, but Bobby Joe skimming money was hardly a murdering offense, only something worth firing him over. A slim possibility existed that Donald had confronted Bobby Joe about the theft, lost his temper, and hit him so hard it killed him. But that was as likely as Ashlee wearing white after Labor Day.

Still, I had one more person mad at Bobby Joe. But had Bobby Joe really stolen from the station? The ATM statement in his room had showed such a low balance that he could definitely have used the extra money. I'd have to ask Ashlee if he had carried a lot of cash on their dates.

I climbed the stairs and walked back across the concourse, remembering to stop and grab Ashlee a soda. As I stood behind a sweaty guy with thinning hair, a thunderous roar erupted from the crowd. I whirled around and tried to look over the retaining wall but couldn't see what the crowd was cheering about. The announcer babbled about a catwalking wheelie, but I could barely hear him over the rest of the noise.

Great, the one big moment at the rally, and I was stuck in line. I picked up my drink a moment later, but by then, the audience had already settled down. "You're a Grand Old Flag" started playing, another patriotic reminder that tomorrow was the Fourth of July. I should already be in bed, getting a good night's sleep. With so many guests staying at Esther's, I was bound to be busy in the morning.

When I returned to our seats with the soda, a grungy-looking guy in his early twenties sat in my spot, his lank body hunched over as he and Ashlee whispered to each other.

"Ahem," I said.

Guilt flashed across Ashlee's face.

"Dana, you're back," she said.

I held the cup aloft. "Here's your soda."

The man jumped up and into the aisle, his ponytail swinging from the movement. "Your throne, milady."

"Yeah, thanks." I squeezed past him and sat down, handing Ashlee her soda.

Ashlee giggled. "Isn't he something?"

"He's something, all right." I watched as Ashlee put her thumb to her ear, her pinky to her lips, and mouthed, "Call me," to her suitor. He blew her a kiss and clomped up the stairs.

I'd only been gone fifteen minutes, and Ashlee had already picked up a new man. Guess he hadn't heard about Bobby Joe. Or if he had, he didn't care.

"What was all the excitement about?" I asked.

"He saw me when we went down the stairs to our seats and waited for a chance to talk to me. So romantic."

"I'm not talking about your love life. I meant what was the crowd cheering about a few minutes ago?"

Ashlee shrugged, losing interest. "I didn't notice. I was talking to Rusty."

Did people really name their kids Rusty these days?

"The announcer mentioned a catwalking move," I prompted.

Ashlee gave me one of her signature looks that let me know I was a total idiot. "Seriously, Dana. This is a truck rally, not a fashion show. There's no catwalk."

Sometimes I wondered why I spoke to my sister at all.

But I needed information about Bobby Joe. As I opened my mouth to ask about his finances, I noticed a new truck enter the field, the base coat a shiny black with a fist made out of boulders appearing on the side. On the hood, the word "Crusher" was spelled out in letters shaped like rocks. I sat up straighter and leaned forward, watching as Crusher paused at his starting position. When the green light popped on, he raced around the track, a Rottweiler truck zipping around the other side, dust billowing up from the track. The announcer declared Crusher the winner, and I cheered along with the crowd.

Beside me, Ashlee played a game on her phone, casting occasional glances over her shoulder, no doubt to see if Rusty was watching her.

After a few more rounds, in which Crusher won twice more, the trucks drove off the field. When no new ones came on, I stood up and reached my arms over my head, feeling the muscles in my back loosen.

"Guess that's it." I nudged Ashlee with my knee. "Ready to go?"

"It's not done."

I leaned down, thinking I'd misheard her. "Wait, what?"

She gestured toward the track with her phone. "The show's only half over. Freestyle's up next."

"What's freestyle?"

"You know, they'll jump over those cars, spin doughnuts, do whatever they want."

Freestyle sounded pretty fun. I'd seen bits and pieces of it on TV before and always liked watching the jumps.

"Guess I'll stretch my legs before they start," I told Ashlee. "Want anything?"

"I'm good."

I made my way up the stairs, wondering who would be in my seat when I returned this time. Night was descending, but the stadium lights scattered the shadows. An occasional breeze drifted through the stands, a brief respite from the heat.

Wandering along the concourse, I noted the people

in line at the hot dog stand and averted my eyes when I saw a couple making out under the staircase leading to an upper level. If Jason had come with me, maybe we'd be the ones making out right now. Or not. Who knew if Jason and I would ever make out again?

I turned to head back and saw a petite girl with long dark brown hair walking in my direction. Where had I seen her before?

She got closer, and I realized it was Maria. Why had I been running all over town trying to talk to people when I could have just questioned everyone at the truck rally?

As I raised my hand in greeting, a loud group of men barreled in between us, laughing and jostling each other. When the group had passed, Maria was gone. But where?

I scanned to the left, then the right, wondering how she'd disappeared so fast. People loitered near the snack bar, and I craned my neck to see around them. I finally spotted her up ahead, scurrying like she was being chased. Had she spotted me after all? But why run?

Darting after her, I threaded my way through the bystanders as she headed farther away from the crowds. She glanced once over her shoulder and sped up to a trot, then passed through a doorway cut in a cement wall. The circle on the wall designated it as a women's bathroom.

She could try to hide in a stall, but I'd wait her out. I focused on the bathroom, the sounds of the crowd dying away as I headed toward the far corner and the doorway I'd seen her go through. I neared the entryway and heard a footstep behind me. Before I could turn around, someone shoved me forward, and the cement wall was directly before me.

I didn't even have a chance to throw up my hands. My head thumped against the wall. Everything went black as I fell to the floor in a heap.

15

My head throbbed, but I knew I should get up. I pushed my palms against the rough floor and propelled myself to a standing position. I had a second to notice all the graffiti on the cement wall before someone whirled me around and held my arms.

As I struggled against the firm grip, I looked into a man's face, level with my own. The clear lenses of his glasses reflected the overhead lights, and his brown hair was cropped close to his head. I felt a flicker of recognition, but my brain was working at only half speed. I couldn't remember where I'd seen him.

Blindly, I threw my weight forward, hoping to knock him off balance, but he shoved back, pinning me like a grocery list on a corkboard.

"Stop fighting me. I just want to talk." His voice was gruff.

"Let go!" This time when I lurched forward, he released my arms and stepped to the side. I almost fell down, but managed to regain my balance.

I swayed slightly as I faced the man who had pushed me, wondering what my options were. He was my height and had a slight build, but I doubted I could outfight him. Could I outrun him?

The man held up his hands. "I'm not trying to hurt you."

Well, he could have fooled me. I was almost positive he did indeed want to hurt me. "Is that why you shoved me into a wall?"

"You were chasing after my wife. I had to stop you."

His wife? The wooziness in my head abated a bit as I realized where I'd seen him before. He'd been arguing with Maria the day I'd stopped at the Breaking Bread Diner. So that *was* her husband. What was his name? Todd? What exactly did he have planned for me?

I took a step back, noticing how little I could hear the people back at the rally. The area we were standing in was remote. In my haste to catch Maria, I hadn't realized how far away I'd walked from the crowd. And where was Maria anyway? Still in the bathroom?

Todd eyed me but made no move.

"I needed to talk to her about something," I said slowly, as though I was trying to soothe a wounded animal.

Based on his stiff back and unblinking stare, he wasn't soothed.

"Like what?" he demanded.

"Girl stuff. You know how girls like to gab," I said, not willing to admit I wanted to ask her where she was Thursday night when Bobby Joe was murdered. I looked over his shoulder to see if anyone was headed our way. Nope.

He straightened his glasses and peered at me. "Then why did it look like you were chasing her?"

I managed to fake a laugh. "Chasing her? That's a good one. She didn't hear me calling her name, what with this crowd and all, so I was trying to catch up to her."

"I thought I knew all of Maria's friends. How come I've never seen you before?"

"We recently met." Maybe it was from my head banging into the wall, maybe it was the sudden exhaustion, but I couldn't stop myself from saying, "I met her through a mutual friend. Maybe you know Bobby Joe Jones, too."

Todd reeled back as if I'd physically punched him. His already wan complexion paled even more as he shook his head. "No, no, I don't. I've never heard that name, and neither has Maria."

Speaking of Maria, where was she? She must be able to hear us through the open doorway. Why hadn't she come out?

Todd raked his fingers across his neck, and lines appeared on his skin. He'd gone from irate to panicked at the mere mention of Bobby Joe's name. In that moment, I felt I'd taken control of the situation.

"Really?" I continued. "I thought you were at the fairgrounds Thursday night, watching Bobby Joe practice." A total lie, but Todd didn't know that.

Todd scratched his neck again. "Wasn't me. I was at home. With my wife."

"Huh, my mistake. Guess I'll go find Maria now." I turned and marched into the bathroom, praying he didn't follow me.

When I'd gotten inside, I stopped by the sink and sagged against the stainless steel, trembling. What an idiot I'd been. If I was going to help solve Bobby Joe's murder, I needed to be a lot more alert. I couldn't just run after people and put myself in danger like that.

I shoved off from the sink and looked down the row.

All three doors of the regular stalls were ajar. Only the handicap stall was closed. I strode up to the door and knocked. No response.

"Maria? Are you in there?"

Still no answer. I looked behind me to make sure Todd hadn't snuck in, then pulled the handle. The door swung open, revealing an empty stall. I pushed the doors all the way open on the other three stalls, but I already knew no one was there.

While Todd had knocked me to the ground and I'd struggled to regain my senses, Maria had escaped.

I splashed cold water on my face, the throbbing having dulled to a mild ache, and patted my skin with a paper towel. Should I call the police? I was no expert, but Todd's shove might be considered an assault. However, Todd would claim he'd been defending his wife, even if I hadn't been doing anything wrong. That might change how the police treated the situation. And the fact that I was chasing after the mistress of my sister's boyfriend might make Ashlee look awfully guilty, as though she was trying to interfere with the police investigation. Detective Palmer had already warned me to butt out.

I studied the square piece of metal that was supposed to be a mirror on the wall. The surface was too blurry and scratched to see clearly, but my face appeared pretty normal, with no telltale signs that I'd been in a scuffle. Calling the police would only cause trouble. Decision made, I tossed the paper towel into the trash and paused at the doorway.

Was Todd waiting for me, ready to pounce again?

Hearing Bobby Joe's name had obviously upset him. Had he decided I was some sort of threat?

Maybe I could call for help. I pulled my phone from my pocket. No signal. Great. The one time I'd actually remembered my phone, and the thing was useless.

Well, I couldn't stay in the bathroom forever. And Todd sounded pretty secure about his alibi. If Maria had been with him at home, neither one could have killed Bobby Joe, unless they were covering for each other. Of course, if Todd was telling the truth, that messed up my entire suspect list, but I'd worry about that after I'd escaped the confines of the fairgrounds' bathroom.

I poked my head out the door to scout the area and let out my breath when all I saw was a giant expanse of concrete. In the distance, people milled about. I homed in on them like a moth drawn to a porch light.

The crush of people and constant chatter were a welcome sensation as I passed the concession stand. Even the scent of exhaust drifting up from the track thrilled me, because it meant I was back in civilization and no longer alone. I had no idea if Todd or Maria were still lurking around, and I didn't want to find myself alone with either of them again. I just wanted to sit down.

As I came in sight of the stairs, the crowd exploded into a frenzy, and I rushed forward until the arena came into view. Crusher's monster truck, mighty rock fists still clenched, idled in the dirt. The crowd stood, clapping and whistling, yells and screams joining the mix as Crusher stuck a hand out the window and waved before motoring toward the gate.

I trotted down to where Ashlee sat, with no male companion this time. I'd already decided not to mention my run-in with Todd. She'd tell Mom, who would then worry about my safety and feel guilty because she suggested I look into Bobby Joe's death. I'd rather skip all that drama.

I plopped into my seat. "What did I miss?"

Ashlee whirled on me. "Jesus, Dana, where have you been? I thought you'd left me and gone home." She peered at me a little harder. "Why do you have a big bump on your forehead?"

Guess my attempts to hide the lump with my bangs hadn't worked. "I was hurrying back here and tripped. Now what happened?"

She immediately jumped from her seat, my banged-up forehead forgotten. I hadn't seen her this animated since Coach released their latest line of purses. "A totally crazy stunt. Absolutely nuts."

"What was the stunt?"

Ashlee stood over me, waving her arms. "I can't even describe it. You had to see it."

Great. I'd missed both big stunts tonight while investigating Bobby Joe's death and getting shoved around by an angry husband. Meanwhile, Ashlee had sat here, flirting and relaxing. Totally not fair.

"Did you see that Crusher was the driver?" Ashlee asked.

"I'll have to congratulate him if I see him at the spa tomorrow." Not that I had any idea what exactly I was congratulating him for.

Ashlee snapped her fingers and pointed at me. "Thanks for the reminder. I might have to stop by tomorrow. Give Crusher my congratulations in person."

I hung my head in mock defeat. "Have you forgotten about poor Bobby Joe?"

"Of course not, but you can't expect me to be in mourning forever."

"He died two days ago." I felt like we'd already had this conversation, but really, the poor guy deserved some respect. Even if he was possibly a cheater, a thief, and a pothead. "What about a funeral? Do you know if he has any family who might plan a service?"

Ashlee sat back down, sobering. "Bobby Joe's dad died a few years ago, and his mom passed away when he was a teenager, but he's supposed to have a brother somewhere. Maybe he'll do something."

"How sad," I said. I'd hate to be so alone in the world that I'd have to worry about who would bury me.

"If the cops can't locate the brother, I'll ask Stump to take care of Bobby Joe. Or maybe his boss at the gas station," Ashlee said.

Donald might not be a big Bobby Joe fan, but I hoped he'd at least spring for a burial.

We sat in silence for a few minutes while the trucks came out one by one and jumped over the cars, the announcers hollering "big air" after the higher jumps. The ghost truck backed up a few feet, then hit the gas, accelerating all the way to the ramp and clearing both mounds of dirt and cars. The announcer screamed something about "the double" as the truck landed with a thump, then bounced back up on its overinflated tires.

The tiger truck spun doughnuts, generating a cloud of dust that reached the stands, until his truck tipped over. Track crews helped the driver out while a bulldozer rolled onto the course and righted the truck. Another guy's tailgate fell off.

The announcer declared the next truck to be the last, thank goodness. My head was pounding harder than the guy banging on the bench behind us. After the last truck jumped a couple of mounds, the driver rolled to a stop. The crowd clapped, whistled, and stomped once more, then everyone headed for the exits en masse.

From our seats near the bottom of the stadium, I watched people struggle up the clogged stairs, then leaned back in my seat.

"Let's let people clear out for a minute."

Ashlee glanced up from her phone. "That'll give Rusty a chance to get my number. He forgot."

I closed my eyes, the pounding louder now. "I thought you were interested in Crusher." The bump on my head felt like it had grown to a gargantuan size, although a little probing with my fingers told me it was pretty small.

"I am. But I like to keep my options open. Crusher might have a girlfriend. Or be gay. Or be headed to a monastery after he's done competing."

I opened my eyes to see how serious she was. She popped gum into her mouth, offered me a piece, then stuck the pack in her purse when I declined. "Plus," she added, "he's probably going home tomorrow, and long-distance relationships are a drag."

The crowd had noticeably thinned, the mass of humanity on the stairs shifting to a mere inconvenience as opposed to an impenetrable block. Still too early to move, though. The parking lot was bound to be jammed, and my car was stuck in the back.

Now would be a good time to find out how much Ashlee knew about her deceased boyfriend. I thought about my conversation with Tara.

"How were Bobby Joe's finances?" Maybe that ATM

receipt was for one bank account, and Bobby Joe had another.

Ashlee snickered. "If our dates were any sign, his finances stank. Why?"

"Tara, Donald's wife, said Donald thought Bobby Joe was stealing money from the cash register."

"Bobby Joe? No way." Ashlee swept her arm toward the arena. "He was broke because of this stupid place right here. Every dollar he made went into his truck. New parts, new paint job, entry fees. But he'd never steal. He was too honest."

Apparently Bobby Joe's death had affected Ashlee's memory. "How can you say that after he cheated on you?"

"I'm sure it was a one-time thing. We all make mistakes."

I wanted to argue the point, but to what end? Bobby Joe was dead. It didn't matter now if he'd cheated. Unless that cheating somehow got him killed.

I decided to switch topics. "What would you say about pot, then?"

Ashlee shrugged. "Sure, I've tried it, but it wasn't really for me. For one thing, you can't rock in a bikini if you're always getting the munchies."

I was starting to think Ashlee was the cause of my headache, not my close encounter with the cement wall. "I'm not asking if you've used it." Although I had to admit I was a bit surprised that she had and that she'd so readily admit it. "I want to know if Bobby Joe was a pot dealer."

"Geez, Dana, what kind of guys do you think I date?"

I skipped right over that question. "Remember when you stole my car to get ice cream? While I was waiting for you to come back, I talked to Yolanda, Bobby Joe's neighbor. She said Stump and Bobby Joe were big-time pot dealers."

"That old lady is nuts. I told you she was always spying on Bobby Joe. And she watches those judge shows all day. She thinks everyone is guilty of something."

I was getting two completely different pictures of Bobby Joe here. On the one hand, his boss thought he was a thief and his neighbor thought he was a drug dealer, while on the other, Ashlee thought he was too honest for anything other than cheating on a girlfriend, not that that was exactly honorable. Who was right?

The crowd had almost completely disappeared, and the cleaning crew was roaming the aisles, stabbing trash with their pointed sticks and depositing everything into garbage bags.

"Come on, let's go." I was tired, sore, and a little cranky. I'd missed most of the rally, and I wasn't sure I was any closer to finding the killer. I hadn't even talked to any drivers, and right now, I didn't feel like tracking them down.

But one thing I was almost sure of. Todd absolutely knew about his wife's affair with Bobby Joe.

16

Few cars remained in the overflow lot by the time we climbed up the cement stairs and walked down the other side. The sky was dark, the moon new, but the stadium lights illuminated our path to the car.

Traffic through town was heavier than normal, most likely people hitting the fast-food joints for a late-night snack after the rally. But I had to work in the morning and couldn't afford to stay up any later than I already had. Six o'clock would be here soon enough.

Once home, I changed into PJs, brushed my teeth, and scrubbed my face. Out of habit, I checked my cell phone and saw that I had a voice mail. I punched the button and listened to the automated lady. Then the message started, and my breath caught as I heard Jason's voice.

"Hey, Dana, Jason here. I wanted to apologize for what happened at lunch. I know Ashlee would never hurt anyone. Being a reporter makes me forget sometimes how difficult it is for the people involved. Anyway, give me a call."

It was already past eleven. Too late to call. And I had

no idea what to say anyway. I'd been so angry at lunch, but now I felt deflated. I'd lashed out at Jason over my frustration at not making more progress. I knew Ashlee hadn't killed Bobby Joe, but the police had every reason to think she might have. And Jason had every right to point that out. I needed to work harder at finding the real killer, so I could get back to my nice, quiet life.

I switched off the light, crawled into bed, and stared at the ceiling in the glow from my alarm clock. After a while, I drifted off into a restless sleep.

The next morning, I dragged myself out of bed and assessed my health. My head no longer hurt, and my arm muscles protested only a little when I moved. A glance in the mirror showed the bump on my forehead had dwindled to the size of a large zit. Guess I'd live.

I stumbled into the shower and went through my usual morning routine automatically. Khaki shorts and work shirt on, I stopped in the kitchen for a bowl of sugar-free oatmeal, wishing Mom would occasionally splurge on the yummy kind, before getting in the car.

Downtown was blocked off for the Fourth of July parade, so I maneuvered through a series of side streets until I reached the freeway on-ramp. Too bad I had to work instead of watching the parade. Of course, my interest had dimmed once I was too old to collect the candy thrown by the Lions Club members as they rode around in their little cars. Parades weren't as fun without free candy.

At the farm, the birds chattered noisily in the trees as I followed the path past the cabins and walked through the back door of the kitchen. Zennia, dressed in a muumuu, daisies woven through her braid, was adding fresh blueberries from a strainer to a bowl of white goop.

"Dana, I heard some people in the dining room a moment ago. Can you take the custard out while I prepare the bacon and eggs?"

I eyed the bowls. "Is that real custard?" I knew the bacon was veggie bacon, but maybe the custard was actually custard.

She set the empty strainer in the sink. "Of course the custard is real. How can you have fake custard? I mean, it's made from tofu, but it still counts as custard."

No, it didn't.

I kept that thought to myself as I grabbed two bowls and carried them into the dining room.

Horace and Darlene Steddelbecker sat at the table closest to the French doors, loudly discussing their plans for the day.

"Hikes, bikes, what am I supposed to do with my bum knee?" Darlene asked Horace as I approached the table.

I set the bowls before the couple. "The beach isn't far from here. You could sit and watch the ocean."

Horace picked up a spoon and pointed it at me. "Forget it, missy. When one of those big earthquakes California is always having hits, I'm not getting sucked into the ocean."

"We really don't have that many earthquakes," I said, straightening the roses that sat in the vase between them.

"Bull pucky," Horace said. "We've seen the movies."

And movies were always so accurate. "How about shopping? Blossom Valley has some lovely stores downtown."

"Too much walking," Darlene said, tapping her knee.

I momentarily missed the Bickersons and the meals where they never spoke. Too bad they'd checked out instead of the Steddelbeckers.

Horace poked at the custard with his spoon, then set the spoon back on the table and shoved the bowl away. "I reckon we oughta stop at one shop. You know Susan will be expecting something, what with sending us on this trip and all."

Darlene banged her own spoon on the table. "You're right. She's always wanting something, that one."

I didn't think one little souvenir in exchange for a free vacation was asking too much, but the Steddelbeckers seemed like the type who would begrudge a dehydrated and dying man a glass of water if they had to hand it to him.

"Well, missy," Horace said to me, "where can we pick up souvenirs on the cheap? I don't want none of these shops that jack up the prices when they see a tourist walk in."

I thought about the new antiques shop, the wine bar, and the accessories store that had all opened on the main drag. None of those would suit the Steddelbeckers. But I knew of one place that would. I'd seen a whole shop full of cheap trinkets and knickknacks just yesterday.

"Running on Fumes is a gas station on the other side of town. The owner also runs a souvenir shop, and he sells all types of gifts from the area, like redwood burls, abalone jewelry, and seashells."

Horace raised his hand like we were in math class and not a dining room.

"At reasonable prices," I added.

He put his hand down.

I gave them brief directions on how to find the station. "I'll be back in a minute with your bacon and eggs."

Darlene held out both custard bowls. "Take these with you. We don't want them."

I accepted the bowls without a word and took them to the kitchen, where I set them on the counter. Zennia looked up from where she was plating the eggs at the other end.

"Let me guess. The Steddelbeckers?"

"Good guess."

Zennia shook her head and slapped a pile of scrambled eggs on the plate. "I can't believe those people. They kicked up such a fuss last night over dinner that I eventually had to make them peanut butter and jelly sandwiches. And then they wouldn't eat those because I used organic, all-natural peanut butter, and they only like Skippy. I can't wait until they go home."

"At least they'll be out shopping this morning. Maybe they'll even eat lunch in town."

"I wouldn't be so lucky," Zennia said.

"You're probably right. They'd need to spend money if they bought lunch."

Zennia laughed as I grabbed two plates and returned to the dining room. Another couple had shown up for breakfast while I'd been in the kitchen and now sat across the room.

I set the plates down in front of the Steddelbeckers, and Darlene immediately jabbed the eggs with her fork, much like Horace had poked his custard.

"These aren't none of that egg substitute nonsense, are they?"

"Nope, the eggs were laid by chickens right here at the spa."

"Good, 'cause I'm getting tired of all this healthy

food. I need something with preservatives. If you can keep food fresh that long with preservatives, think about how long you could keep your body fresh."

I almost laughed at her convoluted logic. Before she could ask if the bacon was from a pig, I escaped to the kitchen for more custard for the new guests.

The rest of the guests arrived, and I got busy serving them. When people had shuffled back out of the dining room, I helped Zennia with the dishes, then went to the office to work on the day's blog.

As I was typing the last few words, Gordon popped his head in. "Dana, did you get those spa visitor demographics I asked for?"

My fingers hovered over the keyboard. "Demographics?"

Gordon stretched out an arm and tugged on the shirt cuff peeking out from his suit jacket. "I asked you on Friday to supply an overview on the age, sex, and ethnicity of most spa guests."

I searched my memory for the infrequent conversations I'd had with Gordon over the last couple of days, but nothing relating to visitor stats came to mind. "I don't recall you asking me for that, but I'd be happy to pull something together for you."

Gordon glanced over his shoulder and stepped all the way into the office, lowering his voice. "You better not let your personal life interfere with this job. You know how important the success of this spa is to Esther. To all of us."

"I'll have that information for you later this morning."

"See that you do. And you've got a woman coming in at two o'clock to interview for the yoga instructor position. Be ready." He spun around and strode out of the room.

How could I have forgotten Gordon's request? I thought I'd been handling both my job and investigating Bobby Joe's murder pretty well, but maybe I was slipping.

Trying to settle my sudden unease, I concentrated on posting my blog, then started on the demographics Gordon had asked for. I finished the task quickly, and I wondered if I'd pushed it out of my mind because I knew it wouldn't take long. That still would be no excuse for forgetting altogether.

When I finished collecting the information, I leaned back in my chair. Too early to help Zennia with lunch prep. I could always wander around the grounds and see what needed tidying. But first . . .

I checked my cell phone. The screen was blank. No new calls. I waited a full minute, staring at the screen, on the off chance it would ring by some magical coincidence. When nothing happened, I punched in Jason's number. He answered on the second ring.

"Jason Forrester speaking." His tone was brisk and businesslike.

"Uh, hey Jason, it's Dana. I got your message."

Silence was my only response, and I plunged ahead.

"I wanted to apologize for yesterday, too. I'm worried about Ashlee, but I shouldn't take it out on you."

"Sorry, I can't talk about this now. I'm working on a major story. I'll call you later, promise."

Click. He hung up.

I pulled the phone away from my ear and stared at the length of the call. Thirty-two measly seconds. I knew when Jason was working on a story that he blocked out the rest of the world, but I'd been apologizing. He could have at least acknowledged that.

I tossed my phone in the drawer with my purse. If he called back, he could talk to my voice mail. I had things to do, too.

My internal voice started lecturing me on my immaturity, but I shut it down and went into the hall. The kitchen was empty, and I grabbed an apple from a bowl on the counter. Munching away, I strolled through the herb garden, the scent of rosemary and thyme heavy in the air. A squirrel darted up the nearby oak tree, an acorn stuck in its mouth, while honey bees hovered over the lavender. I wondered if they'd sting me, like Jason had stung me a moment ago. Or maybe I was being melodramatic.

I wandered over to the pigsty and chucked my apple core in the direction of Wilbur and his pals. As he made a grab for the core, I leaned on the rail.

"What a day, Wilbur. Gordon is all over my case about doing a better job."

Wilbur snorted twice.

"I know, he's always demanding, but what if he's right this time? I have been focusing on Bobby Joe's murder quite a bit."

No response this time.

"And to top it off, I called Jason to apologize, and he gave me the brush-off. Isn't that rude?"

Wilbur snorted.

"I thought so." Sure, a pig was the one agreeing with me, but as long as somebody validated my feelings, I was okay with that.

Wilbur went back to rooting in the mud, and I straightened up. "Thanks for listening."

I strolled by the chicken coop, but the yard was empty

and quiet. No doubt the chickens were hiding inside the coop to escape the mid-morning sun.

"Dana, yoo-hoo."

Esther trotted down the path toward me, her peach-colored cotton skirt rising and falling as she moved.

"Esther, how are you?"

"Right as rain, thanks." She glanced up at the blue and cloudless sky. "Speaking of rain, I wouldn't mind a little these days."

"You and me both." I heard a chicken cluck from within the hen house. Guess she agreed.

Esther wiped her forehead with the back of her hand, strands of one gray curl sticking to her skin. "I'm glad I ran into you. Zennia mentioned she needs tomatoes for today's lunch. Could you pick them for her?"

"You bet." I gestured toward the cabins. "It's nice having so many guests here, isn't it?"

Esther nodded and fiddled with a button on her white blouse. "The summer's been slow, that's for sure. This truck rally has been a boon for the town, but it's only one weekend. We need more events to bring in guests."

Guess I shouldn't have been handing out those bottles of shampoo to the Steddelbeckers so freely, what with business being slow.

"How's your Blossom Valley Rejuvenation Committee?" I asked. "Coming up with any new projects?" The committee, all three members of it, tried to promote the town and increase tourism through a hodgepodge of events, including the cricket-chirping contest I'd helped with a couple months back.

Esther pulled her blouse away from her skin and fanned herself with her other hand. "We've got a few ideas going." She patted my arm. "I've got to get inside now. I'm melting like my favorite praline ice cream."

I followed her back to the kitchen and snagged the large basket from its usual spot on the counter, then went back out and stopped by the toolshed for a pair of gardening gloves. After Gordon had pointed out those tomato worms, I wasn't taking a chance on accidentally touching one. The temperature was rapidly approaching triple digits, so I threw on an old straw hat I found hanging on a peg.

As I headed out, the pool water shimmered in the light, a mild breeze making the ripples twinkle like the stars I still occasionally wished upon. Crusher wasn't hanging around the pool as usual, but he might be resting after his big rally performance last night. Or maybe he'd already packed up and gone home.

I followed the path past the cabins and down the walkway until I reached the vegetable garden. I stopped at a tomato plant and set the basket on the ground. No giant green worms waited for me, thank goodness.

I squeezed a few tomatoes before finding one that wasn't too firm and snapped it off the vine as Zennia had shown me once upon a time. Three more followed, and I moved to the next plant. As I searched for the ripest tomatoes, I heard voices moving in my direction.

The Steddelbeckers came around the curve and stopped when they saw me.

"You," Horace said, sending a chill down my back, despite the heat.

I deposited a tomato in the basket and straightened up. "Did you enjoy your shopping?" I asked, though their grimaces already told me the answer.

"I don't know why you sent us to that godforsaken place. Are you just mean-spirited?" Darlene asked.

Was the gas station gift shop really so bad? I'd thought it'd fit their style—cheap and cheaper. "I suggested Running on Fumes because they have such a good selection of unusual items at low prices. Did something happen?" Had the three-dollar glow-in-the-dark plastic octopus been too much for them?

"I'll say something happened." Darlene thumped her wooden cane on the ground. "We were almost killed!"

17

Almost killed? Had I somehow endangered the Steddel-beckers?

In response to Darlene's outburst, Horace reached over and covered her hand on the cane with his own. "Don't get yourself riled up. Remember your heart."

After a mini wave of panic and a flash of guilt, I had to wonder if they might be exaggerating. They certainly looked fine. "What happened? Did someone rob the store?"

Horace shook his head. "We found ourselves in one of those domestic disputes. You know how they can turn ugly."

"Who was fighting? Customers?" I asked.

"I don't know their names," Horace said. "Some heavyset feller with a bad-looking toupee and some chesty floozy in a tight shirt."

Was he talking about Donald and Tara?

"What were they fighting about?" I asked, wishing he'd get to the part where they were in actual danger.

"Hollering at each other something fierce," Horace said. "When we first got there, they were in the back, but we could hear them clear as day. He was shouting about her sleeping around with some other feller who worked there. And she yelled back that he musta killed the guy, hit him with a tailpipe or something."

Darlene chimed in. "If it weren't for this here cane, I'd about fell over when she said that."

Holy cow. Had Tara been sleeping with Bobby Joe? That guy sure got around. First Bobby Joe steals from the business, then he steals Donald's wife?

"Did they say anything else?" I asked, almost forgetting the sun that beat down on me.

Horace nodded. "You bet. The man said he wished he'd had the chance to kill the guy, but he wouldn't use a tailpipe. He'd strangle him with his own two hands."

Hmm . . . that comment implied Donald might not have known about the affair before Bobby Joe died, if there even was an affair. Or else he was bluffing to convince Tara he hadn't killed Bobby Joe.

Horace and Darlene stared at me, waiting for me to speak.

"And then?" I prompted.

"Isn't that enough?" Darlene snapped. "Then those two came out from the back, and we hightailed it outta there, ran for our lives."

I imagined them hobbling toward their car, screaming bloody murder, and had to suppress a smile.

"Something funny, missy?" Horace asked.

I forced a frown. "No, of course not, but I don't quite see when your lives were in danger."

"After what we heard?" Darlene said. "We're lucky that guy didn't follow us. And here you're the one who sent us out to that place in the middle of nowhere. Anything could have happened, and no one would ever know."

"Well, I'm glad you made it back safe," I said, hoping

they wouldn't whine about their imagined danger all day. "Now, I need to finish collecting these tomatoes for lunch."

Darlene harrumphed. "At least that's one food we've eaten before." She tapped her husband's ankle with her cane. "Come on, Horace. I need to lie down after all that excitement."

I removed my hat and wiped the sweat off my forehead as they made their way down the path. When they were out of sight, I planted the hat back on my head and finished collecting the tomatoes, all the while wondering if Donald and Tara had really said those things or if Darlene and Horace had misinterpreted what they'd heard. Did Tara really believe her husband had killed Bobby Joe, or had she suggested that to distract him from her possible affair?

As I picked up the basket, it sagged under the weight of the fruit, and I sagged right along with it. Why did the vegetable garden have to be so far from the kitchen? I lugged the basket toward the house, sweat pooling under my arms and trickling down my back.

When I was a few yards from the cabins, Crusher stepped out from his door in a T-shirt, longboard shorts, and Crocs. He gestured toward the basket. "Let me carry that for you."

I had a two-second internal struggle between proving that girls didn't always need some burly guy helping them out and dropping the basket right there. My screaming muscles made a good argument, and I let Crusher take the basket from me. I tried to ignore how easily he toted the tomatoes while my fatigued arms hung limply at my sides.

"Were you taking these to the kitchen?" he asked.

"Yes, thanks." We walked around the side of the

cabins and past the pool. "By the way, congrats on the truck rally last night. I missed your big move, but everyone was talking about it." I didn't mention that I'd been busy struggling with an over-protective and abusive husband outside a bathroom while spying on Bobby Joe's mistress. That sounded like a scene from *Days of Our Lives*.

Crusher grinned, and I was reminded once more of how darn charming that smile was. "Sorry you didn't see the trick. It was unreal. A scout already contacted me this morning about finding a sponsor."

"Wow. Congratulations. You must be thrilled."

Crusher flashed his teeth again. "You bet. Last night made my entire future."

"Does that mean you're packing up and heading home?" With the rally over, I didn't see any reason for him to stay.

"Not yet. I'm meeting with the scout this afternoon, and I don't know if anyone else will be contacting me. Figured I'd stick around for a couple days. Lucky for me, you guys aren't booked up."

Esther had probably done a hoedown routine when Crusher extended his stay. I knew most of the guests were leaving today or tomorrow, and she'd need the extra revenue. We reached the back door, and I grabbed the basket handles, my fingers brushing Crusher's.

"Thanks for the help."

He held onto the basket for a moment. "No problem. I've been wanting to talk to you. I thought we could have dinner tonight."

My thoughts started spinning like a kid on a merry-go-round. Was he asking me out on a date? Or did he want to have dinner because he didn't know anyone else in town? Why, oh why, couldn't Jason and I have a defined relationship? Were we exclusive or not? Was he even still interested in dating me? He'd given me the brush-off on the phone this morning, and things hadn't exactly ended well at the cafe yesterday.

Crusher watched me, his smile drooping at the corners.

"Um, let me check my schedule," I said, stalling for time. I already knew I had exactly nothing planned for the night, but I needed a few more minutes.

Crusher let go of the basket and shrugged. "Sure, no biggie. Just an idea."

"And a good one. I'll get back to you." I felt myself blushing as I stepped in and set the basket on the table. When I turned back, Crusher was gone.

I poured myself some lemonade from the pitcher in the fridge and held the glass to my sweaty forehead. God, I was so lame when it came to the dating scene, so unlike Ashlee. Why did I have to overthink everything? Jason and I weren't married. We weren't even an official item. If an eligible guy wanted to take me to dinner, then I should go. I wasn't especially attracted to Crusher, but it still might be fun to have dinner with the guy. I only wished I didn't feel so guilty.

Zennia entered the kitchen, distracting me from my dilemma.

"Good, you brought the tomatoes. I'm about ready to plate lunch." She grabbed two tomatoes and rinsed them under the faucet, patting them dry with a towel.

I handed her the next two. "I've got some bad news," I said in a solemn voice.

Zennia paused with her hands under the faucet. "Nothing too serious, I hope."

"The Steddelbeckers are back early, so they're bound to be here for lunch."

"Then I'll give them an extra helping of this bulgur wheat salad." Zennia let out a cackle at her own deviousness. She gestured toward the basket. "If you'll finish rinsing these, then core them, I'll put the finishing touches on the salad."

I took her place at the sink as she moved to the fridge and retrieved a Tupperware bowl. I rinsed a tomato. "Has your nephew heard anything about Bobby Joe's murder?"

Zennia popped the lid off the bowl. "Now, you know my nephew would never share confidential information with me, especially since this isn't the sheriff department's case." She winked at me. "But if he did, he'd tell me that the police are taking a closer look at some guy named Todd."

I hadn't even known how tense I was until I heard that. My breath came out in a whoosh. "Thank goodness they're not focusing on Ashlee." I grabbed a serrated knife out of the block and jabbed the top of the tomato, twisting the knife to extract the core. "And I don't mind telling you that I have my own suspicions about Todd."

Zennia leaned toward me, the smell of vinegar following her. "You didn't hear this from me, and I didn't hear this from my nephew, but Todd's alibi is shaky."

I gave the knife an extra twist and spattered my shirt with tomato juice as I lost focus. "Get out of here." I snatched up the dish towel and wiped off my shirt.

Zennia nodded, then put a finger to her lips.

I gave her a two-fingered salute back, then scooped out the insides of the tomato, my mind whirring.

Todd had claimed he was with Maria the night Bobby

Joe was murdered. But if the police doubted his alibi, they might focus on Todd and forget about Ashlee. He had as much motive as she did if he knew about the affair, maybe even more. After all, he and Maria were married, and Ashlee and Bobby Joe were only dating. And judging by how hard Todd had shoved me against the wall, he was easily strong enough to crush Bobby Joe's skull. I practically hummed aloud as these thoughts ran through my head.

My euphoria lasted until I started coring the third tomato. If the police really had evidence linking Todd to the murder, they would have arrested him by now. Was there no evidence because Todd was too careful or because he wasn't guilty? Could I afford to stop poking around while I waited for the police to make an arrest? They might arrest Ashlee instead, while I sat back and did nothing. I shook my head at this thought.

"Something troubling you?" Zennia asked.

"Only thinking." I couldn't stop poking around now. I'd be letting Ashlee down. And Mom. After what Horace and Darlene had told me, I wanted to find out if Tara was really sleeping with Bobby Joe and if Donald knew. I also didn't know if Bobby Joe was really dealing drugs. Another visit to Stump might be in order. After I stopped by the gas station, of course.

I finished the last tomato, then watched Zennia fill each one. I tried not to wrinkle my nose at the piles of bulgur wheat that spilled onto the plates.

With everything ready, I made sure guests were seated in the dining room, then took the first two plates in. I set them before a brunette in her mid-forties and a silver-haired man two decades older. A few other tables were occupied.

I retrieved two more plates and delivered one to a

woman in her thirties whose lunch companion was a steamy romance novel, based on the cover with a long-haired, bare-chested man and a maiden in a corset. The woman was so engrossed in her book that she barely acknowledged me. I took the other plate to Crusher.

"Check that schedule of yours yet?" he asked, draping one arm over his chair and stretching out his long legs.

I hadn't decided about the date, so I took the easy way out. "Looks like I have to work."

Crusher crossed one ankle over the other. "All night?"

Okay, maybe that wasn't the easy way.

"We could always meet for coffee after your shift ends," Crusher said, offering me that slow smile of his.

Coffee sounded harmless. You never saw long tapered candles and white linen tablecloths at a coffeehouse. And he couldn't exactly whisper sweet nothings in my ear while the espresso maker hissed and shrieked.

I felt like smacking my forehead as a thought popped up. I shouldn't be looking at this as a date. I should be looking at this as an opportunity to find out more about how well Crusher knew Bobby Joe and where he was the night Bobby Joe was killed.

"That might work," I said. "I should be done here by seven."

"Great. I'll meet you in the lobby then. We'll grab some coffee and maybe watch the fireworks later."

Without answering, I went to retrieve more plates. The guy was smooth, I had to admit. He'd downplayed the evening by switching from dinner to coffee, then managed to ratchet it back up by throwing in the fire-works. I'd already imagined watching the fireworks with Jason, snuggling up on a picnic blanket, but I needed to adjust that picture, considering we weren't getting along right now. And stretching out the evening would give me extra time to ask about Bobby Joe.

I delivered the rest of the meals, then helped myself to a plain tomato in the kitchen, wishing I had some tuna salad or seasoned bread crumbs to stuff it with. I kept trying to build up the courage to sample more of Zennia's creations, but that bulgur wheat salad could stay right where it was in that Tupperware bowl.

Once the guests finished their meals, I cleared the tables and stopped in the office to update my time sheet before I took my lunch break.

I waved to Gordon on my way through the lobby, and he scowled in return. You had to love the guy's consistency.

But he could scowl all he wanted. I had things to do.

18

As soon as I opened the lobby door, a wave of heat washed over me, sucking the air out of my lungs. The temperature must have increased at least ten degrees since I'd collected the tomatoes.

I'd rather have gone back inside and avoided the heat, but the argument between Donald and Tara that the Steddelbeckers had overheard sounded too important to ignore. It couldn't hurt to see if either one was willing to talk, even if Donald had basically kicked me off his property the last time I'd been out there. Maybe the man had a bad memory and would have forgotten by now.

As I made my way down the walk, I shooed two ducklings back toward the pond, then crossed the sweltering parking lot. I started the car and drove down the highway, bypassing Blossom Valley and taking the off-ramp for the gas station. A pickup truck was pulling away from the gas pumps as I entered the driveway. I parked and walked into the store. The bell chimed overhead.

As my eyes adjusted to the dim lighting, I heard the

cash register door slam shut. Tara stood behind the counter. She grimaced when she saw me.

"You again," she said.

Wow, that welcome was about as warm and cozy as a cactus blanket. "Yep, it's me."

Tara stepped away from the register and crossed her arms. I noticed again how defined her biceps were. Was she strong enough to beat a man to death with a tailpipe?

"Donald won't like it if he sees me talking to you," she said.

Guess I wouldn't be getting a discount on gas anytime soon. "I'll make it fast. I heard you and Donald had quite the blowup this morning."

Tara smirked. "You friends with Tweedle-Dee and Tweedle-Dum? You should have seen those two running out of here. Donald thought they were stealing the store. Never mind that they're both so skinny they couldn't hide a Slim Jim under their shirts."

"They ran because they overheard you accuse Donald of killing Bobby Joe after he said you two were fooling around." I waited for a volatile reaction, maybe shrieking, maybe slapping, but all I got was an amused look.

"Donald didn't kill Bobby Joe."

"That's easy to say, but is it true? Maybe Donald found out that you were sleeping with Bobby Joe and slugged him with that tailpipe out of jealousy."

Tara brushed a strand of brown hair away from her face. "But I wasn't."

"Wasn't what?"

"Sleeping with Bobby Joe."

I raised my eyebrows. "Then what was Donald so mad about?"

Tara peered around the store like she thought more

customers might be hiding in the aisles. "Donald and I knew each other for only a month before we got hitched. I was waitressing at this dive down in Bakersfield when Donald came in one day and asked me out. He's about twenty years too old and a thousand hairs too bald, but I wasn't making it on my own, and I was tired of trying." She drummed her fingernails on the countertop. "So I went out with him, and when he asked me to marry him, I said yes."

I studied her nonchalant attitude, wondering if it was a front. "That's all well and good, but that still doesn't mean you weren't sleeping with Bobby Joe. I'm not saying you're the kind to cheat, but I know Bobby Joe was."

Tara gave me a world-weary smile. "I know which side my bread's buttered on. I'm not gonna risk what I have here for a quick roll in the hay, even for a guy as cute as Bobby Joe."

"So Donald is just insecure?" I suggested.

"You got it. I mean, I'm way closer to Bobby Joe's age than Donald's, and Bobby Joe did flirt with me. He'd try to be sneaky about it, but I'm sure Donald noticed."

I felt like slapping my forehead. Why had Ashlee dated Bobby Joe as long as she had? The guy was a total player.

"If you're really hell-bent on finding out who killed Bobby Joe," Tara said, "I'd look at all the boyfriends and husbands of the women Bobby Joe slept with. But trust me, I wasn't one of them."

Tara stretched her arms over her head, her boobs squeezing together and almost spilling out of her V-necked T-shirt. She tugged at the seams along the shoulder to pull up the front and gave me a defiant look. "Donald likes it when I dress this way. Now, you need to get out of here before he sees you."

The door to the back room swung open, and Donald barreled through. Too late.

Tara swallowed hard, then pointed a finger at me. "I was telling her to get out of here. We don't have anything to say."

Donald put his hands on his hips, his toupee slightly off-kilter. "Aren't you that troublemaker? What are you doing back here?"

Interviewing your wife about her extramarital affairs? Wondering if you killed a man in a jealous rage? "I saw a seashell magnet in your store the other day that I thought would be perfect for my aunt's birthday. She loves seashells, and that bright pink and yellow one is right up her alley." My aunt's birthday wasn't coming up and even if it was, no way would I buy her such an unattractive trinket, but the shell was so ugly it was the first thing that popped into my head.

Donald still frowned at me. "We're all out." Apparently the idea of a four-dollar sale wasn't enticing enough for him to forget his anger.

"Really? 'Cause I'd swear there were a good dozen on that back shelf." I craned my neck to peek around the corner. "I see a whole basket right there." Why was I harping on a seashell that I didn't even want?

"They've been recalled. Lead in the paint."

His attitude was making me ornery. I felt like grabbing that dead animal on his head and yanking it off. "Then perhaps I can find something else. A seashell night-light. Or a bottle-cap opener."

"I don't know what you're after, but I'm closing the store for a lunch break."

All I was after was answers, but clearly I wouldn't be

getting any from him. Why didn't he want me poking around?

Donald stalked across the floor, Tara watching him. I thought he was going to ram right into me, but he sidestepped me at the last minute. He went to the door and flipped the sign from OPEN to CLOSED.

"See. You need to leave."

From the obstinate look on Donald's face, he wouldn't be talking to me now. I nodded to each of them and went out to my car. I hopped in and turned on the air-conditioning, thinking. If Tara and Donald were arguing this morning, they might start up again now that I'd angered Donald. Perhaps I shouldn't be in such a hurry to leave. My lunch hour wasn't over for a while.

I sat for a few minutes, waiting for Donald to step away from the door. Instead, he stood there, immobile. With a sigh, I backed out of the space and drove across the lot, keeping an eye on the storefront in my rearview mirror. When I reached the surface road, I flipped a U and drove back past the station. Donald still waited at the door, arms crossed. So much for that plan. My little trip out here had netted me a little bit of information and a whole lot of anger. At least it had saved me from another spa lunch.

Maybe I'd have better luck with Bobby Joe's roommate. If Yolanda was right that Bobby Joe and Stump had been arguing, it might have turned physical. Pot smokers were rumored to be exceptionally mellow, but what happened when a smoker ran out of pot? Maybe he'd snapped once he'd sobered up.

The glow of the evening sun on my first visit to Bobby Joe's apartment complex must have blinded me to its many faults, because the place looked one broken window away from being condemned now that I saw it in broad daylight. Paint peeled from the buildings, the fences were faded from years in the sun, and cracks ran through the sidewalk.

All the shaded parking spots were taken, so I pulled into the same slot as on my earlier visit and parked next to a dark blue Crown Victoria. As I passed Yolanda's back patio, I saw movement through a gap in the fence planks and wondered if she was spying on me. I waved in her direction, but she didn't pop her head over the fence and wave back. Just as well.

As I neared Stump's apartment, the door opened and Detective Palmer walked out. Crap. I thought about running back to my car, but before I could, he caught sight of me. He nodded good-bye to some clean-cut guy in the doorway and walked over to me.

"I wasn't expecting to see you here," he said by way of greeting, giving me a cop stare that probably made suspects weep in fear. Lucky for me, I wasn't a suspect. At least, not yet.

"Um, yeah, I didn't expect to see you, either." The little hamster wheel I liked to call my brain spun around and around as I tried to think up a reason for my appearance. "I wanted to ask Bobby Joe's roommate about a possible service," I finally blurted out.

Detective Palmer continued to stare, and I felt my heart rate pick up.

"You couldn't call him?" he asked.

"Didn't have his number."

"Wouldn't your sister have it?"

Ack, I hadn't thought of that. "She only had Bobby Joe's cell number." Based on my ever-increasing heart rate, this lying to the cops business was definitely bad for my health. I didn't know how criminals did it.

"Say now," he said, "you wouldn't be here to ask questions about Bobby Joe, would you?"

I let out a nervous giggle. "Me? No, don't be silly."

"Good, because this is an ongoing investigation."

"Well, now, that's the problem. It's still ongoing, and my sister needs her name cleared. Have you guys made any progress at all?"

Why did I ask that? I really needed Yolanda to come out and spray me with her hose to shut me up.

"Why don't you let me worry about this investigation? I've been hearing some rumors that you're sticking your nose in this whole business. Let me make it clear that the police department does not like people interfering with a homicide case."

I didn't know who was spreading the rumors, but I'd bet it was Donald. He seemed like the type who would whine about my visit. "I would never interfere," I lied, my heart pounding so hard now that I expected to keel over any second.

We stood around in the sun for a moment until I broke the silence. "Guess I'd better let you go."

He grunted in response, gave me one last hard look, and headed toward the parking lot. I took a moment to let my heart rate slow, then approached Bobby Joe's apartment. At least I didn't have to worry about the apartment being full of pot smoke like on my first visit. Otherwise, Detective Palmer would have already hauled Stump off to jail. I rapped on the door.

The clean-shaven man I'd seen talking to the detective answered, dressed in a polo shirt and khakis. I double-checked the number on the front of the building to make sure I had the right apartment, even though I knew I did.

"Uh, hi, is Stump here?"

The guy squinted at me. "You're Ashlee's sister, right? We met a couple nights ago." He stepped to the side and gestured inside the apartment with his arm. "Won't you come in?"

I blinked, then blinked again to make sure my vision was clear. Could this possibly be the same pothead that couldn't even get off the couch when I was here before? Feeling like I'd gotten caught in an episode of *Fringe*, I moved past him into the apartment and took a sniff. Pine with the underlying scent of cannabis. I wondered if Detective Palmer had picked up on that.

A woman in a cream-colored silk blouse buttoned to the throat and an ankle-length black skirt stood up from the couch. Her hair was in a bun and a silver cross hung on the chain around her neck. She held out her hand, and I stepped forward to shake it.

"I'm Mrs. Davenport, Andrew's mother."

"I'm Dana."

She looked at me expectantly, no doubt waiting for an explanation for my presence.

"I knew Bobby Joe," I said. "My sister dated him."

Mrs. Davenport sniffed like she had suddenly noticed that pot smell. "I won't speak ill of the dead," was all she said.

Oh, boy.

"I didn't realize you had company," I said to Stump. "I can come back."

"Nonsense, little lady," a loud voice boomed from down the hall. A large man in slacks and a plaid shirt emerged from where I knew the bathroom to be, hitching up his pants as he walked. "We're not company, we're family. I'm Andy's father. Pretend we're not here."

That would be next to impossible since I wanted to ask their son about his drug habits, but I smiled all the same.

Mrs. Davenport gasped, and I turned back toward her as she covered her mouth with her hand, her pale skin darkening to crimson. She was staring at her husband, and I whipped back around in time to see Mr. Davenport zip his pants.

"You wouldn't believe how often I forget that part," he said to me. "Now what brings you by today?"

Time to improvise. "I stopped by before to pick up my sister's iPod, but she's worried she may have left other things here." If I could have given myself a trophy for such an outstanding lie, I would have.

"Why didn't she come herself?" Mr. Davenport asked.

The trouble with lying was that sometimes people asked follow-up questions. "Um, this place is full of memories of Bobby Joe, and she didn't think she could handle it. She's so heart-broken over his death." Ha! Not bad. "Say, is a funeral planned?" I asked, to keep Mr. Davenport from asking any more questions. My excuse hadn't worked so well with Detective Palmer, but maybe the Davenports were a softer touch.

"Bobby Joe's brother in Texas is arranging the funeral," Stump said. "He's having it back there as soon as he can ship the body out."

"I'm glad someone made arrangements," I said.

Stump pointed toward Bobby Joe's bedroom. "I packed up his stuff last night and found a couple things that belong to Ashlee. Hang on a second." He disappeared down the hall.

As soon as he was out of sight, Mrs. Davenport grabbed my hand. Her touch was cool and sent a shiver up my back. "I'm sorry Bobby Joe is dead, but thank heavens he doesn't live here anymore," she said in a low voice. "That boy was nothing but trouble, such a bad influence on my Andrew."

So much for not speaking ill of the dead.

"In what way?" I asked.

"He was a druggie, the little sinner," she whispered fiercely. I could almost see the fire and brimstone light up her eyes.

"You don't say?" I was guessing that Mrs. Davenport didn't know about her own son's extracurricular activities.

She nodded. "Why, we popped in for a surprise visit one time, and there was an actual bong sitting right there on that coffee table. Of course, I didn't know what it was, but Mr. Davenport recognized it."

"I watch *Cops*," Mr. Davenport said, puffing up his chest as if that made him an honorary deputy. "And you can bet I mentioned that bong to that detective who was here."

"We tried to get Andrew to move out right then, but he said rents are too high everywhere else, and he couldn't afford it. We offered to pay the difference, but Andrew always was too proud to let his parents help him."

Or maybe all of Stump's customers knew exactly where to find him, and he didn't want to inconvenience anyone by moving.

A rustling sound came from the hallway, and Stump walked out, a plastic bag in one hand. "Here are those things I mentioned." He held the bag out to me.

Before I could step forward and retrieve it, Mr.

Davenport reached over and grabbed the bag. "What have we here?"

He dipped into the bag and held up a cherry red bra, the same color as Ashlee's Camaro. He let out a whistle. "Don't see this every day."

Mr. Davenport smiled at me. I looked over and found Mrs. Davenport's mouth agape, her skin once more reddening.

"Uh, well, uh," I stammered. I grabbed the undergarment and stuffed it back in the bag. "How did that get over here?" I turned toward Mrs. Davenport. "It must be from that time Ashlee fell in the pool over here, needed a change of clothes." Did this dump even have a pool?

I backed toward the door, clutching the plastic bag to my chest. "Nice meeting you both. Thanks for the stuff, Stump, I mean Andrew. 'Bye now." I groped behind me for the doorknob, yanked the door open, and stepped out backward, almost falling. Then I pulled the door shut.

That had been a colossal waste of time. And a huge embarrassment to boot.

I stared at the door. Now what?

19

I opened the plastic bag I'd grabbed from Stump and saw a tube of lip gloss, a pack of gum, and, of course, the flaming red bra. He shouldn't have bothered. I squashed the bag in my hand and headed for my car. As I reached the curb, I heard a "psst." Yolanda stood in the doorway to her apartment, holding up one finger.

She trotted down the walk, clutching her housedress closed at the throat, her bunny slippers scraping the sidewalk. Her hair was up in curlers, and she smelled vaguely of Ponds cold cream, a smell my brain had trouble dealing with in the middle of the day.

"What are you doing back so soon? You an under-cover cop?" she asked, breathless.

"Not a cop. I just needed to check on something," I said vaguely. Who knew if her gossip grapevine was comprised of a single plant or an entire vineyard. I didn't need my business spilled like wine from a tipped-over bottle.

She glanced over her shoulder in the general direction of Bobby Joe's apartment. "Did you see those two druggies while you were there? Awful old to be smoking dope, but maybe they were flower children."

"Actually, they're Stump's parents."

Yolanda raised her hands toward the sky, causing her housedress to fall open and reveal a whole lot of wrinkled flesh. I averted my eyes.

"I should have known they were all druggies. The apple never falls far from the tree."

I started to correct her, then stopped. What was the point?

"I need to get back to work now," I said. "Have a good day."

"Come visit me sometime. I'll make you tea." She shuffled into her apartment while I got back in my car.

Once in the driver's seat, I stared out the windshield for a moment, the patch of dead grass to the side of the path a perfect metaphor for my visit. Not only had I failed to ask Stump about Bobby Joe selling drugs, but now I had to doubt everything Yolanda told me. If she assumed Stump's parents were users, especially when his mom dressed almost like the Amish, then she might assume anyone was a user. Even me. Maybe Ashlee was right, and Yolanda saw a felon everywhere she looked.

I drove out of the lot, sweaty and out of sorts. Would I ever figure out who killed Bobby Joe and keep Ashlee from going to jail?

I thought about this question as I sped to the farm. My conversations at Bobby Joe's apartment had taken longer than expected, and my lunch hour was long over. I entered the lot and slipped into the first open slot. I'd barely gotten out of the car before I heard, "Dana!"

Gordon strode toward me, back straight, arms held

stiff at his sides. My stomach lowered a notch as I wondered what I'd done now.

"Where have you been?" Gordon barked as he neared me.

My internal temperature shot up a few degrees, and not from the heat. "At lunch."

"Did you forget about your two o'clock interview for the yoga position?"

Oh, crap, was that today?

When I didn't speak, Gordon moved closer and pointed toward the house. "That woman has been in the lobby for twenty minutes, chanting and standing on her head. We can't let the guests see that nonsense."

"I lost track of the time. I'll talk to her right now." I hurried toward the lobby, Gordon puffing behind me.

"Get your mind on your work, or we're going to have a problem," he threatened.

I didn't respond, but Gordon was right. First, I'd apparently forgotten about the demographics report, now this yoga interview. I couldn't afford to lose my job. I'd have to look into Bobby Joe's murder during non-work hours, even if I was trying to keep my sister from being arrested.

Inside the lobby, I stared at the woman in the neon green leotard, legs folded into the lotus position at right below eye level, her head on the floor. I could hear her repeating "ohm" over and over.

Gordon caught up with me and shoved a paper into my hands. "Her résumé, not that we're going to hire her," he muttered.

I scanned the sheet. "Ms. Mansfield?" I said to the upside-down woman.

The humming stopped. The woman unfolded her legs, swung them to the floor, and stood up. I pegged her age at somewhere in her early sixties. She certainly had good form and muscle control—better than me, in fact, and I was half her age.

Ms. Mansfield practically glided across the room and grasped my hands, crinkling the résumé that I still held. "My child, we are kindred spirits. I sense it already. Call me Lightsource."

Lord, another quack.

She released my hands and began stroking my hair. "Our chakras are spinning in unison."

I nodded, at a loss for words as I tried to feel my chakra spinning, wherever my chakra was.

Out of the corner of my eye, I saw Gordon with his fist covering his mouth, fighting back laughter. The man almost never laughed. At least one of us was having a good time.

His mirth snapped me back to attention. "Ms. Mansfield, er, Lightsource, why don't we sit down, and you can tell me how long you've been practicing yoga."

I led her to the empty dining room, where I settled in a chair. She moved the chair across from mine aside, spread her feet apart, and stretched to one side until her hands rested on the floor next to one foot.

"What are you doing?" I asked.

"I think better this way, with all the blood flowing to my brain, fueling my thoughts. Perhaps you'd like to try it."

"I'll pass. Why don't you tell me about your yoga experience?"

And she did. For a good ten minutes. Nonstop. I wasn't sure where to look during her monologue. I couldn't see her face at all, so I eventually built towers out of the forks and knives on the table, panicking each time the silverware clinked, but I guess Lightsource couldn't hear me with her ears so close to the floor, because she never stopped talking.

As I tried to balance a knife atop my fork tepee, I noticed that Lightsource had gone quiet.

"How interesting," I said, hoping that fit with what she'd just said. "Do you know anything about Pilates, by any chance? We'd like to offer that to the guests as well."

Lightsource's head popped up, her kinky gray hair springing out in all directions. I laid the silverware down.

"Do you mean real Pilates, or that Hollywood tripe?" she asked.

I actually didn't know the difference, but her question made the correct answer clear. "The real version. We pride ourselves on authenticity here at the spa."

She tried to smooth down her hair, but several sections refused to obey. "I felt that prideful aura as soon as I walked in. Some of the townsfolk feel this spa is cursed, but I only sense lightness and joy here."

"Cursed?"

"Blossom Valley was always such a safe place, but the same weekend this spa opened, someone was killed. Now, all these weeks later, another life has been stolen. People blame the O'Connell farm for the murders. Things like that never happened before you opened up."

I felt personally insulted that people were gossiping about Esther's farm. It wasn't our fault people were being murdered. We weren't killing anyone.

"The O'Connell Organic Farm and Spa is not responsible for anyone's death."

Lightsource patted my hand. "I can feel the innocence here. I know I'll fit in."

That was my signal to wrap this interview up. "You certainly know your yoga. Thanks for coming in." I escorted her out to the lobby, where she hugged me as though we were best friends and she was going away on a spiritual retreat for the next year.

From behind the counter, Gordon watched Lightsource leave and spoke as soon as the door closed. "Good riddance. Why are only yahoos applying for this job?"

"Lightsource has a lot of yoga experience. If she wouldn't spend the entire class standing on her head, she might be a good fit."

Gordon grunted. "We'll keep trying. Someone normal's bound to apply."

"Well, keep her on the potentials list until that happens." We definitely needed a new yoga instructor, even if she stood on her head. Other than yoga and Pilates, soaking in the hot springs was the only other spa service offered at the O'Connell Organic Farm and Spa. If we didn't hire someone soon, we'd have to change the name of the place to just the O'Connell Organic Farm.

I wandered down the hall toward the office and spent the afternoon working on the next morning's blog, helping with the laundry, and cleaning out the pigsty. After I'd put the rake and shovel back in the toolshed, I washed my hands at the outside faucet, then went into the kitchen and checked the clock. Not quite five.

Since I'd taken a late lunch and had to meet Crusher here at seven, I'd been planning on helping Zennia with dinner. But I couldn't go to coffee smelling like a pigsty, even if this wasn't a date. At least I kept telling myself it wasn't a date. Who knew what Crusher thought.

I clocked out, raced home, and jumped in the shower,

then ran a brush through my hair and frowned at my reflection. I added lip gloss, mascara, a touch of eye shadow, and a swipe of blush. Not bad.

Now to figure out what to wear. For a non-date, I was certainly putting effort into my appearance.

I stood before my closet and examined my options. It was never more apparent how few clothes I owned than when I was going out for the evening. I still owned several business outfits from my marketing days in San Jose, but I hadn't done much to restock my casual clothes since my return. I reached for one of only a handful of dresses, a light, floral, knee-length number, then drew my hand back. Too fancy for a non-date. Instead, I donned a pair of black leggings and topped them with a flowy baby-doll blouse that dipped in the front. A pair of ballet flats completed my ensemble. That would do fine.

My alarm clock glowed the time, half past five. Still time for dinner.

In the kitchen, Mom waved away my offer of help, so I slid onto a bar stool to keep her company. I could hear the faint strains of the television drifting in from the living room and wondered what show Ashlee was watching.

Mom pulled a package from the refrigerator and set it on the cutting board. We were having chicken. Again. Sometimes I half-expected to cluck instead of speak when I opened my mouth.

"How are you doing, Mom?" I asked, feeling we hadn't spent much time together lately. I flipped open the day's edition of the *Herald* and scanned it for any new articles on the murder.

Mom cut open the package. "Can't complain. I had lunch with my bunco group today."

"I didn't realize you guys socialized outside your games."

"We don't usually, but we wanted to welcome the new members I told you about."

Her voice sounded funny, and I glanced up. She held the knife over the chicken but didn't move.

"Mom?" I prompted.

She lowered the knife and laid it on the board. "I don't want to upset you girls, but I have to tell you something. I might have dinner with one of the new members."

"Why would that upset us?"

"He's a man."

If I hadn't started gripping the counter so hard, I would have fallen right off the bar stool. "Are you talking about a date?" I asked, my voice barely above a whisper.

"I suppose you could call it that."

"But what about Dad?"

Mom came around the counter and rubbed my back, much like whenever I was sick as a child.

"I loved your father so much," she said. "I still do. But I miss the companionship of a man. Having someone to dine with, to dance with, to laugh with. It's not like Lane and I will get married. He's simply asked me to dinner."

"And you said yes?" I couldn't quite get a handle on what Mom was saying. She was a grieving widow. Right? Why would she accept this man's dinner invitation?

Mom rubbed my back faster, sensing my resistance. "Yes, but now I'm wondering if I should go. With everything that's happening with Ashlee, you girls need me here at home."

I let go of the counter edge and faced her. "I'm glad to hear you say that. Ashlee's really suffering right now."

As if on cue, Ashlee let out a loud laugh from the living room.

"She's good at hiding her pain," I said.

Mom studied my face. "I'll call Lane after dinner and tell him no." She went back to preparing the chicken.

I laid my head on the counter, the tile cool against my forehead. Instead of feeling relieved that Mom would cancel her date, I felt like a big, fat turd. How could I begrudge Mom a little happiness? If she was ready to start dating again, shouldn't I support her?

"Dana, are you feeling all right?" Mom asked.

I lifted my head. "Forget what I said, Mom. You should go to dinner with Lane. Ashlee and I will be fine."

Mom raised one eyebrow, her way of saying she suspected I was lying.

"Seriously, go. You caught me by surprise, is all."

"If you're sure." But I could tell she was pleased, and I felt a tiny bit better. But only a tiny bit.

Not wanting to talk about Mom dating anymore, I went into the living room and saw that Ashlee was watching a *Real Housewives* show. I had no idea which one.

She glanced at me, then did a double take and muted the TV. I'd almost forgotten about my prep work for my non-date and wished I'd stayed in the kitchen. Couldn't she ignore me like she usually did?

"Hot date with Jason tonight?"

I dropped into the recliner and decided to play dumb. "What makes you say that?"

"You're wearing makeup. And not only eyeliner or

lip gloss." She made a circular motion around her head with her hand. "You did your whole face."

Ashlee couldn't see a four-foot pothole in the middle of the road when she drove, but she could detect the faintest trace of eye shadow with no problem.

"I'm going out later, that's all. Maybe watch the fireworks."

Ashlee stared at me, a smile starting to grow.

"What?" I demanded.

"You're going out with somebody, but it's not Jason."

"So?"

Ashlee giggled. She actually giggled. "You're always so prim and proper. It'll do you good to date around, play the field."

But I didn't want to play the field. "Calm down. I'm only going out for coffee."

Ashlee leaned over the arm of the couch, her interest in the dueling housewives gone. "With who?"

"Crusher."

Ashlee clapped her hands. "He's so cute. You should totally go for it." She reached for my arm. "And don't worry about me. I'd already decided I didn't want him."

"I wasn't worried about you. It's not even a date."

"Of course it is."

I straightened in the chair, the springs in the worn cushion shifting under me. "For your information, I'm helping you. I've tried talking to Crusher before about Bobby Joe, and he's always changed the subject. This could be my chance to figure out what he's hiding."

"Oh, stop," Ashlee said. "You're only pretending to question Crusher because you don't want to admit you're on a date."

"I am not."

"Dinner!" Mom called from the other room.

I glared at Ashlee as I rose from the chair. Between Mom dating and me not dating, I'd had just about enough date talk.

"Not another word," I warned her. I stalked into the kitchen, my thoughts full of fireworks and murder.

20

By the time I'd finished dinner and cleared the table, seven o'clock was fast approaching. I brushed my hair one last time, spritzed it with hairspray for no other reason than I saw Ashlee do it all the time, then drove to the spa. As I thought about what questions to ask Crusher, the dinner in my stomach jumped and flipped and wouldn't stay still. Surely it wasn't nerves. Must be the wild rice Mom had served with the chicken.

As soon as I entered the lobby, Crusher stood up from the love seat. He wore faded jeans with the knees torn open and a T-shirt that was thinning around the collar. Thank God I'd skipped the dress.

"Ready?" he asked, moving past me and opening the door I'd come through.

"Yep." I followed him across the parking lot to his Chevy truck. From a distance, the truck had looked fairly normal. Up close, it was a younger brother to his professional monster truck, big tires and all.

Crusher swung open the passenger door, and I stood there for a moment, looking up, then up some more. I put my foot on the side step, gripped the inside door handle, and pulled myself in, Crusher giving me a butt shove to make sure I made it.

"Gee, thanks," I called down to him. He grinned, then went around to his side and clambered in like a Cirque de Soleil performer.

The truck rumbled to life, and he drove us to The Daily Grind, Blossom Valley's coffeehouse. Crusher parked and jumped out, but I managed to find my way to the ground before he could rush around and help. Who knew what he'd grab this time. We crossed the parking lot and entered the coffeehouse.

If Starbucks and Cracker Barrel ever had a baby, it'd resemble the inside of The Daily Grind. Gleaming stainless-steel espresso makers hissed behind the shiny brown counter while jars of local jams and pickled vegetables vied for attention on the display stands that lined the front.

We ordered our coffees at the counter. Crusher pulled out his wallet, held it open, and turned to me with a sheepish grin.

"I forgot to stop by the ATM. You mind paying?"

I didn't bother pointing to the debit card swiper attached to the counter. I'd already pulled out a few bills for my own coffee, and a few more wouldn't cause too much damage. I handed over the money.

"I'll pay next time. I get that check for winning the rally in another week or two," Crusher said, grabbing a stack of napkins off the counter.

"It's really no problem," I said.

We found a vacant cafe table to wait for our drinks. The table next to us held a couple of teenagers, the gangly guy tapping his foot and running his tongue over his braces, the girl glancing between her date and the table while twirling her hair around her finger. I felt awkward just watching them.

The barista called Crusher's name, and he retrieved our beverages, his a triple-shot espresso, mine a white chocolate mocha. Crusher smiled at me while I fiddled with a stirrer. I sipped my coffee, burning my tongue, while Crusher smiled some more. I glanced at the teens next to me. Awkwardness must be contagious.

"How long have you been doing the monster truck thing?" I asked, wanting to end the silence and get down to business.

"Since I got my license way back when."

I blew on my coffee. "You must be good to be in the business so long."

"I started like gangbusters. After I apprenticed for a couple of years and got a special license, I got a chance to get behind the wheel and started winning rallies left and right. I love to hear the cheers, even the boos. Means I'm grabbing people's attention."

"So you see this as a long-term career?" I wondered how much money a monster truck driver made if they weren't one of the big names with all their sponsors and endorsements.

"You bet. I hit a rough patch the last couple of years. My ego got in the way. But now I'm back on track."

At least he admitted his shortcomings. "Didn't you say you were meeting that scout today? How did that go?"

Crusher leaned back in his chair, all swagger. "Great. He can get me a deal with Charging Bull Soda. That'll mean some big bucks."

"Maybe you can decorate your truck like a matador to go with the bull theme."

"El Toro Loco's already cornered that market, but

we'll come up with something as rad." Crusher tossed his head to flip a lock of hair out of his eyes. I bet he practiced that in front of the mirror.

"What about you?" he asked. "You worked at that spa long?"

I grabbed one of his napkins and swiped at a drop of coffee on the table. "Only a few months. I used to live in the Bay Area, worked for a computer company in the marketing department. But with the recession and layoffs, I had to move back home. Plus my mom needed me."

Crusher leaned forward, his eyes softening in concern. "Why's that?"

"My dad passed away, and she wasn't handling it well."

"Sorry about your old man."

"Thanks." Talking about my dad reminded me that Mom had a dinner date this week. I changed the subject before Crusher could ask anything more about my parents. "So where'd you grow up?"

We chatted about Crusher's upbringing in San Diego with his military father and his three older brothers. As we talked, the sky out the window faded from oranges and reds to grays. The coffee level in my cup got lower and lower.

When we'd reached present day in Crusher's history, I managed to steer the conversation around to Bobby Joe. "I didn't notice people talking about Bobby Joe's death at the rally. I thought the announcer might say a few words."

Crusher turned his cup around and around in his hands. "He didn't have a big enough name in the sport yet. But you can bet us drivers were talking about it."

"What were you guys saying?"

"Just shooting the shit about who might have crushed his head like that. Someone must have been pretty damn mad."

I felt the stirrings of interest. Finally, an inside opinion.

"Did you come up with anyone?"

Crusher drained the last drops of espresso. "Not much. Some of the guys were there the night he died and saw some girl yelling at him."

The stirrings in my stomach sped up. "That girl is my sister."

Crusher reddened. "You mentioned that."

"Did you hear her yelling yourself?"

"Naw, I was back at the spa pretty early that night. Most people don't realize how hard driving a truck that size is. We have to be in shape like any other athlete. I try to get to bed early the week of a rally."

I couldn't equate driving around in a circle with tackling a quarterback or swimming a hundred meters. "How about the drivers? Any of the others dislike Bobby Joe?"

Crusher popped the top off his coffee cup and peered inside, making me wonder if he was looking for the answer in there.

"Everybody gets along on the circuit. We're like a big family, and Bobby Joe was a pretty cool dude. He didn't have any enemies."

Apparently Crusher hadn't heard about the spurned husband or the angry boss.

He gestured toward the window, where we could see the sidewalk crowding up. "What's with all the people? Is it for the fireworks?"

"Probably. That used to be the big thing around here

when I was a teenager. Not much has changed in the
ten years I've been gone."

"We should grab a spot. Where's the best view?"

He hadn't officially asked if I wanted to join him for
the fireworks, but it seemed ridiculous to go home now
that they'd be starting any minute.

"The park. We can walk from here."

Crusher followed me out of the coffeehouse, and
we stepped onto the sidewalk, merging with a staggered
line of people headed toward the town park and its
large lawn area. A little girl, dragging her mom by the
hand, brushed past us, clearly intent on getting a
good seat.

The lawn was already half full, the largest clump of
people sitting in the middle section away from the trees.
We threaded our way through the picnic blankets and
lawn chairs, searching for a patch of vacant grass. As we
passed a group of women about my age, one of them
nudged her companion and pointed. Then all the
women leaned close together and started chatting.

They must have recognized Crusher from last night's
rally. I felt momentary pride at being seen with a
pseudo-celebrity.

He stopped at a small area between a row of ice
chests and more blankets. We settled onto the grass together while two women to my right noticed us and
started whispering. Guess he was a bigger draw than I'd
realized.

The sky was darkening quickly. I plucked at the grass
and listened as he told me more about San Diego and
what a big shot he used to be. Finally, the sky was black,
the park lit by nearby streetlights. The crowd's mur-
murs grew louder in anticipation, everyone knowing
the show was about to begin.

"This is it," Crusher said, straightening up and staring expectantly at the sky.

As I shifted from kneeling to a cross-legged position, my gaze picked out a familiar shape. I froze. Jason moved among the spectators on the grass, notebook in hand, stopping to chat with the occasional John Q. Citizen.

Shoot. I didn't want him to see me here with Crusher. He might misinterpret the situation. I hunkered down, hoping he wouldn't spot me in the dim light. He weaved among the blankets, getting closer.

"Man, I can't believe how excited I am over a bunch of fireworks," Crusher said.

"Yeah, me too," I practically whispered, though Jason couldn't possibly hear me.

When he was still a good twenty feet away, he glanced over just as I looked at him. He noticed Crusher next to me and visibly frowned, then turned and headed in the opposite direction.

The pain from the guilt and disappointment in myself was so acute that I momentarily thought my appendix had burst. I half-rose, prepared to go after him, explain that this wasn't a date, that I only wanted to ask Crusher about Bobby Joe.

One of the fireworks exploded in the night sky. The people in the crowd lifted their faces, murmuring oohs and aahs, and my own gaze was drawn to the sight. I watched the smiley face collapse into a line of sparkles, then wink out, the smell of gunpowder drifting in the air.

I looked back to where Jason had been, in time to see him disappear among the trees on the edge of the park.

Crap. I was too late.

21

The fireworks show streamed by me in a blur. Every time I tried to focus, my mind replayed Jason's face when he'd caught sight of Crusher and me. The grand finale arrived, full of horsetails and clusters, but even that couldn't hold my attention.

As the last sparkler faded away, Crusher rose and brushed off the seat of his pants, then held out a hand. I grabbed it and stood, twisting from side to side to loosen my muscles.

"Great show," I said, even if I barely remembered any of it.

"Yeah. It's been a long time since I saw fireworks."

We moved with the rest of the crowd across the park and back onto the sidewalk. Groups of walkers turned onto side streets, while most stayed on the main drag.

When we reached Crusher's truck, he opened the passenger door and helped boost me inside once more, making me realize I could never seriously date someone who drove such a tall truck. I felt like a damsel in need of rescue, a ridiculous feeling for something as simple as getting into a car.

I started to pull the door closed but stopped when I heard someone call Crusher's name. A man was making his way through the throng of people, heading toward the truck. Gold chains dangled around his open collar, and a gold bracelet flashed under the streetlight. He wore nice slacks and dress shoes, his attire in sharp contrast to everyone else's tank tops and shorts.

"Crusher," he hollered again as he maneuvered around a stroller, "we need to talk."

Crusher jumped into the driver's seat and slid over to where I sat, sticking one hand out the still-open door. "We'll get together," he called to the guy. "Don't worry."

The man pushed forward faster, his expression obscured by the darkness as he moved away from the streetlight. "Wait right there," he yelled.

"I'll call you, man." Crusher moved back to his side and slammed his door shut. I followed suit, and he fired up the truck. The exit on the other side of the lot was free of foot traffic. He roared onto the street and away from the coffee shop and pedestrians.

I looked in the side mirror and saw that the man had disentangled himself from the crowd. He stood in the parking spot we had vacated, staring after us.

I glanced at Crusher, who was breathing a little heavily. "What was that about?" I had to practically shout to be heard over the engine.

He shrugged, loosening his grip on the steering wheel and draping one wrist over the top. "He's an old friend."

"Do you always run from your old friends?" Maybe that guy was an old friend like Kimmie was an old friend. God knows I wanted to run from her half the time.

Crusher forced out a laugh. "I wasn't running." He adjusted the rearview mirror. Checking to see if we were being followed, maybe? "He's a nice guy, but he's a drinker. I didn't want him to ruin the evening."

The man hadn't looked drunk, but I'd only seen him for a moment, and the area wasn't well lit.

We rode without further talk to the farm, me thinking about Jason, Crusher probably thinking about that guy in the parking lot. Or his next monster truck event. Or ham sandwiches. I really didn't know the guy.

Once Crusher parked, I opened the door and slid to the ground, already digging my keys from the depths of my purse. I pulled them out with a jangle as Crusher came around to my side.

"This place have any booze?" he asked. "Maybe you can dig some out of the kitchen and join me in my room for a nightcap."

Either he didn't notice my keys or he was trying to change my mind. Either way, I wasn't interested. Crusher was definitely charming in a surfer boy way, but this wasn't a date. Besides, we had no connection. That realization had been cemented the moment I saw Jason at the park and knew I'd rather enjoy the fireworks with him.

"Thanks, but I have an early day tomorrow." I was careful not to say, "Maybe next time." I didn't want to give him false hope.

Crusher twisted to the side a little and surreptitiously cupped a hand in front of his mouth to smell his breath, like bad breath was the only reason I might turn him down. Then he turned back with a slight frown. "Sorry to hear that. This is good-night then." He stepped toward me at the same time I stepped back, keys held up as a blocker.

"Right. Good-night."

Crusher shrugged. "It was worth a shot." He gestured across the parking lot. "At least let me walk you to your car."

"I'm a big girl. I can make it." I offered a smile to take the sting out of my words.

I walked to my car alone and slid behind the wheel. When I looked back, Crusher still stood next to his truck, checking his reflection in the side mirror. Guess he wasn't used to being rebuffed.

Traffic was light, and I pulled into my driveway minutes later. As soon as I got inside, I slipped into my room and tried to call Jason. No answer. I debated leaving a voice mail, then decided against it. I'd try again in the morning.

I changed out of my leggings and top, threw on a T-shirt and pajama shorts, brushed my teeth, and climbed into bed.

The next morning, my alarm blared at six. Why did I insist on torturing myself by getting up so early? The spa had no set work hours. I needed to learn to sleep in.

My brain felt foggy as I slogged my way through high-fiber cereal and an overripe banana. In the light of day, my guilt from last night had faded like the shadows caused by the moon. We were all adults here. Jason and I weren't exclusive. And besides, I hadn't even been on a date.

I slipped on my Keds, waved good-bye to Mom as she emerged from her bedroom, and drove to work.

The branches of the pear trees that lined the highway drooped as if too exhausted to hold up the weight of the fruit. Even the dragonflies that usually buzzed along the highway had taken the morning off. Now that the three-day weekend was coming to a close, most guests would be leaving the spa this morning, and I was looking forward to a slow and peaceful workday.

In the parking lot, a young couple loaded a rolling suitcase into the trunk of their Subaru, no doubt anxious to get on the road before the temperature soared. I parked in my usual spot and went straight to the office to post the spa's blog, then opened a marketing document I'd started a few days ago. I'd decided to target niche markets to promote the spa. Writers-retreats ads would appear in *Writer's Digest* or *The Writer,* family-fun trips would be advertised in *Parents* magazine, and healthy-living vacation ads would appear in *Whole Living* and *Health*—provided Esther's budget could handle the cost. Esther was so concerned about money that we currently only advertised in a handful of papers, all small and independent. I spent the next hour or so fleshing out my ideas and fine-tuning the proposal for each magazine.

Satisfied, I leaned back in the desk chair and contemplated how to spend the rest of the day. Swim in the pool under the guise of cleaning it? Help Zennia in the air-conditioned kitchen? Maybe I could convince her to make soy ice cream. I might even eat some. Or maybe, instead of thinking up ways to pretend to be working, I should be worried about how little work there was for me to begin with. I'm sure Gordon hadn't missed that detail.

The office door opened, and Esther poked her head in.

"Dana, my favorite peach."

I crossed my fingers that whatever project she was

about to dump on me wouldn't involve manure, compost, or ducklings.

"What's up?" I asked.

"You remember the other day when I mentioned the town's Rejuvenation Committee was thinking up ideas?"

I nodded slowly, wondering where this was going.

"We've picked our project, and you're just the person for this little job."

I bit back a groan. The last time I'd helped the committee I'd set up chairs for the cricket-chirping contest. Not exactly a bullet point to add to my résumé. "What's the project?"

She clasped her hands together. "Window painting at local businesses."

Sometimes I wondered if the committee members were drunk when they thought up these plans. "Where do I fit in?"

"You'll be doing the painting, silly. Several of the downtown shops have signed up. They figure cute little window paintings will draw in the tourists. Get people to stop and come in their stores."

I held up my hand like I was under oath. "I'm not an artist. I can barely paint over scuff marks on the walls."

Esther waved her hand as though my concerns held no more weight than a helium balloon. "We have stencils. You don't need talent."

Good thing. "Did George or Bethany consider doing the painting?" I knew Esther's arthritis bothered her, but the other two committee members were fit and able the last time I'd seen them.

"You know what a fusspot George is. He can't possibly leave that teenage helper of his to run the tire shop, and Bethany works by herself. She can't afford to close the flower shop for even one day with business so slow already."

I sighed in resignation.

Esther took that as consent and beamed. "I knew you'd do it. I've left the supplies in the toolshed. We really should have done this before the holiday weekend, but that egg's already hatched." She toddled off, humming.

So much for my relaxing workday. Oh well. I wasn't getting paid to be lazy.

I looked down at my work shirt, wondering if Esther had included a smock in the supplies, then rose to my feet. I stopped in the kitchen long enough to let Zennia know I wouldn't be helping with the lunch service, and went out the back door to the toolshed. As promised, a large cardboard box containing several paint cans, brushes, and other odds and ends sat on the floor of the shed, wedged between the lawn mower and the edger.

I dragged the box across the floor until it was free of its neighbors, then hefted it up, the cans clanking against each other. With back arched and knees slightly bent, I staggered down the path to my car and dropped the box on the pavement near the trunk.

My clothes already felt sticky, and I hadn't even made it out of the parking lot yet. I swiped my arm across my forehead before I popped the trunk and loaded the box. A sheet of paper tucked to the side of the paint cans caught my eye, and I pulled it out. Five downtown businesses were the lucky recipients of my stenciling skills today. Get the Scoop would be my first stop. How hard could it be to draw ice cream cones, with or without stencils?

I drove into town and down Main Street. As I approached the ice cream parlor, a man backed his Oldsmobile from a spot in front of the shop, and I swooped in, studying the storefront as I shut off the engine.

GET THE SCOOP arched across the top half of the large plate-glass window, the empty bottom half beckoning me to fill it with bright colors and yummy treats.

I spread the drop cloth on the pavement before the window, set the paint cans on top, and grabbed the stencils. A dog. A horse. A unisex person. Not the widest selection, but I'd have to make it work.

Armed with only a vague idea of what to paint, I stared at the blank windowpane that was no longer beckoning me. Now it was blatantly mocking me. Stupid window. The list of businesses didn't mention what I was supposed to paint for each, but an ice cream sundae should be easy enough. I used a screwdriver I'd found at the bottom of the box to pop the top off the paint can marked "Pink."

With a shaky breath and even shakier hand, I dipped in a brush and stuck the paint on the window, smearing it into a circular shape. One strawberry scoop down. As I worked, people walked in and out of the shop. Business was brisk on such a hot day, even before lunch.

I wiped my brush clean, dipped it in the white paint, and painted a circle shape with it next to the pink one, then stepped back.

Not the best scoops. But they'd be more recognizable after I painted the dish underneath and the cherry on top. I crouched down to add the finishing touches.

Down the block, a bell tinkled as someone opened a door. I glanced over and saw Kimmie emerge from For

Richer, Not Poorer, the high-end boutique that had opened two weeks ago in the space once occupied by a video store. The handle of a sky-blue shopping bag hung over one forearm as she pushed a stroller before her. As far as I knew, Kimmie didn't have children. Maybe she was babysitting. I wouldn't trust her with small children, but others might.

As Kimmie headed in my direction, a battered brown Nissan Altima with that boxy style from the eighties pulled into a parking space and sputtered to a stop. Maria stepped out of the car, dressed in her waitress uniform, the pink matching the color of my ice cream scoop.

I sucked in my breath. The moment I'd been waiting for had arrived. Maria might abandon her work in the middle of a shift or pull a disappearing act in a bathroom, but she couldn't escape me this time.

Maria was going to answer my questions.

Right now.

22

Before I could drop my paintbrush and tackle Maria to question her about Bobby Joe, Kimmie let out a sound that was half squeal, half cry. Maria stepped back so fast, she almost stumbled off the curb. She swayed a little as she regained her balance.

"Maria, you poor dear," Kimmie said, abandoning the stroller and grabbing Maria's elbows before she could escape. "You must be so upset."

"What do you mean?" Maria asked in a high-pitched voice that bordered on hysteria.

They stood only a few feet away, and I leaned my ear toward the two, my body partially blocked by the ice cream shop's sandwich board.

"You know, with Bobby Joe dead. And you being the other woman." Kimmie stage-whispered the last part, adding to the drama she was creating.

Guess Kimmie would be questioning Maria for me. I dipped the brush into the white again, pretending to work while I listened to the two women.

"I had nothing to do with Bobby Joe's death," Maria squeaked. I risked a peek in her direction. She reminded me of a kitten trying to avoid a bath, twisting side to side while Kimmie kept a solid grip.

"Well, not directly. No one thinks you killed him yourself, but everyone knows about your husband's temper."

At the truck rally, Kimmie had implied that everyone thought Ashlee had killed Bobby Joe. Either she'd changed her mind, or she just liked to say things to upset people.

"Todd doesn't have a temper," Maria protested. "What are you talking about?"

"Your mom told me about how he . . . I don't even want to mention it." I assumed Kimmie was referring to Todd's abuse.

Maria went from a distressed kitten to an enraged tiger. She gave a rather vicious twist and managed to free one arm. "My mother needs to mind her own business," she snapped.

Kimmie let go of the other arm, her blue bag rustling. "She cares about you, like any good mother. If Todd killed Bobby Joe, he'll go to prison, and he won't be able to harm you anymore. You can get away from him."

Maria's face paled, and her demeanor shrank back to kitten status. "Todd didn't kill anyone. He was home, with me. That's what I told the police, and you can't prove any different."

My ears perked up at the uncertainty in her voice. Was Maria lying to protect her husband? I leaned farther into the sandwich board and loosened my grip on the paintbrush. It slapped against my leg. I let out a grunt as I jumped to my feet, grabbing a corner of the drop cloth to swipe at the white smear on my bare calf.

I noticed the voices had gone silent and looked up to

find both women staring at me, Kimmie's lips forming a smirk, Maria's mouth agape.

"Dana," Kimmie said, "I didn't see you hiding there behind the sign." The delight in her voice was obvious.

I straightened up, trying to muster a hint of dignity. "I wasn't hiding. I was painting. Volunteer work for the Blossom Valley Rejuvenation Committee." I gestured to the window.

Kimmie squinted at my drawings. "Are those butt cheeks? Why are they two different colors?"

What was wrong with Kimmie? Why would I be drawing butt cheeks on a window? "They're ice cream scoops."

Kimmie scoffed. "If you say so."

Maria had remained silent during our little exchange. Now she backed off the sidewalk, felt behind her for her car door handle, and wrenched the door open. "I gotta go." She slipped into the car, started the motor, and backed into the street before she even shut the car door.

Was she trying to escape Kimmie's clutches or avoid me? She sped down the street, once more managing to get away before I could ask her a single thing.

I turned to Kimmie, who was now my only option for finding out anything. "I couldn't help but overhear what you two were saying."

There went that smirk again.

"Do you really think her husband was home that night?"

Kimmie pursed her lips, already savoring the delicious morsel she was about to hand me. "Not according to her mother, Rosa."

"Really," I said, prodding her along. This information

jibed with Zennia's comment that Todd's alibi might be shaky.

"Rosa knows that my husband and I hire only the best, and that includes lawyers. She asked my advice on whether Maria needs an attorney since she lied to the police." Kimmie brushed her long hair away from her face. "Of course, Rosa couldn't afford our lawyers, not on a paltry maid's salary."

Far be it from me to point out that Kimmie was providing that salary and that she should give Rosa a raise if the money was so paltry.

"And Rosa said Maria had lied about the alibi?" I asked.

"Are you still trying to solve the murder? I figured you'd give up by now. Let the police take care of it."

I set my brush on the edge of the paint can. "I'm not stopping until the police arrest the killer. Did Maria lie about Todd's alibi or not?"

Kimmie patted the baby in the stroller, and it whined, an odd sound for a baby. "Rosa didn't admit that in so many words, but it was pretty clear." A large crowd came down the sidewalk and moved inside the ice cream shop. Kimmie eyed them. "I'd better get in there before the next herd of people shows up. I don't have time to waste in line."

She wheeled the stroller past me, and I glanced inside. A miniature poodle peered back at me, bug eyes watering, body trembling. A bonnet was tied under the dog's chin, like something an actual baby might wear. Leave it to Kimmie to take dog pampering to the next level.

Through the window, I watched as she tried to sidle up to the front of the line with her stroller, then retreated to the end of the queue when no one let her in.

I went back to painting. I needed brown for my Neapolitan sundae. I added that scoop, then drew a clumsy dish under the three scoops. Now no one else would mistake my masterpiece for a rear end.

I grabbed the person stencil out of the box and lined it up so one hand appeared to be holding the dish. While I filled in the arms and legs, I thought about what I'd overheard and what Kimmie had told me. Between Todd's abuse of Maria and his physical assault on me at the truck rally, he clearly had a bad enough temper to kill someone in a rage. That gave him means. And Bobby Joe's affair with his wife was a solid motive. If he'd lied about his alibi, that gave him opportunity, too.

I colored in the stenciled face and cleaned my brush.

Of course, if Todd hadn't been with Maria that night, then she didn't have an alibi either. Maybe Bobby Joe had threatened to expose their affair. Maria might have been afraid that her husband would take his anger out on her, and she killed Bobby Joe to protect herself. But would a victim of abuse be able to murder someone else? Other than when talking about her mom, Maria seemed too meek to attack someone, let alone kill them.

I added a shirt and shorts to the pale figure on the window as I thought about other possible killers.

Donald thought Bobby Joe was not only embezzling gas station funds but sleeping with his younger wife, too. That gave Donald a double motive. Tara said they'd both been at the station that night, but if she was watching TV in the house, she couldn't possibly know if Donald was really manning the store.

Or maybe Tara was the one with a reason to kill Bobby Joe. She swore they weren't having an affair, but she might have worried that Bobby Joe would ruin her meal ticket with Donald if Donald became too jealous over the flirting. With him working at the station, Tara could have easily slipped out to the fairgrounds without being missed.

And then there was Crusher. Ashlee was positive he was Bobby Joe's biggest competitor. With the dropped sponsors and his fade from the limelight, maybe he'd killed Bobby Joe so he'd have one less person to battle with. But he must have known his big trick would wow the audience and any scouts, so he didn't need to kill Bobby Joe.

I was putting jet black paint on top of the head to create hair when Kimmie emerged from the shop, pushing the stroller with one hand and holding a cup of sherbet with the other.

She stopped and ate a spoonful. "Mmm . . . pineapple. And fat free. We have such upscale clientele in our restaurant, I always watch my figure. If people see a fat restaurant owner, they'll worry about their own weight."

I didn't buy into her reasoning, so I only offered up a "huh" in response.

Kimmie scrutinized my latest handiwork. "Why are the ice cream scoops the same size as the guy's head?"

I dropped the brush in the bucket, almost spattering black paint on Kimmie's fancy sandals with the pearl and rhinestone-covered strap. Wouldn't that be a shame? "Get the Scoop is generous with their portions. I wanted to emphasize that." I wiped my hands on a rag. "Don't you have a restaurant to run?"

Kimmie raised her diamond-encrusted watch. "Goodness, where did the time go? I can't believe I let you talk to me for so long."

It was typical of Kimmie to blame someone else for her tardiness. "Gee, sorry about that." The sarcasm flew over her head and slapped the window behind her.

"The staff is probably pilfering from the cash register already," Kimmie muttered to herself as she trotted to her Mercedes and opened the car's door while juggling her shopping bag, the stroller, and the sherbet. She carried the dog to the passenger side, placed it on the seat, and strapped it in with what looked like a harness of some type.

I turned back to my ice cream painting, realizing I should add a dog to the window, mostly because I had the stencil. I used the white for the main body, then added black paint for spots. Instead of a dog, the creature looked like a miniature cow. Oh well, this was farm country. People might bring their cows to get ice cream, not that I'd ever seen that. At least the picture would draw attention to the parlor, which is what the owner wanted.

Even with the awning covering the sidewalk, the sun's heat rolled off the nearby blacktop and over me like smoke from a campfire. Rather than pack up all the supplies to move next door to Raining Cats and Dogs, I grabbed two corners of the drop cloth and dragged everything the twenty feet, careful not to let the paint cans tip over.

Since Raining Cats and Dogs sold pet accessories, a dog was the obvious choice for the window, but I'd already painted one at the ice cream parlor, and I wanted each store to have a different style. A crouched cat, ready to pounce on a toy, sounded easy enough, or maybe this heat was melting my brain. I dipped my brush in the white paint and got to work.

I was adding the final dabs to the feet when I heard a snort behind me.

Ashlee stood on the curb, dressed in her work smock and khaki pants, her hair in a French twist. "I didn't expect to see you downtown this time of day. Is that supposed to be an otter? Why is it white?"

"It's a cat."

"Are you sure?"

I blew a stream of air off my bottom lip and sent a ripple through my bangs. When had everyone in town turned into art critics? "Slow day at the vet office?"

Ashlee smiled, knowing she'd rankled me. "We had a break between patients, so I'm taking an early lunch."

"And you came to admire my artwork?"

"As if. I came for one of those mocha shakes they sell next door. If you get it with skim milk, it has less calories than a turkey sandwich."

Maybe Ashlee and Kimmie should compare diet notes.

Ashlee regarded the window again. "You know, if I tilt my head and close one eye, I can almost see a cat. How'd you get stuck with this dopey project anyway? You get a second job when I wasn't looking?"

"Esther's Rejuvenation Committee, making Blossom Valley a better place." I used the tone of an infomercial host. "With these adorable paintings, tourists can't help but stop and shop."

"They'll stop all right, trying to figure out what this is. You might even cause an accident out in the street when people slam on their brakes."

I refused to let Ashlee annoy me, though it took all my willpower. "As long as people buy something at one of these shops, I'm okay with that." I squatted down to clean my brush.

Two women came out of the ice cream parlor and stopped when they saw Ashlee and me. At first, I thought they were checking out my artwork, but then the dark-haired one leaned toward the blonde and loudly whispered, "That's her, the one who killed Bobby Joe."

"She should be in jail," the other woman whispered.

Ashlee gasped and whirled on the women. She narrowed her eyes and thrust her hands onto her hips, clearly ready to do battle.

Before she could speak, I rose to my feet in a flash, pointing the dripping paintbrush at them. "My sister did not kill Bobby Joe. You'd better keep those remarks to yourself."

The blonde stepped back and tugged on the other's sleeve. "I think she's the one that works at that funny spa. We didn't have murders in this town before that spa opened. That place is cursed."

The brunette nodded. "Let's get out of here before she puts a hex on us." They both strode away, the blonde casting one last glance over her shoulder.

I glared at them until they rounded the corner, then looked at Ashlee. Her eyes were rimmed with tears, her hands visibly shaking. I gave her a hug, careful not to let the brush touch her clothes.

"Don't pay any attention to those losers. No one else thinks you're guilty."

Ashlee flipped her hair back and swiped at her eyes. "But they do. People whisper about me everywhere I go. I try to tell myself they're just jealous of my looks, but it's getting harder."

I didn't know what to say. In my cocooned world, where I spent most of my time at the farm or at home, it never occurred to me that the townspeople would be so vocal with their gossip. Here I'd thought those women at the fireworks had been whispering about my being with Crusher, but they'd probably been whispering about how I was the sister of Bobby Joe's girlfriend. How disgusting.

"Ignore them all," I said. "They'll feel like crap when the real killer is caught."

"If that ever happens," Ashlee said in a quiet voice. "Guess I should get going."

I watched her walk toward her car, shoulders hunched. "But what about your shake?" I asked.

Ashlee opened her car door. "I'll throw together a sandwich at home. I need to save my money anyway."

I gaped at her. Ashlee's philosophy was to burn through money faster than a Duraflame log. The rumors were definitely affecting her.

She got in her car and peeled out, leaving the smell of burning rubber hanging in the already stifling air. I returned to my work, wishing I'd never witnessed those women being mean to her, but at the same time, I was glad I was reminded of what my sister was dealing with.

The one bright spot was that two people had now mentioned Todd's flimsy alibi. The police must be close to arresting him.

I had my fingers crossed.

23

I dragged my paint supplies down the sidewalk to Don't Dilly-Dahlia, the flower shop, and set to work on the third window. I used the stencils where I could and freehanded the rest. Occasional passersby would comment or even snicker, but I focused on my work, more interested in finishing up and getting out of this heat than defending my lack of artistry.

After what felt like a week but was probably no more than two hours, I finished the last window and put the lids back on the paint cans. My back ached, and my wrist was sore. I loaded the cans, brushes, and stencils into the trunk and went back for the drop cloth. As I rolled the material into a ball, I heard a car pull into the slot before me. I recognized Jason's Volvo and tightened my grip on the cloth, remembering last night's fireworks.

He stepped out, dressed in a blue dress shirt and Dockers, and looked past me at my recent handiwork. "Do these store owners know you vandalized their windows?" he asked with a smile that could melt my insides.

And unlike when I talked to Crusher, I knew Jason's smile was sincere.

I held up the cloth. "That's why I'm making a run for it before they realize what happened."

He pointed a couple stores down. "I might need to make a citizen's arrest based on your drawing of an albino alligator over there."

"It's a cat," I said, not able to keep all the exasperation out of my voice. I forced a softer tone. "I saw you at the fireworks last night, but you left before I had a chance to say hi."

Jason stuffed his hands in his pockets. "Had to get the story ready for last night's printing. You were busy anyway. Didn't want to interrupt." His tone was flat, providing no insight to his emotions.

"I agreed to meet Crusher for coffee so I could ask him questions about Bobby Joe. Then all the people were headed to the fireworks. It's been years since I've seen them, and Crusher was interested, and they were starting any minute . . ." My voice trailed off.

He poked at the sidewalk with one loafer. "Sure, I get it."

"Really, I did talk to Crusher about Bobby Joe, but he didn't have much to add. How about you? Any news on the murder?" Jason might think the question was my attempt to change the subject, and it partly was, but after seeing Ashlee turn tail and run home a few minutes ago, I was really hoping the police had made a breakthrough.

Jason stepped aside to let a woman and her toddler pass, then moved back into the shade. "That's why I stopped by when I saw you out here painting. To fill you in on the latest. I know it's been worrying you."

I put a hand on his arm. "Then the police have found something?"

"Donald is apparently in danger of losing his business. He took out a new mortgage a few years ago to carry him through the recession, but he's missed several payments."

"I've heard rumors Bobby Joe was stealing, but I can't imagine he was taking so much that Donald would kill him."

Jason shrugged. "Hard to say what sets people off. Otherwise, the detectives are verifying alibis and trying to track down witnesses. Somebody mentioned overhearing Bobby Joe arguing that night at the fairgrounds."

"Think they were talking about Ashlee when she was yelling at Bobby Joe?"

"No, this was later. But the witness only heard Bobby Joe, not anyone else, so he might have been on the phone. The cops are pulling his records."

"That's a pretty slim clue. But I might have a clue of my own." I set the drop cloth back on the ground, not wanting Jason to think a barrier, physical or otherwise, existed between us. "I heard a rumor that Maria lied about Todd being with her the night of the murder."

A notebook and pen appeared in Jason's hand so fast that I wondered if he'd been holding them the whole time. "How reliable is the source of this rumor?"

I'd use a lot of words to describe Kimmie, but reliable wasn't one of them. "Maria herself hinted at it when I was eavesdrop . . . I mean painting."

Jason smiled but didn't comment on my little slip-up. "A scorned husband is always a good choice for a killer." He flipped his notebook closed. "I gotta run, but we should definitely get together soon. I don't want you having any more coffee with the out-of-towners, even if it is to gather information."

Hang on a second. Was Jason jealous? "I've been trying to cut back on my caffeine anyway."

"Even if I were to ask you to the Daily Grind some time?"

I tucked a lock of hair behind my ear, wishing I wasn't so sweaty from painting. "For you, I'd make an exception."

He kissed me on the cheek, then got back in his car and drove off.

I automatically touched the spot where his lips had been. Maybe our relationship was more solid than I realized.

I picked up the drop cloth and stuck it in my trunk on top of the paint cans. Time for lunch. After all that work, I deserved a high-calorie treat.

Once in the car, I saw that it was already after one. No wonder I was hungry. I drove to the other end of town, down by the gas stations and fast-food restaurants. The line at McDonald's was shortest, so I pulled up behind a silver Cadillac sedan with tinted windows.

The driver motored up to the pickup window while I yelled my order for a salad and an ice-cold McFlurry at the speaker, then followed the Cadillac. As I watched, a clerk handed a stuffed bag to the driver. A moment later, another bag appeared at the window and disappeared into the car. When the third bag came out, the clerk released it too soon, and the bag dropped to the pavement.

The driver opened his door and bent down to retrieve the bag. A jolt ran through me as I recognized Stump and realized I hadn't included him in my list of suspects. If Bobby Joe hadn't approved of Stump's profession—

and I was using the term "profession" loosely—Stump might have removed his roommate from the picture so he didn't interfere with future sales. No one would do business with a dealer whose roommate might turn into a snitch. And clearly business was good if he could afford such a fancy car, although he must not have used any of his profits to decorate his apartment. Maybe he didn't want to tip off his parents.

Stump threw the bag into the passenger seat and pulled away. I had a momentary urge to bypass the takeout window and follow him, but wasn't sure what I'd accomplish. I already knew where he lived. I was almost positive he was dealing drugs. What could I possibly gain by stalking him?

My stomach rumbled so loud, I could hear it over my car engine, making my decision for me. I retrieved my food and drove home, aiming my air-conditioning vent at the McFlurry to keep it in a semi-solid state before I devoured it.

The driveway was empty, Ashlee already gone. I entered the house, clutching my salad and dessert, and set my meal on the kitchen table. As I sat down, I spotted Mom through the sliding-glass door, filling the bird feeders at the picnic table.

I stuck the McFlurry in the freezer, grabbed a real fork from the silverware drawer, and carried my salad outside.

Mom glanced up from the bag of regular seed. "Dana, I didn't expect you home for lunch."

"Esther gave me a project in town, so I figured I'd grab a bite before I head back."

Mom eyed my takeout container. "At least you got a salad. But watch that sodium."

I speared a piece of chicken. "I promise to drink five

glasses of water when I'm finished eating to dilute all that salt."

"I don't think that's how it works."

Neither did I, but no way was I throwing out this salad with its yummy cheese and crispy tortilla strips.

Mom finished filling the copper feeder shaped like a parachute and rolled the top of the seed bag down. Her tone grew serious. "Your sister came home a while ago."

"Yeah, I saw her downtown earlier. A couple of women were whispering about her and Bobby Joe."

Grabbing the sack of finch food, Mom angrily tore at the top. "Sometimes I can't stand the small-minded people in this town. Why, yesterday at the grocery store, I could hear the clerks talking about Ashlee, and with me standing right there. They know full well I'm her mother."

"I had no idea people were gossiping so much." Though I should have known better.

Mom wrenched the bag the rest of the way open, spilling thistle seeds onto the patio. "That's why the police need to solve Bobby Joe's death. And from what I've heard through the grapevine, that's not going to happen anytime soon." She pressed the open bag to the lip of the finch tube and poured, the seeds pattering to the bottom like drops of spring rain. "How about you? Are you having better luck?"

"I've almost convinced myself that Todd killed Bobby Joe when he found out about the affair with Maria."

"Who's Todd?"

Guess I hadn't been keeping Mom up-to-date on my discoveries. "Todd Runyon. He's married to Maria, the same girl Bobby Joe cheated on Ashlee with."

Mom set the finch food down. "Runyon. Why does that name sound familiar?" She slapped the bag top.

"He was a few years ahead of you in school. I knew his mom from the PTA. He was quite the troublemaker. The principal used to suspend him for fighting. Barely managed to graduate, and then he got a job at the steel factory. I think his father had to pull some strings."

He'd gone from hitting other students to hitting his wife. Great. "All I have are suspicions. Nothing I can take to the police. I need evidence."

"Then you really need to find some, Dana," Mom said, an edge to her voice.

Didn't she realize I was doing the best I could, even at the risk of my job? I made a show of looking at the patio surface around the picnic table. "None over here." I looked toward the lawn. "Or over there. Guess evidence isn't just lying around for people to trip over."

Mom screwed the top on the finch tube and rubbed her temple. "I know you're trying to help, but I'm so worried about Ashlee. The longer this goes on, the more likely her reputation will be permanently ruined. Ours, too."

Mom hung the feeder up on the hook and dusted off her hands. "What do you know so far about Todd? Anything that would help you find evidence?"

I shook my head. "I know practically nothing, only that he has a bad temper. Maria's mom, Rosa, works for Kimmie and told her that Todd abuses Maria."

Mom put a hand to her mouth. "Oh my, he doesn't sound like a very nice man."

"No. And anyone who would beat his wife would probably kill someone who was sleeping with her. It's all part of that possessiveness and jealousy you hear about. But I really need to find out more about him."

"You know what you should do," Mom said. She

grabbed the broom that was leaning against a wood beam of the gazebo.

For a moment, I thought she was going to instruct me to sweep the patio, like some kind of Karate Kid learning exercise. But she just leaned on the handle.

"Look up that Web site my shows are always talking about. Facebook, isn't it? Apparently people are always getting in trouble with that. Girls put up naked pictures of themselves, or people talk about how they're playing hooky at the beach when they're supposed to be at work, then they can't figure out why they got fired. Maybe Todd's put something on there that could help you."

Had it come to this? Was my mom giving me tips on using social networking sites? "I doubt he confessed to the murder on his wall, but it's worth a look," I said. "As long as his profile's public."

Mom gave me a blank look. "I have no idea what you just said, but it sounds like I helped."

I gathered up my salad remnants and stood, leaning forward to kiss Mom on the cheek. "You did. Thanks, and sorry I sassed you earlier. I need to get back to work now, but I'll try to find out more at my afternoon break."

"Good, and then you can pass anything you find on to the police. I don't want you talking to this man yourself. He sounds too dangerous."

I was now double-glad I'd never told Mom about my altercation with Todd at the truck rally. She would have grounded me on the spot, which would have been highly embarrassing at my age.

I returned to the house, dumped my trash in the can, and got back in my car, not bothering with my McFlurry still in the freezer. I rolled down the windows to flush out the stifling air and hummed to myself as I drove back to work, excited about my new research project.

Only three cars sat in the parking lot. I'd have to check with Esther on how reservations looked for the next couple of weeks. She was functioning on a tight budget as it was, and she always worried about being able to keep the farm open.

Gordon wasn't at his usual post behind the front desk, and my step instantly lightened. I didn't have any pressing work this afternoon. Was five minutes after I finished my lunch break too soon to take my afternoon break? I could slip into the office right now and see if Todd had a profile on Facebook.

As I hurried down the hall, a figure appeared in the kitchen doorway at the other end. Gordon. I tried to keep the guilty look off my face, since I hadn't actually done anything wrong, but Gordon's gaze picked up my expression.

"Finally back to work, I see," he commented, pulling at his lapels.

Like a light switched from off to on, my feelings switched from guilt to anger. "Yep. All done painting the downtown windows, like Esther asked. I'm sure she told you about that."

Gordon sneered. "Another Rejuvenation Committee idea that will go nowhere. That group should give up."

"Yoo hoo, Dana," a voice that could only belong to Esther called behind me. Sure enough, Esther trotted down the hall. As she approached, I noticed she wore one navy blue and one black shoe. Sometimes I wondered what she'd do if she had to run the farm without Gordon, much as he annoyed me.

Esther stopped before me, slightly out of breath.

"Dana, I'm glad I caught you. I've been getting so many calls about your window paintings."

Uh-oh. I knew the paintings weren't great, but I hadn't expected the complaints to start so soon. "Esther, I can explain," I started, but she cut me off.

"Everyone loves them, can't stop raving about them."

"What?" I blurted out, as I heard Gordon echo, "What?" behind me.

Esther nodded, her gray curls bouncing. "People can't get over your artistic technique, especially your use of disproportion, how the ice cream is the same size as a man's head, or how you combined features of different animals to keep people guessing. The owner of Raining Cats and Dogs told me that every customer who came into the store commented on the pictures."

My face was flaming hot, and I hoped Esther mistook that for humility, rather than embarrassment that everyone thought my mistakes were intentional.

"I'm glad the paintings are such a hit," I said. "Maybe the town council will take the Blossom Valley Rejuvenation Committee a little more seriously now."

Esther's eyes widened, and she slapped a hand to her chest. "Wouldn't that be a la mode on the pie? Imagine if they talked us up at a town meeting. Everyone would want to join then and help put Blossom Valley on the map."

Behind me, Gordon mumbled something under his breath.

Esther chuckled at him. "Someday you'll see how important this committee is."

"Unless it brings in more guests, I'm not interested. And from what I've seen so far, the committee hasn't helped this spa one bit."

I turned and caught his glower before he stomped back into the kitchen.

"Poor Gordon," Esther said with a sigh. "Our reservations are drying up, so he's worried. I am, too."

"Sounds like we need to beef up our advertising," I said. "If we expanded to the national magazines, we'd attract more people. I've been putting together a proposal that I'd like to show you."

Esther fiddled with a button. "Oh, dear, that sounds expensive. Find out how much it'd cost, and I'll talk to Gordon. He's so much better with numbers than I am."

I crossed my fingers that Gordon approved my plan. I didn't know how much longer Esther could find me these odd jobs to fill my work hours.

Esther touched my shoulder. "Speaking of Gordon, he was talking about this Tweeter thing some of the kids are doing. Do you think that would be good for business?"

"Twitter? Not a bad idea." And one I should have thought of. "Plus, it's free. I could set up an account."

Esther fingered her button again. "I hate to correct you, dear, but I think it's Tweeter. Gordon was talking about tweeting and it reminded me of Tweety Bird."

"Right. You tweet on Twitter."

"But Dana, that doesn't make any sense. Wouldn't you twit on Twitter and tweet on Tweeter?"

Oh, boy. This conversation could go on all day. "I'll double-check when I set up the account."

Satisfied, Esther toddled down the hall.

I placed my hand on the knob to the office door and noticed brown paint specks all along the edges of my fingernails. Shoot. I'd left the paint cans in my trunk. While I didn't really mind having the paint there, I wasn't sure what the heat in an enclosed space would do. Did paint cans explode? I definitely didn't want to find out.

I exited through the French doors, crossed the vacant patio, and followed the path past the vegetable garden. I spotted Zennia across the way, bending over the zucchini plants, and waved hello. She raised her head, her straw hat giving the impression of a flying saucer taking off, and waved back.

A black BMW pulled up to the curb in front of the house. Esther hadn't mentioned any new guests today, and I watched the car out of the corner of my eye while I popped my trunk and tried to cram the drop cloth into the box, eager to carry everything in one trip.

As I worked, a man emerged from the BMW. With his dark suit and conservative tie, he could have been Gordon's brother. He glanced around the nearly-empty parking lot, then disappeared inside the lobby.

Maybe he was a salesman, stopping for the night. But Blossom Valley had a chain hotel to handle business travel, and I couldn't recall any businessmen ever staying here before.

I grabbed the box, almost folding under the weight, and closed the trunk with my chin. A slamming door drew my attention back to the house. The man in the suit practically jumped off the curb in his haste to reach his car, red splotches clear on his cheeks. He yanked open the car door, threw himself in, and slammed the door shut.

Yikes. What had set him off? We had plenty of room at the spa. Had he stopped for another reason?

My arms ached in protest as I stood there, forcing me to abandon all thoughts of the mystery man as I carried the box toward the lobby. If I cut through the house, I might reach the shed before I dropped the supplies.

Gordon was staring toward the door when I entered, but his gaze was off in the distance, as though he was thinking.

"Who was that guy?" I asked. I rested the box on the love seat, my muscles completely useless by now.

He snapped to attention and shuffled the papers on the counter before him. "Some guy named Vince. A friend of Crusher's. At least that's what he said."

Why would a guy in a suit visit a California-casual monster truck driver? "Do you think he was lying?"

"Don't know. But I wouldn't want any friends like that. About had a stroke when I told him Crusher had just left. I've never seen someone's face get so red."

I shivered, not sure why I found that so concerning. That man had definitely looked angry. Maybe he was another scout, trying to pitch to Crusher before he signed any papers. "Think he'll be back later?"

"I hope not. I didn't like the looks of that guy." Gordon turned back to the computer, once more absorbed in his work.

I hoisted the box, my arms protesting, and headed toward the toolshed before my body failed me. That chore done, I retreated to the office and sat down in the desk chair. I needed to get those numbers to Gordon, and then I'd do a little Todd research.

I spent the next couple of hours mostly on hold as I tried to track down advertising prices for the magazines I was interested in. After several rounds of transfers and the occasional hang-up, I finally got all the information I needed and added it to the proposal I'd been working on. Now it was time for a break.

My first stop was Facebook. Wasn't everyone on Facebook now? Well, maybe not my mom. Or Esther. But I'd seen Todd with a smartphone, so the odds were in my favor. I entered "Todd Runyon" into the search box and clicked the little magnifying glass.

A surge of excitement rushed through me as his page appeared, for all the world to see. As I scanned the Farmville-related posts, from Todd sharing fuel to needing to harvest his crops, frustration replaced my hope. His only personal posts involved places he'd eaten and pictures of his *Star Wars* memorabilia. And nothing was posted the day of Bobby Joe's murder, or even the day before. So much for that great plan.

I drummed my fingers on the desk in front of the keyboard, then brought up Google. My search for Todd immediately resulted in a link to Facebook, but the second hit made me pause. Todd belonged to Twitter. Was it the same Todd Runyon? Did he actually post personal information or did he only Twitter about Farmville?

I clicked the link, and a page full of posts populated my screen. The first post, from today, read, "Late 4 work. Boss gonna kill me. So much 4 Steel Works employee of the week."

Bingo. Mom had mentioned that Todd worked at Steel Works. I scrolled through the page. The guy liked his Twitter way more than his Facebook. He posted at least half a dozen times a day.

I got to the entries for the day of Bobby Joe's murder and started at the bottom. If I hovered my cursor over the date, a time stamp appeared. Todd had eaten a breakfast burrito at six that morning. Argued with a coworker at nine, then ate a Snickers. Had a cheeseburger and fries for lunch. Saw a red-tailed hawk on his way back to work.

My fingers twitched with impatience as I continued through his day. Where was the proverbial smoking gun? Didn't this man do anything besides eat and bird-watch? I scanned through his dinner selection, then froze at the next entry, my mouth sapped dry, my breathing halted.

There, at ten that night, he'd posted, "Betrayed by wife. Gotta take care of that."

A chill ran down my spine. It seemed obvious exactly how he'd taken care of his wife's betrayal.

By killing Bobby Joe.

24

I scanned the next few entries for any insight into what had happened after ten on Thursday night, but the posts only contained more food lists. No references to the betrayal, no admissions of a guilty conscience. I wondered if Todd had posted that comment in a fit of anger and then decided he'd shared too much. Surely he could delete a Twitter post. Unless he'd been so busy killing Bobby Joe that he forgot.

But that didn't matter. I'd found his admission that he knew about his wife's affair. Now all I needed was proof that he'd killed Bobby Joe. Detective Palmer wouldn't exactly do cartwheels when I showed him this Twitter posting, but if I could find one more piece, the detective would have to take my suspicions seriously, maybe even arrest Todd. Then my family could get back to our normal lives where people didn't gossip about us.

I checked the clock on the computer. Almost time for Todd to get off work, assuming he worked the standard nine-to-five shift.

I had no idea where Todd and Maria lived, but I knew where Todd worked, so I'd start there. Maybe I'd be able to follow him home. But what would I do once I got there? As much as I wanted to clear Ashlee's name, I wasn't prepared to break into someone's house, even if I was fairly positive that person had committed murder. Maybe I'd come up with an idea on my drive into town.

I updated my time card, made sure to put my cell phone in my pocket, and headed out. I nodded at Gordon on my way out the door, and he held up a hand in acknowledgment as he focused on a paper on his clipboard.

When I reached the outskirts of town, I kept an eye out for the sheet-metal factory. While I knew the general location, I wasn't positive on how to get there. I spotted the STEEL WORKS sign and took the next exit, then followed the service road back the way I'd come. The factory had been in business for decades, long before the town council dictated that every new store needed a cute name. Besides, it'd be hard to think of an adorable label for this plain, brown building with its boring brown door. Not even a window livened up the drab facade.

The parking lot was half full, pickup trucks and an occasional sedan taking up the spaces. I drove up and down the rows until I spotted Todd's green Ford. I wasn't one hundred percent sure I had the right truck, but it was the only green Ford in the lot, and it had a bumper sticker like the one I'd noticed when I'd seen him at the diner. He was parked between a beat-up van and a large SUV.

I looked around for an inconspicuous parking spot, preferably one in the shade, but the lot was free of trees and provided no cover. I settled for a spot three rows over, next to a pickup, hoping my little car would go undetected. Then I settled in to wait.

After five minutes, I turned the key and rolled the driver's-side window down, sweat dewing along my hairline.

After another five minutes, I rolled down the passenger window, but that didn't help. You needed a breeze to cool off the inside of the car, and the only air movement was when I'd inserted the key in the ignition.

Five more minutes, and I got out to search the trunk for any water bottles I might have forgotten. The trunk smelled faintly of paint and dirt. I slammed it shut.

Back in the car, I felt under the seats for water and glanced occasionally at the main building, but Todd hadn't exited. In fact, no one had left, making me worry that these guys worked a swing shift and I'd be sitting here for hours. In this heat, I'd melt faster than the Wicked Witch of the West when you threw water on her.

I thought about what I was doing here. I needed evidence, no matter how flimsy, that would connect Todd to Bobby Joe's death. Since Bobby Joe was killed at the fairgrounds, Todd would have had to drive there, presumably in his truck. Maybe he'd dropped something on the floorboards, or absentmindedly thrown trash into the truck bed that could place him at the scene. Hmm . . .

No one had driven into the parking lot. No one had left the building. Might as well use the time and solitude to snoop around Todd's truck. If anyone saw me, I'd claim to be waiting for Todd. Unless it was Todd who saw me. Then I was screwed.

I shut my car door and wound through the parked cars until I reached Todd's truck, all the while listening for the sound of a car pulling into the lot or the door of the building opening. I stopped at his tailgate, using the van to partly shield me, and looked in the bed. Scraps of paper and an empty plastic bag clung to the corners nearest the tailgate. I picked up each piece of paper, then dropped it back; most were receipts from the liquor store.

The rest of the bed was empty, save for the tool chest at the front. I moved to the side of the truck, stood on tippy-toe and, not spotting a lock, lifted the lid. The tool box squeaked open, and my gaze locked on the building, sure everyone inside had heard the noise.

When no one came out, I lifted the lid higher and peered inside. Wrenches and screwdrivers lay scattered in the large box, gleaming in the evening light. In the far corner, somewhat obscured by a hammer, rested a dull black handgun.

I stared at the gun as though it was a rattlesnake coiled to strike, a combination of fear and fascination mesmerizing me. What was Todd doing with a gun? Why hadn't he used it to kill Bobby Joe? Of course, when you found out your wife was cheating on you, crushing a man's skull with a tailpipe might be more satisfying than shooting him.

Did the police know about the gun? Would they care? If he had a permit to carry it, I wasn't sure it mattered. Knowing Todd had a gun didn't really help in my search for evidence.

I eased the lid back down, wincing at the squeak, and stepped back from the truck. A total strikeout. Then I noticed the lock was not engaged on the driver's-side door. Did I dare open it? I wasn't willing to sneak into Todd and Maria's house in search of evidence, but I wouldn't technically be breaking into Todd's truck.

That unlocked door was practically an invitation for me to snoop around. If he was going to be that careless about his personal property, then it served him right if someone opened the door. And that someone was going to be me.

With a shaky breath, I rested my hand on the door handle, then curled my fingers under it and pulled. The door came open, releasing a cloud of pent-up summer air. The faint odor of stale cologne wafted out. I leaned inside.

The area between the seats held a plastic coffee mug, a handful of papers that looked like they related to his work, and a *Maxim*. I ran my hand under the seat on the driver's side, but came up only with a dime and three toothpicks.

I started to pocket the dime, then dropped it back on the floor. There was a big difference between opening an unlocked truck door and stealing from the owner, no matter how small the denomination.

The passenger side called to me, and I debated between going around to the other side and actually climbing into the cab. In the interest of time, I pulled myself onto the seat and slid in front of the glove box. I dropped open the door and pawed through the papers, but all I found was a current registration, an old parking ticket, a travel brochure for Mendocino, and a pack of Kleenex. Not the most incriminating assortment.

By now, I suspected I was wasting my time, but I'd come too far to quit. I reached down under the passenger seat, and felt along the floor, my hand brushing against more paper. I stretched a little farther, bringing my shoulder down so it almost touched the plastic mat. As I captured the paper between two fingers, I heard a footstep land directly outside the truck. My heart beat triple-time, and my fingers went numb. With a slowness that belied my absolute panic, I pulled my arm back from under the seat, raised my upper body, and turned.

A whimper escaped my lips.

Todd stood at the open driver's door, a shiny silver buck knife in his hand.

25

Todd raised the knife, his eyes unreadable through the clear lenses of his glasses. I scooted on the truck seat until my back hit the passenger door, my mind motoring. If I could pop the door open, I could jump into the truck bed and grab the gun. But would I be fast enough?

"What the hell are you doing in my truck?" he asked, his voice loud, the anger obvious.

I stared at him, my mind no longer motoring. Now it was idling. All I could think was, "Please don't stab me. Please don't stab me."

"Answer me!"

He reached into the truck and swiped at my leg with his free hand. I scrunched up farther against the door, not sure I could get out before Todd grabbed me.

"I was . . ." I tried to think of any plausible reason I might be sitting in the truck of a likely killer. "I wanted to leave you a note," I blurted out.

Todd gestured toward the windshield. "You couldn't leave it under my wipers?"

"Nothing to write with. I was looking for a pen and some paper." Sweat poured down my temples, and I wanted to wipe the mess away, but my brain no longer had control over my arms. Or my legs. All I could do was sit frozen in the corner.

A burly man not much smaller than Shaquille O'Neal came into view. "Need any help, Todd?" the man asked.

I didn't know whether to be scared or relieved. Surely Todd wouldn't try to kill me with a witness present, would he? Then again, in some states, you could beat a robber to death with your shoe if he broke into your house, and the police wouldn't arrest you. Did the same apply if someone broke into your truck?

Todd glanced at the man, who probably couldn't see the knife behind the door. "I've got it covered, thanks."

The man moved past the truck and on his way. I almost yelled to him for help, but I wasn't sure whether he'd help me or Todd.

Todd lowered the knife. A positive sign.

"So if you *had* left me a note, what would it say?"

Good question.

"Um, to meet me at the Watering Hole after work." What the hell made me pick a bar as a meeting place? I didn't hang out in bars.

Todd folded the knife and stuck it in the back pocket of his jeans. "Wow, you'd break into my truck to set up a rendezvous? Sorry, honey, I'm married. Guess you couldn't stop thinking about me after we met at the truck rally."

I shot up from the corner without thinking. "I'm not hitting on you."

Todd reached for his back pocket, and I tensed. When his hand reappeared, it held a bandanna. He whipped off his glasses and rubbed the lenses. "Then what did you want to meet for?"

"To talk about Thursday night. You know, the night Bobby Joe was killed."

What was wrong with me? Here I thought Todd killed Bobby Joe, and I was provoking him while trapped in his truck, while he stood outside with a knife. What an idiot!

Todd's hand froze for a second, then he resumed cleaning his glasses. He slid them back on his nose and folded up the bandanna before stuffing it in his pocket. "What about Thursday night?"

"You know," I said, "it's pretty hot in here. I'm just gonna step outside."

Todd reached over and hit the lock button on the driver's-side door. I heard a click in response from the passenger door behind me. My breathing grew shallow, my lungs begging for more oxygen. I grabbed my St. Christopher medal and pressed the smooth surface to my lips.

"The hell you are," he said. "Why do you keep asking about Thursday night?"

"You're right. Forget I said anything."

I had to get out of this truck. Maybe I could honk the horn with my foot. Someone might notice and come help me. But I hadn't seen anyone in the lot except that Jolly Green Giant. Of course, I'd been so focused on Todd that a band of trumpeters could have marched through and I would have missed them.

"Sounds like you think I had something to do with Bobby Joe's death," Todd said. "Now I know why you were chasing Maria at the rally. You thought she'd tell you I had a hand in it."

My arms finally started working, and I reached out to him, palms up, like a beggar in the street seeking a handout. "He seduced your wife. No one could possibly blame you for killing him." Well, other than twelve of his peers, but I didn't mention that.

Todd placed a foot on the side step and rested one elbow on the armrest inside the door. "I didn't kill him."

"Of course you didn't," my lips said. But my mind screamed, "Yes, you did."

"Then why do you keep pestering me about where I was?"

I sized up Todd's threat level. He wasn't much bigger than me, but he was most likely stronger. If I ever wanted to escape this truck, honesty might be the best approach. "My sister was dating Bobby Joe, and I'm worried the police think she did it."

"So you decided to play Little Miss Detective and point the blame somewhere else. You planning on sticking something in my truck, then calling the cops with an anonymous tip?" He snarled the last two words, like it wouldn't be the first anonymous tip pointed his way.

"Don't be silly." But darn, that would have been a good plan.

Todd straightened up and put his foot back on the ground, creating a small draft that I lapped up. At this rate, I was going to die of heat exhaustion. Todd wouldn't have to lift a finger.

"Hate to disappoint you, but I've got an alibi."

Someone near the building called Todd's name. He looked in that direction and raised a hand in acknowledgment.

It was now or never.

I twisted around, jerked up the door lock, grabbed the handle, and pushed. The door opened so fast, I almost fell onto the pavement. I managed to swing a foot out and bounce down from the truck, slamming the door shut at the same time.

I looked at Todd over the truck bed.

"You got out," he said. The small smile on his lips implied more amusement than surprise or anger. He rubbed at the brown stubble on his chin.

I couldn't help but notice how relaxed he was for a killer, and I felt a tickle of doubt. Could I have been wrong about Todd? But what about his Twitter post?

Now that I wasn't locked in his truck, I could afford to rile him up a little. I rested my forearms on the side of the truck, dangling my hands toward the bed, matching his calm attitude. "Your alibi might not be as good as you think."

He scowled, and I stiffened. Not only did he have that knife in his pocket, but the gun still sat in the tool box. It was closer to me than to him, but the difference was that Todd probably knew how to use it.

"You sure think you know a lot," he said.

"I know your wife lied about your alibi to the police." Okay, so I didn't know for a fact, but the implication had been there.

"Maybe I have another alibi."

That stopped me. Why would Maria need to create a fake alibi if Todd already had one? Where was he that night? Anger management class? Wifebeaters Anonymous?

"Tell me about it," I said, trying not to drool in my eagerness to find out.

"You tell me, since you know so much."

"You posted on Twitter that your wife betrayed you. That was the same night Bobby Joe was killed."

Todd's face reddened. "And what would you do if

you found out your wife was cheating on you with some loser?"

"Um, kill him?" I said. "I think I already mentioned that."

"Or maybe you'd run to the nearest bar and pick up the first chick you saw to get back at your two-timing spouse."

My mouth dropped open. Literally. "You were with another woman?"

"You got it. Not that anything happened. I couldn't bring myself to cheat on my wife, even if she did it to me." Todd adjusted his glasses. "Maria has no idea where I was that night, but she lied to the cops to give me an alibi."

"But why would she even protect you? I heard that you beat her." An image of the knife in his pocket popped into my head, and I wondered if I should be keeping my mouth shut.

Todd harrumphed. "My mother-in-law tell you that?"

"Well, not directly."

"She's said a lot worse, believe me. Can't stand the fact that her daughter married a gringo, as she likes to call me. Talks shit about me every chance she gets."

"Sounds like the mother-in-law from hell." For a moment, I felt sorry for Todd, even if he might be a killer.

Todd jutted his chin out. "You don't know the half of it. Tells people I'm a child molester, that I'm running from the law. She had a husband all picked out for Maria, and she never got over it when Maria married me instead."

So that was it. A bitter mother refused to accept her son-in-law and instead spread lies about him. I felt more deflated than a Macy's parade balloon the day after Thanksgiving. I'd based all my assumptions about Todd's guilt on the fact that he beat his wife. And he'd just told me that not only did he not hit his wife, but he had a solid alibi for Bobby Joe's murder.

Todd flicked a fly off his forearm. "Looks like you'll have to find someone else to blame Bobby Joe's death on."

I swallowed hard, trying to quell my sense of despair as I grasped at the one thing that had been nagging me since my chat with Kimmie.

If Maria hadn't been with Todd the night Bobby Joe was killed, then where was she?

He might be lying about Maria's alibi, he could be too...

26

Before I could ask Todd about Maria's whereabouts that night, he slapped the side of his pickup. "I gotta get home. Make some dinner for Maria before she gets off work."

Todd climbed into his truck and slammed the door shut as I half-heartedly raised a hand to stop him. There was really no point in asking him about Maria's alibi. If he'd been at a bar the night Bobby Joe was killed, then he couldn't verify where his wife had been. He could only tell me whatever she'd told him, which might not be the truth.

When Todd started the engine, I jumped back. Considering I'd broken into his truck, he might run over my toes to show his unhappiness with me.

As he drove away, I waved exhaust fumes from in front of my face, relieved to have survived the confrontation. Then again, I wasn't sure I'd ever been in danger at all. The poor guy, going about his regular day, got off work and found his truck door open. It was somewhat understandable that he'd pull out a weapon in defense, in case I turned out to be a homicidal maniac.

Which apparently Todd wasn't. He wasn't even a wife beater, for crying out loud. He was a loving husband who cooked dinner for his wife.

I groaned and rubbed at my sweaty temples. I'd been so sure that he was the killer. The motive fit, he was definitely strong enough to land a fatal blow, and his Twitter page had hinted at revenge for his wife's affair. He might be lying about his alibi, but he'd sounded too cocky for me to believe that. And that meant I was back at square one, minus one suspect.

Well, I wasn't going to solve the crime standing in a hot parking lot, feeling sorry for myself. I got back in my car and drove home, trying to shake off how wrong I'd been.

Ashlee's Camaro hogged the driveway. As I looked for a spot on the street, I saw a dark blue Crown Victoria slide away from the curb, Detective Palmer behind the wheel. He lifted his hand in acknowledgment, but all I could do was stare. What was he doing here? Had something happened?

I parked as quickly as I could and hopped out, only partially aware of the evening's lingering heat. I hurried up the walk and into the house. Even from the entryway, I could hear Ashlee's wails. I ran into the kitchen to find out what had happened.

Ashlee sat at the table with her head on her arms. Mom stood behind her, rubbing her shoulders and offering reassuring noises.

"Mom, what's going on?" I asked.

Before Mom could answer, Ashlee lifted her head.

"That policeman was here again. I think he's about to arrest me." She laid her head back down, a sob escaping.

"Is that true?" I asked Mom.

"I'm sure he just needed to ask a few more questions."

Ashlee's head popped back up. "Then why did he ask the exact same questions as last time?"

"Maybe he forgot to write down the answers last time," Mom said.

I started to comment on how ridiculous that statement was, but Mom cut me off. "Dana, you told me you knew who the killer was. Did you have any luck finding the proof?"

Her question brought back the realization that I'd completely failed at solving Bobby Joe's murder. "Sorry, a dead end." I winced at my choice of words as Ashlee broke into new sobs.

"Oh, God, they'll lock me up for sure," she said.

Mom frowned at me, and I flushed.

"You wouldn't believe how mean he was to me." Ashlee sniffed. "He didn't even smile this time."

Detective Palmer was probably feeling threatened by my superior investigating skills and wanted to take his bitterness out on Ashlee. Maybe I shouldn't have suggested that they weren't making any progress in the case.

Mom squeezed Ashlee's shoulder. "We'll be right back." She walked over to where I stood, took me by the elbow, and led me into the other room.

"I didn't want to say anything in front of your sister," she said in a low voice, "but I think she's in real trouble now. This visit from the police was much more serious than last time. He was quite stern with her. Made several veiled accusations."

Her hand still rested on my elbow. As she spoke, her grip tightened, but that was nothing compared to the invisible hand of worry squeezing my innards.

"Did you call your lawyer?" I asked.

"Of course. He said not to answer any more questions and call him if she's arrested. But I don't want it to get that far. Your sister is much too fragile to be arrested." Mom released her grip on my arm. She stared at the picture of Dad on the mantel for a moment, then turned back to me. "Who else could be the killer, Dana?

I threw up my hands. "I don't know. It could be anyone. Even someone I haven't thought of yet. I still can't believe how wrong I was about Todd."

She gestured toward the kitchen. "Keep your voice down. We don't want to upset her any more than she already is."

"But how can the police possibly think she did it? It's absurd."

"She found out that very night that Bobby Joe was cheating on her. She had that big argument with him in front of all those people. And she doesn't have a good alibi."

I rubbed my eyes, but the vision of Ashlee in prison garb didn't go away. Did they at least let you accessorize in prison?

"There's no one else?" Mom asked.

"I still have some possibilities. Bobby Joe's boss was definitely hiding something last time I was out there, but I don't know if it has anything to do with the murder."

"Great. Go talk to him again." She gave me a critical

look and adjusted the collar of my polo shirt. "See what you can find out."

I stared at her. "And what if he's the killer? You want me to pester the guy at that lonely deserted gas station where he could kill me, too?"

"You know I'd never ask you to put yourself in danger. Use your judgment. Make sure other customers are there when you talk to him." Mom glanced at the mantel clock. "If you go right now, you can still catch the tail end of the commuter traffic."

"Right now?" I said. A look out the window confirmed that the sun was still shining, which meant it was still hot. Another wail erupted from the kitchen. Maybe being out in the heat wasn't such a bad option.

I sighed. "All right, I'll go."

Mom reached over and brushed down my hair. "Perfect. And I'll have the cabbage rolls ready for dinner by the time you get back."

Couldn't we have chicken again? I grabbed my keys from the kitchen, offered Ashlee a reassuring pat on the shoulder, which she ignored, and headed back out.

I hadn't been in the house long enough to cool off, and the air-conditioning in my Honda did little to help. But my bit of discomfort was nothing compared to how poorly Ashlee would feel if she was carted off to jail.

On the drive to the gas station, I wondered how much I could actually accomplish out there. Whatever Donald was trying to hide, he wasn't going to tell me. He'd made it clear he didn't appreciate my questions. But maybe I could hit up Tara. She'd been more open on earlier visits and might let something slip if I pushed hard enough.

Three parking spots in front of the mini-mart were already taken, and a teenage girl was pumping gas when I pulled into the lot. I parked in the last available slot and made my way inside. Donald looked over at the sound of the bell and gritted his teeth when he saw me. If it hadn't been for the customers already in line, he might have thrown me out right then.

I grabbed a bag of Fritos and stood in line. Donald couldn't kick me out if I was a paying customer. That WE RESERVE THE RIGHT TO REFUSE SERVICE sign on the back wall was merely for show. I just hoped Donald knew that.

The old man at the front paid for his chewing tobacco and girlie magazine and left the store. While I waited for Donald to ring up the woman who was next in line, I studied the back of the guy in front of me. His hair reached halfway down his neck, the strands greasy.

The woman accepted her change and her paper bag full of goodies and exited through the doorway, the bell ringing in accompaniment. That left the guy in front of me, and I still had no idea what I was going to say to Donald.

I almost laughed when the customer placed a pink and yellow seashell with green polka dots on the counter. How on earth did those ugly little four-dollar tchotchkes sell so well?

I shifted to the side to get a better look at the guy and watched as he handed over a twenty-dollar bill. Donald's hands trembled as he reached in the till and handed back six dollars.

The guy took the change, snatched up his trinket, and turned to go.

I couldn't believe it! Donald was short-changing the guy, and he didn't even notice.

"Hey," I said, touching the man on his forearm, "I think you got cheated."

He jumped a little and looked at me. His ice-gray eyes locked on mine, and I recognized him as the guy I'd spotted at Stump's apartment the first time I'd gone there. Coincidence?

"What?" He stared at my hand still on his arm, and I pulled it back.

I pointed to Donald. "He only gave you six dollars back for a four-dollar item. He shortchanged you ten bucks."

Donald was licking his lips and staring at us.

The guy shook his head. "No, that's right. I gave him a ten."

"I saw you give him a twenty."

The guy looked at Donald, who still hadn't moved, other than his flicking tongue, then shook his head again. "You must have seen it wrong."

What was going on here? Didn't this chump care that he was getting cheated? Was he embarrassed that he hadn't caught the mistake himself?

The guy and Donald exchanged a look I couldn't quite read, but I suddenly got the impression they knew each other more than a casual gas station customer and owner might. The only other place I'd seen this guy was at Bobby Joe's apartment. And Donald always got weird around those seashells.

I snatched the shell out of the guy's hand.

His eyes flew wide. "Hey, give that back."

"I'll give you the four bucks," I said.

I smashed the shell on the counter.

It shattered, pieces scattering.

Among the broken bright pink and yellow shards sat a little plastic bag of green leaves.

Holy crap. That was definitely worth more than four dollars.

27

Donald's hand snaked out and closed around the baggie of pot before I could grab it. The guy next to me muttered, "I'm outta here," and bolted for the door. Donald and I faced each other.

"Guess this explains why you got upset when I tried to buy a shell magnet," I told him.

Donald dropped his closed hand behind the counter. For a second, I wondered if he had a shotgun or base-ball bat under there to ward off robbers, but his hand came up empty. No weapon and no pot.

"Now before you get all high and mighty, let me say all my customers have medical marijuana cards."

I laughed. "Is that why you hide their medicine in those ugly souvenirs?" I put emphasis on the word "medicine," but Donald was sweating so much by this point, the sweat was probably dripping onto his eardrums and he couldn't hear me.

But he couldn't miss the fact that I was laughing at him. His face grew red. "You better keep quiet, or I'm gonna . . ." His threat trailed off.

"You're gonna what? Kill me like you did Bobby Joe? Did he find out about this little operation?"

His flushed face paled at the accusation, and I wondered if I was right. Before I could get too smug, I noticed the empty store and vacant gas pumps, and realized that I was alone with Donald. Maybe I should have kept my suspicions to myself.

Donald moved toward the gap in the counter faster than I'd thought possible for a man of his girth. My previous humor evaporated as panic took its place. I ran for the exit, his footsteps pounding behind me.

I escaped the store and yanked open my car door, glad I'd forgotten to lock it. I threw myself inside, pulled the door shut, and slapped down the lock as Donald stomped off the curb.

He jerked the door handle, putting his other hand on the car to brace himself. He glanced past me and stopped tugging at the handle. I looked over my shoulder and saw a car pull into the driveway and up to the pumps. A man in some type of worker's uniform, maybe a mechanic or an electrician, got out and unscrewed his gas cap.

I turned back toward Donald, who was a sweaty mess.

"I didn't kill Bobby Joe," he yelled through the glass of the car window, the hairs of his toupee swaying in the breeze. "I didn't kill him."

Without a word, I dug my keys out of my pocket, started the car, and backed out of the space. I glanced at the man pumping gas and found him staring at us. I wondered how long it'd take for news of our little conversation to travel through Blossom Valley's grapevine.

As I drove out of the lot, I mentally lectured myself. How many times could I put myself in danger in one day? Somebody murdered Bobby Joe. I needed to take my safety more seriously, or I might meet the same fate as my sister's boyfriend.

Internal lecture over, I moved on to the next issue. Had Bobby Joe stumbled across Donald's pot activities, and had Donald killed him to keep him quiet? But that didn't make any sense. Stump had his own pot business, in which Bobby Joe might have been a partner. Was it some type of turf war?

Maybe I should visit Stump. If I caught him in one of his zoned-out moods, he might tell me all kinds of things. But did I dare go over there alone after what had already happened to me today? First, Todd had pulled a knife when he found me in his truck, and then Donald had chased me out of his store.

I'd just told myself to stop sticking my nose in dangerous places, and I was already thinking about doing it again. If only the cops hadn't questioned Ashlee a second time. They obviously had no idea who had killed Bobby Joe. If I didn't work faster, my little sister might be carted off to the big house. No way could she survive those sparse conditions with limited access to makeup and hair-care products. And no way could I survive knowing she was in there.

Besides, Stump was most likely too stoned to hurt me. I could knock on his door and see what kind of mood he was in, then leave if he appeared sober enough to cause harm.

I skipped the street that would take me home and headed for the train tracks instead. All was quiet in the Palm Villa Apartments complex when I pulled into the parking lot.

I knocked on Stump's door. No answer. I knocked again. Still nothing. A window beckoned from my right, and I stepped off the pavement and into the shrubbery, twigs poking my legs as I moved to the window. I cupped my hands on the glass and peeked in. The blinds were open enough that I could look through the slats into a room empty of furniture.

"He moved out," a voice said behind me.

I jumped and turned around. Yolanda stood on the path, wearing her same housecoat and a pair of plastic gardening clogs.

"When?" No one had said anything about moving when I'd been here yesterday.

"After you left. His folks helped him pack everything into his dad's truck. He mumbled something about not being able to afford the rent on his own. At least I think that's what he said. That kid talks like a first grader."

I ignored Yolanda's assessment of Stump's communication skills. "Think he's moving back in with his parents?" He wouldn't be the first guy who'd flown the nest, only to flutter back home to the family tree. I'd done that exact thing, although I liked to tell myself it was for my mom's benefit, not mine.

Yolanda shook her head. "Said he'd be renting a room from his buddy, Donald, the guy who owns that gas station north of town. His folks seemed to think he'd be filling in for Bobby Joe since he got himself killed."

My face must have broadcast my shock.

"Don't look so surprised. You knew his roommate got killed."

That wasn't the part that had shocked me, but I didn't feel like explaining to Yolanda. Instead, I said, "I still haven't gotten used to the idea." I stepped back onto the pavement. "Guess I'll be going then. Thanks for the info."

We walked down the path together until we reached the fork in the sidewalk.

"Let me know next time you stop by," Yolanda said. "I still owe you that tea. And I'll make you my famous ambrosia salad."

The woman must be seriously lonely to keep asking me over. I barely knew her. "Sounds delicious. I'll be sure to do that." I headed to my car while Yolanda went toward her apartment. She stopped at her door and turned back.

I waved good-bye and drove toward home, pondering this new bit of information. Why would Stump move in with a drug rival? The only answer was that they weren't rivals, but partners. Stump must grow or acquire the pot, and Donald distributed it in those painted seashells. Bobby Joe could have been killed if he'd threatened to expose the operation. Either he didn't approve of their business, or else he had wanted a bigger cut and they'd decided his part in the deal was no longer necessary. I should have pressed Ashlee for more details about Bobby Joe's possible pot dealings when Yolanda first mentioned it. Shame on me for not following up more.

Another dilemma was what to do about the drugs. Growing marijuana was a profitable business in Northern California, but you couldn't legally sell it to any pot-head who asked. They needed a marijuana card. And the seller probably needed some sort of license as well.

I should tell the police. But if I contacted them now, they might pull officers off Bobby Joe's case. While they gloated over busting up a drug ring, they'd forget all about finding his killer. Then again, Donald or Stump might be Bobby Joe's killer, and this new information would help the police prove that. My head started to throb as I tried to sort everything out.

As my house came into view, I decided to worry about my latest discovery after dinner. I never made good decisions on an empty stomach.

I parked, grabbed my keys, and hurried up the walk. When I opened the front door, a waft of cabbage-filled air greeted me. Yeesh, I'd forgotten about the rolls. Maybe I should have gotten takeout while I'd been off snooping.

Ashlee ran in from the living room, fresh makeup on her face, her hair blow-dried and styled. "You're back. What did you find out?"

Before I could answer, Mom appeared from the kitchen, drying her hands on a dish towel. "I was starting to get worried. How did it go?"

I'd been feeling pretty good about everything I'd uncovered in the last hour or so, but now I realized I had little to report. "I'm following up on a couple of things," I offered lamely.

Ashlee looked like I'd stolen her favorite lipstick. "That's it?"

"I'm sure you're doing your best," Mom said, though the way she scrubbed her hands with the dish towel implied otherwise. "Dinner will be ready in a minute."

"That'll give me a few minutes to talk to Ashlee." I clasped her hand and pulled her into the living room while Mom returned to the kitchen. I didn't bother cushioning my question. "You said before that Bobby Joe didn't sell pot. Are you absolutely sure?"

"Positive." Ashlee puffed out her chest, the picture of indignation. "I'd never date a guy like that. In fact, he was totally anti-drugs."

"How do you know?"

"Remember I told you that he and Stump didn't get along? It's because he found out that roommate of his was dealing drugs and told him he had to stop."

Now that was interesting. I stepped closer. "When was this?"

"I don't know, not too long before he got killed. He was sure this truck rally was going to change his whole career. He'd be famous. TMZ would follow him, snapping his picture while he bought frozen burritos at the grocery store. And he didn't want some drug bust ruining everything."

From the little I'd known of Bobby Joe, he'd had enough inflated delusions to make this kind of thinking possible. "What did Stump say when Bobby Joe demanded he stop selling pot?"

"He said no. Boy, was Bobby Joe pissed. But Stump said that he'd gotten himself a partner and expanded, so he was making too much money to quit now."

I wondered why Stump was moving out of the apartment now if he was flush with cash. Maybe he figured it'd be easier to live with Donald, who could package the stuff for sale that much faster, and was using the money excuse to satisfy his parents' curiosity.

"Couldn't Bobby Joe kick him out?" I asked.

Ashlee shook her head. "Stump's parents signed the lease, so Bobby Joe would be the one to move. And he'd put all his money in that truck of his." Ashlee pursed her lips at the mention of this, as if remembering all the fancy dates she'd missed because of her broke boyfriend. "He figured he'd start making tons of money after a scout spotted him this weekend."

Man, I wished I lived in Bobby Joe's imaginary world.
I bet it was so nice right up until he was murdered.

"So he was biding his time until he could afford to
move," I said.

"Right. Like I said, once he got his sponsors lined up,
he knew he wouldn't be living there much longer. He
already avoided Stump because Stump spent all his
time smoking weed. Bobby Joe only used the apartment
to sleep and shower."

"Dinner!" Mom called from the kitchen.

Ashlee bounded down the hall to eat. I trailed
behind her, wondering all the while how any of this related to Bobby Joe's death and wishing Ashlee had told
me these details earlier. Maybe tensions had run so high
those last couple of days that the two had argued, and
Stump had killed him. Or maybe Bobby Joe had found
out Donald was the new partner and tried to get him to
quit since Stump wouldn't. If Donald tried to fire Bobby
Joe to get him out of the way, Bobby Joe could rat him
out to the police as retaliation. Donald might have decided the only way to handle Bobby Joe was to kill him.

And what about the missing money Donald accused
Bobby Joe of stealing? Was that a cover Donald had in-
vented to make Bobby Joe look bad, or was he really a
thief? Keeping that truck ready for a rally must have
been expensive, but would Bobby Joe had stolen the
cash, even if Ashlee swore he wouldn't?

I plopped down in my usual spot at the table and
eyed the casserole dish resting on the crocheted hot
pad. The limp, green cabbage rolls lay there, nestled
in a pile of beige sauerkraut. I fought back a grimace
as Mom spooned a pile onto her plate. I added a significantly smaller stack to my own plate, earning a
disapproving frown from Mom.

"What did you do today?" I asked her before she could lecture me on not eating enough.

"I visited your father this morning, and then had lunch with Martha so we could go over some bunco strategy."

I put my fork down. "I didn't realize you were visiting the cemetery. I wish you'd told me."

Mom dabbed at her lips with a napkin. "Sometimes I like to visit by myself. I don't expect you girls to go with me every time."

I had to wonder if she'd gone out there because of her upcoming date with Lane, to tell Dad about her decision. "I haven't visited in a while. I should probably go," I said.

Ashlee twiddled with her fork and stared at her plate of sauerkraut.

Mom shook her head. "You should only go if you want to. There's no right or wrong number of times to visit."

Truth be told, I preferred to remember Dad through the photos around the house and the medallion around my neck. I found the cemetery too impersonal.

With our talk about Dad's passing and my thoughts on Mom's upcoming date, my gut already felt heavy and I hadn't even eaten any cabbage yet. I switched topics.

"Tell me about this bunco strategy. I didn't realize strategy was actually involved."

"Well, it is mostly luck, but Martha and I are going to try different dice-cup-shaking techniques to see if we can change the results."

We chatted about whether that qualified more as cheating than strategy while I nibbled on a cabbage leaf and tried to figure out a way to hide the rest under my napkin or beneath the plate rim. Too bad we didn't have a dog. Sure, I was a grown adult who could decide whether or not I wanted to finish my dinner, but Mom worked hard to make us healthy meals. The least I could do was pretend to eat it.

In the end, I managed to eat enough of the roll that she didn't comment. Ashlee remained noticeably quiet during the meal, probably still worried about the cops. A second visit was definitely a bad sign.

After dinner, I cleared the table and washed the dishes, then settled in the living room for some mind-numbing television. Ashlee joined me, and we listened to the latest celebrity gossip, though I didn't recognize half the so-called celebrities. When a commercial came on, I muted the sound.

"Wait," Ashlee said, "what's that movie they're advertising?"

"They'll show the ad again. I want to talk to you about Mom."

Ashlee's expression grew serious. "What about her? Is something wrong?"

Good question. That's what I was hoping to find out. "I was wondering if she'd mentioned this Lane guy to you. The one who's in bunco."

"You mean about how he asked her on a date?"

My neck felt stiff as I nodded. "That's the one. What do you think about that?" I'd given Mom my blessing, but the idea still made me uneasy.

I expected a wise crack or some flippant remark, but Ashlee surprised me.

"When she first mentioned it, I was really upset," she said. "I mean, how could she possibly betray Dad like that?"

I leaned forward, my head bobbing freely this time. "My thoughts exactly. I mean, if you love someone for that many years, how can you possibly think about dating someone else?"

Ashlee studied the picture of Dad on the mantel. "But then I got to thinking about how much I like dating. I mean, I know I'm not going to marry any of these guys, but it's fun to get out, have someone to do things with. So I asked myself if Mom would be better off sitting at home moping or spending time at the movies or dinner, even if it is with some guy. The most important thing to me is that Mom's happy."

I stared at Ashlee like we'd never met. When had my sister gotten so smart?

"Wow," I said. "I was so worried about Dad's memory that I forgot to think about Mom. She deserves to be happy."

I felt a hand on my shoulder and jerked my head around. I hadn't heard Mom come in the room.

"Thank goodness you girls feel that way. Now I can enjoy my dinner with Lane without feeling guilty."

I rose from the recliner and hugged her. "Please do. I'm sure he's a great guy."

Mom returned my hug, then settled on the couch while I sat back down. With my mind clear, my thoughts immediately turned back to Bobby Joe's death. I felt an underlying sense of panic since I'd removed Todd from my suspect list. Was I any closer to solving the murder with this new information about Donald and Stump, or was I merely grasping at straws?

This question plagued me all evening, even as I got ready for bed, turned out the lights, and got under the covers. And it continued to plague me long into the night.

28

Even though I forgot to set my alarm and woke up an hour late, I still tried to see the next morning as a fresh start, a new day with which to come up with different angles to investigate Bobby Joe's murder. That optimism lasted until I arrived at work.

Gordon paced the sidewalk in front of the lobby entrance, glancing at his watch. When he saw my car approaching, he stopped pacing and tapped his foot until I'd parked and stepped onto the curb.

"Morning, Gordon," I said in a neutral voice, never mind my trembling nerves.

He looked at his watch again, even though he'd checked it fifteen seconds ago. Must have a memory like a goldfish. "You're late."

"Is that possible? We don't have set working hours."

Gordon shook his head. "But you're normally here at seven. Consistency is what makes an employee dependable. Lately, you've been less than dependable."

I started to rebut his accusation, but he talked right over me.

"You left early yesterday, you've been taking long

ALL NATURAL MURDER 273

lunches, and this isn't the first morning you've been late. You haven't been doing your job."

"I always do my job," I snapped, managing to squeeze the words in when he paused for breath.

"Then where are the marketing numbers Esther said you'd give me?"

Crap. I'd forgotten to pass the numbers along to Gordon, like I'd forgotten when he'd asked about those demographics. "I finished the research but didn't have a chance to give you the results yet," I answered with false dignity.

"You could have gotten me the numbers yesterday if you hadn't left early."

I felt my anger brewing. I'd had plenty to deal with this past week. The least Gordon could do was show me some compassion. "My sister's boyfriend was murdered, in case you forgot. I'm trying to find out who killed him before the police arrest her."

"And I'm trying to run a successful farm and spa. I warned you before not to let your sister's problems get in the way. If you can't do your job, then I'll speak to Esther about your taking a leave of absence. As it is, we barely have enough work for you."

I stared at Gordon, my entire body quivering. Did this guy not care that my sister was a suspect in a murder investigation? Did his tunnel vision really allow him to see only what related to the spa?

"Of course I can do my job. You need to be more understanding."

Gordon gestured toward the house behind him. "Being understanding won't keep this place in business." With that, he turned and strode back into the lobby.

I stood on the sidewalk for a moment to gather my

wits, which were scattered all over the cement. I definitely hadn't been putting one hundred percent into my work, but Ashlee was involved in a murder, and that took precedence over a daily blog and chasing ducks. How could I focus on my job when the police were targeting her?

Then again, Esther wasn't paying me to do mediocre work. Considering how much I needed this job, I couldn't afford to slack off any more.

I headed for the lobby, bracing myself for another encounter with Gordon, but the room was empty. Maybe he was bothering Zennia, counting the blueberries in everyone's oatmeal to make sure she was being frugal.

I slipped into the office, shut the door, and flopped into the desk chair. After a one-minute pity party, I printed the figures and set them aside for Gordon. If only I'd done this simple step yesterday, I could have saved myself a lot of aggravation.

Today's blog might as well be about trying to handle too much at once and balancing priorities. I dashed off a few paragraphs, reread the blog for typos and accuracy, and posted it.

As I spun around in the chair to celebrate another blog finished, the office door opened, and I momentarily saw Esther's face before I spun toward the bookcase, then the back wall, then the file cabinet, and then the desk again.

I grabbed the desk edge to stop another rotation. "Esther, I finished the blog and well, never mind." She obviously had something on her mind and wasn't interested in my chatter.

Esther clasped her hands before her, fiddling with the cow button on her denim shirt with the embroidered barn scene. Her mouth opened and closed three times before she croaked out, "Honeybunch, we need to talk."

Oh, no, not that overused line. She couldn't be breaking up with me, so she must be about to fire me. No more help for Mom's bills, no more socking away a few dollars here and there for the day I'd eventually move into my own place again, no more teasing Zennia about her healthy eating or feeling like I was helping Esther launch her business.

"Esther, before you start, I know I haven't been the best employee lately, but as soon as the police figure out who killed Bobby Joe, I'll be back to normal, honest." I bit my lip and waited for her response.

She looked at a spot over my head. "You know I love your work, but Gordon came upstairs a few minutes ago and told me you've been missing assignments and leaving early."

"I've kept a strict record of my hours."

Esther waved her hand. "I'm not worried about that. You're more honest than Abe Lincoln. But your heart's not in it. How can you possibly concentrate with everything that's going on with your sister?"

I held onto the edge of the desk. I felt queasy, and I wasn't sure if it was from spinning in the desk chair or the direction this conversation was taking. "I'll admit I've been distracted, but I'd like to think I'm still doing a decent job here."

Esther sank into the guest chair and pressed her lips together. "Gordon has suggested I find a replacement until your personal life calms down."

Oh, God, she was really going to fire me. Finding a temporary replacement was the first step in my permanent departure. "You don't need to do that. By the time you find someone, this whole situation will be taken care of."

Esther touched my knee in a maternal gesture. "I'd like to believe that. Let's sit on this for a couple of days. If nothing's changed, we'll talk again."

Two days. Not much time. If the police hadn't made progress in the last five days, would two more make a difference? But two days was better than never filling out my time card again.

"Deal," I said.

We stood at the same time, and Esther gave me a quick hug. "I know Gordon can be difficult at times, but he loves this farm almost as much as I do."

"I've posted my blog and printed those numbers you wanted me to run by Gordon. What's next?" I asked, eager to prove my value.

Esther studied me a moment. "Today's Tuesday. You always fill in for Heather on her day off."

So much for my increased attention to my job. "Of course. I meant anything before I start that," I fibbed.

The wrinkles in Esther's face smoothed out as she bought my lie. Her trusting nature made me feel guilty for deceiving her, but I wasn't ready to give up my position here.

"I can't think of anything right off. More businesses have asked if you can paint their windows, but we'll wait until this weather cools off."

Man, I hoped they'd forget all about my painting by that time. Sooner or later, someone would realize that what they thought was artistic brilliance was really lack of skill.

"I'll get started on the rooms." I stepped into the hall and turned into the laundry room next door. The cleaning supplies and fresh towels sat prepped and ready. I wheeled the cart out the door and across the hall to the French doors.

As I crossed the patio, the wheels bounced along the cement, kicking a small pebble into the pool. The smooth surface broke apart as ripples ran through the water. Yet another example of one tiny disturbance causing major waves. But clearly murder was no small disturbance.

I abandoned the cart by the cabins and made my way to the pigsty. Wilbur looked up expectantly, probably hoping I'd have a treat for him.

"Sorry, only me." I leaned on the rail. "Turns out Gordon's right. I am doing a bad job these days."

Wilbur nosed at the mud and grunted.

"It's just that I have to solve this murder. Ashlee's freedom depends on it." I slapped my hand on the rail. "Am I ever going to figure this thing out?"

Wilbur snorted several times in a row. I'd almost swear he was laughing.

I pointed a finger at him. "If you're not going to take this seriously, I'll go talk to Berta." Sure, Berta had pecked my hand the few times I'd collected her eggs, but that proved she was a no-nonsense chicken.

Wilbur lowered his head as if embarrassed by his behavior, but I was the one who should have been embarrassed. I was getting mad at a pig, for pete's sake.

"Sorry, I'm on edge. Guess I should get back to work."

I returned to the cart and grabbed a dust rag. The first three cabins were vacant and still clean from Heather's work the previous day. I ran a cloth over the surfaces, did a quick vacuum, and moved on. The next room belonged to Crusher. My mood perked up when I saw he wasn't there.

I hurriedly cleaned the bathroom, stripped the sheets and threw on new ones, then plumped up the pillows and straightened the items on the coffee table. I was spritzing a burst of homemade lavender water into the air when the cabin door opened and Crusher walked in. So much for avoiding that first awkward meeting after our non-date.

As always, he looked relaxed in his jeans and T-shirt with a surfboard on the front.

I gathered up my cleaning bottles and dust rags. "I'll be out of here in a sec."

"No rush. I always like to see you."

I wasn't sure whether I should take that as a romantic or platonic remark, so I ignored it. "What have you been up to?"

He moved into the room. "I met with my scout again yesterday. He videotaped me performing my trick to show to possible sponsors, even interviewed me to make it like a promo." He grabbed his laptop off the dresser. "You should watch it. It's wicked."

Gordon picked that moment to walk by the open door and peer in. His usual frown deepened when he saw me talking to Crusher, but he kept walking.

"I need to finish the rest of the rooms. Maybe another time." I darted to the door, clutching my supplies.

"Have I done something?" Crusher called as I flew over the threshold and reloaded the cart.

I slipped the air freshener into a vacant slot and glanced around to make sure Gordon wasn't lurking nearby. I spotted him down at the end of the row, and I turned toward Crusher, who had moved to the doorway.

"It's not you. I got reamed by my boss this morning."

Well, technically my boss's right-hand man, but same difference. "I need to focus on my work or else I might be replaced."

Crusher scratched his head. "I had no idea. You could always stop by at lunch to watch the video. I really think you'll like it."

Would I even take a lunch break after this morning's lecture? Should I work through my meals to prove my dedication? If I did take a break, it would be to track down Maria and ask about her alibi, not to watch Crusher's video.

"No guarantees, but I'll try to stop by later today," I said.

"Awesome. I should be around."

I pushed the cart forward a few feet and stopped at the next door. Darlene and Horace were out, probably hiding in embarrassment at the state of their room. Wrinkled socks and underwear were scattered across the sofa, empty Styrofoam coffee cups occupied every surface, and chocolate from half-eaten candy bars oozed onto the wooden dresser top. I straightened up as best I could without manhandling too many of their personal items. I chose to ignore the clear plastic makeup bag full of the spa's little shampoo and conditioner bottles as I wiped down the counters in the bathroom.

Chores completed, I took one more look at the room and cringed. Even after tidying up, the space was far too cluttered. But Horace and Darlene seemed the type to complain if I threw away anything not already in a trash can. Maybe they were planning to stick those Styrofoam cups in their suitcase for a new set of free drinkware. I shrugged at the half-finished room and left, pulling the door closed behind me.

As I stepped behind the cleaning cart, Darlene and Horace came around the corner, Darlene's wooden cane tapping on the cement path. I pushed the cart to the next door, grabbed a handful of cleaners, and hurried inside before they could ask for more toiletries.

I managed to clean the room without interruption and finish up the remaining cabins. I returned the cart to the laundry room and went into the kitchen to see if Zennia needed help prepping lunch.

She sat at the table, sipping a green substance that smelled suspiciously like seaweed and nibbling on a brown square that looked like a muddy hay cake. She set her teacup on its saucer. "Dana, what have you been up to lately?"

Trying to solve a murder, worrying about keeping my job, avoiding the Steddelbeckers. "Too much to relate. But my schedule is open now, and I'm free to help you with lunch."

Zennia sipped her mystery brew again. "As you can see, I'm not exactly swamped. With only three guests, I figured I'd make okra and lima bean vindaloo for lunch."

I suppressed a shudder. "Sounds interesting."

She chuckled. "You're always so diplomatic."

"I try." I poured myself a glass of lemonade and sat down across from her. "Any updates from your nephew?"

Zennia shook her head. "He was passing along most things he heard from the police department, but he's been real hush-hush lately."

"Why's that, do you think?"

She brushed at the front of her tie-dyed dress, where

bits of hay had gathered. "When he gets quiet like that, it means they're about to make an arrest."

The gulp of lemonade I'd swallowed shot back up as fear threatened to close off my throat.

I only knew of one person they could be planning to arrest.

Ashlee.

29

I coughed and spluttered as I forced the lemonade down.

Zennia handed me a napkin. "Goodness, are you all right?"

I nodded, unable to speak.

"Would you like some of my kelp tea? It relaxes the muscles. Might help your throat."

I shook my head emphatically and willed my throat to calm down before Zennia served me slimy weeds from the ocean. I managed to whisper, "I'm fine."

"Whoo, you gave me a scare there," she said.

I swallowed more lemonade to lube my throat before I spoke again. "Any idea who the police are thinking about arresting?"

Zennia laid a hand on my arm. "I am so thoughtless. My chi must be misfiring today. I completely forgot Ashlee was involved in this mess."

"Is that who the police are about to arrest? Please, I need to know."

She looked at her tea cup. "I really don't know.

Maybe it's that Todd fellow that my nephew mentioned before."

I couldn't tell whether Zennia was lying to protect me or really didn't know. But the answer didn't matter. I needed to clear Ashlee's name no matter what. What else could I do to help? I'd interviewed everyone, broken into Todd's truck, and confronted Donald about his drug dealings. I was running out of options.

I realized with a start that Zennia was talking to me. "Sorry, what's that?"

Zennia gestured toward two full boxes of vegetables sitting near the back door that had escaped my attention until now. "I was saying that we've been overrun by tomatoes and zucchini with this hot weather. With so few guests, I can't possibly use everything before it spoils, and I was wondering if you could take the extras to the food bank."

"I'd be happy to." I could use the alone time to figure out my next steps with Ashlee. Maybe I'd come up with a course of action while I was in town.

Zennia took the box of zucchini, while I grabbed the box of tomatoes. We loaded them in the back of my car, and I headed out.

On the drive, I once more struggled with whether I should tell the police about Donald's drug dealings and that he was possibly working with Stump. I'd hesitated because I'd wanted the police's full attention on Bobby Joe's murder. But if the cops were using that time to build a case against Ashlee, maybe I needed to provide a distraction after all. Or maybe the drugs were somehow responsible for Bobby Joe's death.

I exited the freeway, swung through the nearest drive-thru for an iced tea, then pulled into the first shady spot I could find. I dialed Jason's number on my cell phone, crossing my fingers that he wasn't too involved with work. I needed his full attention.

"Dana, it's good to hear from you." The warmth in his voice sent a rush of pleasure through me.

"Jason, I need some advice."

I'd heard typing in the background when he'd first spoken, but the sound ceased.

"Of course. What's up?"

"I've discovered that two of the suspects in Bobby Joe's murder are involved in other illegal stuff, and I'm not sure if I should tell the police. They might forget all about the murder investigation."

"What kind of illegal activity?"

The excitement in his voice leaked through the cell connection. I could imagine the journalist antenna sprouting from the back of his head.

"Drug sales."

Jason let out a low whistle. "You said two. Are we talking a husband-and-wife team here?"

I sucked some iced tea through the straw. "No. It's Stump and Donald. I never would have even realized those two knew each other except I stopped by the gas station yesterday right in the middle of a sale and put the pieces together."

"Stump was selling to Donald? What was it? Meth?"

"Pot. And Stump is supplying the stuff to Donald, who then hides it in this ugly little seashell and sells it to people pretending to buy gas."

A rumble came over the phone. I was so surprised by the sound that it took me a moment to process that Jason was laughing.

"What's so funny? This could be important."

Jason kept chortling while I struggled with the urge to hang up on him. When he spoke, his voice still sounded amused. "Sorry. I was picturing a major meth ring with underworld connections, but it sounds like a small-time pot operation to me. The cops don't care about those around here. They're way too common."

"Even though I caught Donald in the act?" The cops in the Bay Area seemed to focus more on the large marijuana growers, but surely any drug bust was a big deal in this town.

"They might send an undercover officer out there to try and buy a bag, but they're not going to pull anyone off another case. I'm pretty sure even my eighty-year-old neighbor sells pot in her spare time."

Jason laughed again. Good thing we weren't in the same room, or I might accidentally kick him in the shins.

"Huh." Another potential dead end. Then again, Donald had seemed pretty worked up when I'd discovered his secret. Just because Jason felt the cops would overlook Donald's dealings didn't mean Donald wasn't worried about it. I mulled this over.

In the silence, I heard Jason resume his typing.

"Working on a big story?" I asked.

"Article about the cooling centers being shut down due to budget cuts. A timely topic with this heat wave."

I wished he hadn't mentioned the heat wave. The car immediately felt hotter. I turned the ignition key and hit the A/C button, then sipped some iced tea.

"I thought those centers were popular," I said.

"They are. But the city council sees them as a luxury item."

I shook my head, not that Jason could see that. "Tell that to some ninety-year-old sitting at home with no air-conditioning."

"Preaching to the choir." Jason cleared his throat. "Say, how about dinner tonight?"

"Are you asking out of personal interest or as a reporter who wants to interview me about my drug-busting skills?"

Jason laughed. "I'll definitely be off the clock, I promise. And you have to take a break from all this Bobby Joe stuff, too."

I'd been about to laugh, but the sound died in my throat. "I can't guarantee that. Zennia thinks the police are about to arrest someone, and that someone could easily be Ashlee. They stopped by to see her again yesterday."

"I know you're worried about your sister, but you can't obsess every minute. You need a night off to get your head straight."

He had a point. I felt like all I did was think about the information I had, then get confused, then review it all again with no progress. It was like exercising on a stationary bike—all you did was wear yourself out without getting anywhere. "I'll try. That's the best I can do."

"Deal. I'll pick you up at seven."

I hung up, feeling almost giddy. Dinner might be what Jason and I needed to smooth over the week we'd been having.

With a renewed burst of energy, I dropped my cup into the holder and pulled out into traffic. I passed the new downtown shops, pleased to see cars parked out in front of the wine bar, before turning onto a side street and driving by a row of mostly vacant buildings. On the next block, Second Kitchen sat alone. Someone had attempted to paint over the graffiti on the two sides that I could see, but some of the words still showed through. A new blue awning covered the door, and a man in a T-shirt and shorts swept up broken glass in the parking lot.

I pulled around back to where a rolling garage door sat open and popped my trunk. A man in cargo pants and a plaid shirt appeared in the doorway and approached my car as I got out.

"Vegetables from the O'Connell Organic Farm and Spa," I told him. He grabbed the first box without a word. I took hold of the second one and followed him inside.

Three people worked in the large, high-ceilinged room, sorting through boxes, stocking shelves, and breaking down cardboard. I set down my box where the man indicated and straightened up, noting a woman whose back was to me. She turned around, and I sucked in my breath.

Tara.

She caught sight of me at the same moment and glanced over her shoulder as if she planned to run for an available exit. With none in sight, her shoulders sagged a smidge, or maybe that was my imagination. She offered me something that was probably meant to be a smile but looked instead like she'd just swallowed a bug.

I stepped around boxes and bags of canned goods to reach her side. "I didn't realize you volunteered here," I said.

Tara rubbed her hands on her jeans and studied her palms. "I've visited a food bank more than once when money was short. Now that I'm not starving, I like to help out when I can. It's one of the few places Donald lets me go on my own."

"He does keep you on a short leash."

Tara brushed her hair away from her face. "He

likes to keep an eye on his prize. I'm young and good-looking. He's old and not exactly hot."

Did Donald know his wife described him in such an unflattering light?

The man who'd helped empty my trunk came over. "Tara, when you get a chance, we need to box up some lunches for those kids."

Tara nodded and moved toward a shelf on the far wall. I tagged along, knowing I was slowing her down as I tried to figure out why I was talking to her at all. What could she tell me that she hadn't already?

While she grabbed some paper bags and a stack of napkins, I hovered nearby, waiting for her to finish.

She looked at me. "Are you gonna bother me with more questions about Bobby Joe? I already told you everything I know."

"Look, the police still haven't solved his death. I have to figure out who killed him."

"Tara, we got a huge shipment of canned corn," the man called again. "Give me a hand, will ya?"

If I didn't know any better, I'd swear he was trying to keep me from asking questions. Or maybe my lack of progress was making me paranoid.

Tara went to the open garage door, where a large truck now idled, and began pulling boxes off the back. We couldn't exactly talk while she carted boxes back and forth, so I grabbed one myself and stacked it with the others. After several minutes of lifting and hefting, the truck was empty, and I was winded. Tara wasn't the least out of breath, and she smoked. How embarrassing.

As the truck pulled away, Tara nodded at me. "Thanks for the help. Guess I owe you now."

I wasn't one to turn down voluntary cooperation.

"Have you thought of anything useful since we last talked?"

Tara walked back into the building, me right behind her, and returned to the shelves where she'd been working earlier. She grabbed a package of juice boxes and used a nearby box cutter to slice through the plastic. When she didn't answer, I started to wonder if she'd heard my question.

"Nope, sorry," she finally said. She shook out a paper bag and stuffed a napkin inside, followed by the juice box. "But I haven't been thinking about it. I've got my own problems." She closed her eyes. When she opened them, I'd swear I saw tears, but she blinked, and the moisture was gone.

Something was definitely troubling her. Had she found out about Donald's drug activities? Did she disapprove of his pot selling?

With any luck, I was about to find out.

30

I took a paper bag off the stack and shook it open, determined to keep Tara talking. "Let's go back to why Donald didn't like Bobby Joe all of a sudden. He thought you two were sleeping together, plus Bobby Joe was skimming from the till. Anything else?" Like that wasn't enough to make a man mad.

Tara slammed a juice box on the shelf, and I winced. The cardboard bent, but didn't bust.

"I told you," she said. "Bobby Joe didn't steal that money."

"How can you be so sure? You and Ashlee say Bobby Joe is innocent, but Donald believes otherwise. And Bobby Joe was always short on cash, what with his expensive truck and all those parts. It must have been awfully hard working around that money all day, especially alone, and not be tempted."

"He didn't take it."

"How do you know?" I noticed for the first time that Tara had little dark half-moons under her eyes, partly hidden by concealer. Something was keeping her up at night.

She offered a humorless smile. "I've felt bad about Bobby Joe getting blamed ever since he got killed. He doesn't deserve people talking about him, especially when he didn't do anything wrong." She squared her shoulders. "I took the money."

I knocked the stack of napkins to the floor as I brought my hand up to my chest, and scrambled to pick them up. "You were stealing from your own husband? Why?"

"A little insurance."

"Insurance against your husband?"

The same guy wandered past us, humming to himself. I must have appeared awfully threatening if he felt the need to constantly remind me of his existence.

"I'm not exactly new to this game. Donald married me as a trophy wife, nothing more."

I started to interrupt, but she held up a hand.

"I'm sure he loves me in his own way, but our relationship isn't based on deep conversations and shared worldviews." She grabbed a tuna pouch from a nearby box and added it to the bag. "He saw me at that diner where I was working, liked the way I shook my booty, and made me an offer. Keep working in a dive in the middle of nowhere or marry him and enjoy the middle-class life."

"All the more reason not to steal from him, am I right?" I don't know why I was needling Tara, but I had trouble with a woman blatantly stealing from her husband. Did everyone lie, cheat, or steal in a marriage these days?

Tara gave me a smile that said she knew more about the world than I could ever learn. "You can't see it through my jeans, but an expiration date is already stamped on my ass." She slapped her butt, in case I couldn't find it on my own. "I saw some cellulite last week. Any day now, Donald's going to decide I'm old and used up at thirty-two and go find himself a younger model."

A truck rumbled up to the back of the food bank, its brakes squealing as it slowed.

"Is that why you tried to blame the missing money on the other clerk, the young, pretty one you mentioned?"

Tara adjusted her top. "You got it. She has her eye on Donald, and I need to make sure she's fired before she can sink her pretty little nails into him, if she hasn't already."

"You think Donald's cheating on you with her?"

"Something's up. He's been acting squirrely for a while now, making secret phone calls, running errands but bringing nothing back. I know the signs."

I nodded to keep her words flowing. "So you started stealing the occasional twenty."

Tara licked her lips like a lion eying a gazelle. "I was stealing before that, but I upped the amount when Donald started acting different. The man never met a dollar he didn't like. Which is why he made sure I signed a pre-nup. If I leave, I get nothing."

"Surely if Donald's the one who cheats, then you could get a settlement. Doesn't the pre-nup cover situations like that?"

"If I'm the one who asks for the divorce, I get nothing, no matter what. So Donald can sleep around all he wants, and I can either sit there like yesterday's leftovers or leave with my dignity and not much else. Which is why I decided to take that money. I consider it payment for all those times Donald made me dress like a schoolgirl in bed."

Ack! Too much information. "And here Donald

thinks Bobby Joe was to blame," I said, circling back to the reason I was talking to her.

Tara started filling another bag. "He must realize by now that he was wrong. I'm still taking my fair share, even with Bobby Joe dead. But things are going to blow up soon."

"What makes you say that?"

"Donald was totally freaked last night. I don't know if his honey on the side has a boyfriend, or if he figured out I was on to him, but he was jumpier than one of those twitchy Chihuahuas. Kept looking over his shoulder, sweating every time the phone rang. This morning, he was up and out super early. Maybe he's gonna run off with the little tramp."

Or maybe Donald was worried the police were about to arrest him for his drug dealing. Tara seemed completely oblivious to that side of Donald's life. I wouldn't be the one to tell her, but I did say, "I'm sure he's not cheating on you."

Tara went back to her wise smile. "I wish I had your sunny outlook." She glanced toward the front of the food bank, where a few people had entered, and gasped. "Oh crap, here comes Donald to drive me home. You need to get out of here. He'll blow his top if he sees me with you."

Donald was a man who might have already lost a profitable side business, thanks to me. He was bound to be furious when he saw me here.

Was it too late to run?

31

Tara gave me a shove toward the garage door in the
back. "Hurry up, would you? If Donald's thinking about
leaving me, I don't need to give him another reason
when he sees me talking to you."

Given how Donald had chased me out of his store at
our last encounter, Tara's worries might be on the
mark. She hustled me farther back toward the rolling
door.

I literally dug in my heels to stop my momentum and
held up my hands. "All right, I'll go."

"Thanks." Tara gave me another little shove, in case
I changed my mind, then hurried toward the front. I
nodded to the guy unloading a palate of toilet paper
and walked to my car.

As I drove out of the lot, I thought about our conversation. For all that talking, Tara really hadn't helped
much. Now I knew she'd been stealing the money, but
that didn't change things. As long as Donald thought
Bobby Joe was guilty, that still gave him a motive.

Back at the farm, I gave up my usual parking place

for one in the shade and trudged along the side path that would lead me to the kitchen door. Lunch was long over, but Zennia might need my help with a snack. Otherwise, I'd spend the afternoon working on marketing materials.

I hung a left when I reached the cabins and walked toward the pool area. Crusher reclined on a chaise longue, sunglasses planted on his face.

I thought he might be sleeping, but he jumped up when I walked by and whipped off his sunglasses. "Dana, hi again."

"Hey, Crusher, enjoying your day?"

He let his gaze linger on me. "It's better now."

I blushed and tried to think of a conversation changer. As I poked around my empty brain, Crusher spoke.

"How about watching that video now?"

He spoke with such eagerness that I was catapulted back fifteen years to when Mickey, my next-door teen neighbor, invited me to his room to see his comic-book collection. As I'd soon discovered, he'd really wanted to try out his quick technique for removing my bra. Since I already knew I didn't want Crusher removing any of my clothing, his suggestion didn't exactly excite me.

"I'm still working."

He gave me a puppy-dog look, big eyes and all. "It'd only take a minute."

I felt myself waffling. What would it hurt? The guy obviously wanted someone to show off his video to, and he didn't seem to know anyone else in town. I was about to agree when I heard my name. Gordon stood at the French doors of the dining room, waving his arm for me to join him. Drat.

"Duty calls," I said lightly to Crusher. I didn't want him to know my insides were one giant knot. What did Gordon need to talk to me about this time? What had I done wrong now?

"Later, then." Crusher slipped his sunglasses back on and lowered himself onto the chaise longue. I headed to where Gordon waited, checking his watch. If he was in such a hurry, maybe he should have walked over to where I was.

"I didn't want to talk in front of the guests," he said as if reading my mind.

I put my hands on my hips, preparing for battle. "Don't think for one minute that you're going to tell me I'm doing something wrong again. I've been working all day and haven't even taken a lunch break." Well, except those few minutes sitting in my car and talking to Jason on the phone, but that hardly counted.

Gordon narrowed his eyes. "I wanted to apologize," he snapped.

My eyebrows shot up. "Come again?"

"A couple of days ago, I accused you of not giving me the demographics report."

"I remember." I spoke slowly and quietly, not wanting to interrupt a possible admission that he'd made a mistake.

"While looking at my clipboard a bit ago, I noticed there was no check mark next to that particular line item, which means I never actually asked you."

I felt a gloating smile creep its way upward, but I tamped it down. "I see."

"I'm sorry I falsely accused you. You're not quite as incompetent as I accused you to be."

"Gee, thanks." As apologies went, it was certainly

lacking, but for Gordon, this was a breakthrough moment. "Did you happen to mention this discovery to Esther?"

Gordon fiddled with a cuff link. "I did. However, all my other observations were correct. You still need to focus more on your job."

I smiled sweetly. "I always do." Well, I hadn't been lately, but no way would I admit that.

Gordon smiled back at me. "Excellent, because we have another yoga candidate coming in for an interview tomorrow. He hasn't worked in the last ten years, but I'm sure he has a valid reason."

"I'll be sure to ask him." Maybe he was in prison, or living in a monk's cell, or hiking the world with only a backpack and a pair of sturdy shoes.

Gordon's smile widened. "Good, but before that, I need you to do something for me this very afternoon." Uh-oh, a little payback for the apology?

"What is it?" I asked, bracing myself.

"The Steddelbeckers would like to spend their last day here doing something fun. I volunteered you to drive them out to the fairgrounds."

Of all the horrible chores I could have thought up, chauffeuring the Steddelbeckers around wasn't one of them. But it should have been. "What the heck am I driving them to the fairgrounds for?"

"Someone mentioned the old tractor collection. Turns out they're huge tractor fans and want to take a look."

"Those tractors are still there? When is the town going to clean up that place?" The Blossom Valley town council had fenced off an area way back when I was in junior high. It'd been collecting rusted parts and broken-down tractors ever since.

"There's still talk of turning the area into a tractor display one of these years." Gordon adjusted the other cuff link. "Now, I'm sure you can squeeze this trip into your schedule. I don't need to mention how crucial customer satisfaction is right now, with so many vacancies."

I pictured myself ripping off my work shirt, throwing it on the ground, and quitting right then. Who wanted to drive those two around town, listening to them complain? But I needed this job. And with Esther and Gordon watching my work performance, I couldn't afford to refuse. "When do we leave?"

Gordon looked at his watch. "Twenty minutes. They'll be waiting in their cabin." He walked off.

Great. That gave me one minute to walk to their cabin and nineteen minutes to convince myself that I absolutely, positively had to drive them to the fairgrounds. Off to my right, I heard someone singing and followed the sound across the patio to the herb garden. Zennia crouched among the plants, plucking rosemary stems and placing them in a basket. She waved a stalk at me. "For tonight's halibut."

"Wow, halibut's a bit pedestrian for you, isn't it?"

Zennia chortled. "In honor of Darlene and Horace's last dinner with us, I thought I'd present them with something they might recognize." She plucked another stem. "But I'm making a side of seaweed salad with diced prunes for good measure."

"Give them a double dose. Gordon's making me drive them out for a tour of the old tractors at the fairgrounds."

Zennia rose, her knees popping. "You poor child.

Just remember, you're doing it for the spa. Maybe they'll tell their friends about this place."

I was pretty sure we didn't want any of their friends staying here either, but her words reminded me once again about how precarious the spa's livelihood was. We needed a steady stream of visitors to make the place a success. "We could use more guests; that's for sure."

With a few minutes left to kill, I went into the house and stopped by the office to see if I had any e-mail. After sending a handful of replies, I closed the browser and grabbed my purse from the desk drawer. Might as well get this afternoon over with. Then I could enjoy my dinner with Jason.

I mentally sorted the clothes in my closet as I thought about what to wear on our date. I definitely wanted an outfit that showed I was making an effort. Maybe I'd wear that dress I'd rejected for my non-date with Crusher. I'd have Ashlee help me with the shoes, though she'd no doubt lament my lack of selection. But when you slopped food to the pigs and collected chicken eggs, you basically only needed a pair of boots.

At two minutes after three, I knocked on the Steddelbeckers' cabin. Darlene opened the door, dressed in a gold tracksuit and black running shoes. It was way too hot for the sweatshirt, but I wouldn't be the one to tell her.

"You're late," she said.

Already off to a great start. "I was finishing up some work. Are you and Mr. Steddelbecker ready?"

Darlene harrumphed, and I took that as a yes. Horace appeared in the bathroom doorway, his white socks pulled up and his plaid shorts hanging down, leaving only his knees exposed.

"Let's get this show on the road," he said. "Time's a wastin'."

With an internal sigh, I turned and led the way down the path, steeling myself for my time with the Steddelbeckers. This was bound to be a long afternoon.

32

I led the Steddelbeckers down the path and stopped at my Civic. As soon as I opened the passenger door, Darlene swung her cane inside and tapped the seat.

"Awful tight space," she said. "We're not gymnasts."

"Perhaps Mr. Steddelbecker could sit behind me, and we can slide your seat back," I suggested.

When neither one argued with that idea, I flipped the seat forward. Horace crawled in the back, and Darlene eased into the front. She laid her cane on the floor, wedging it beside the seat.

I shut the door, grumbling to myself about my unwelcome afternoon plans as I walked around the car and got in. Sweat gathered along my hairline before I'd even settled into my seat.

Horace leaned between the two seats and tried to hit the buttons on my console. "Good God, woman. Turn on the air conditioner."

"You trying to kill us?" Darlene asked. She removed her gold sweatshirt, revealing a purple T-shirt with a picture of a cheese wedge on the front.

I turned the key in the ignition and started the air

conditioner full blast. We headed out, Darlene fiddling with the air vents so that they pointed directly at her.

She spent the ride complaining about the weather, complaining about the cost of food and gas, and complaining about the long plane ride ahead of them. Horace would occasionally grunt his agreement from the backseat. By the time I pulled into the fairgrounds parking lot, I was wishing that we were headed to the airport instead, so they could get started on that plane ride.

The fairgrounds looked completely different on this visit compared to the last. On Saturday night, the parking lot had been packed with monster truck fans all jazzed up for the rally. Today the parking lot was one giant, empty expanse, save for a lone truck over near the buildings. As I pulled into a slot a few spaces away, I glanced at the green paint job and did a double take as I bumped the curb with my car. If I wasn't mistaken, that was Todd's truck. What was he doing here? Retrieving something from the scene of the crime? Had he lied about his alibi after all?

I shut off the engine, and we all piled out of the car. Darlene fanned herself with her hand, then reached down and retrieved her cane from the car.

"Hotter than blazes out here," she said. "Did you pack any drinks?"

"No, but you'll find vending machines over there." I pointed to the nearest building, where a Pepsi machine glowed.

"I didn't bring my purse."

Horace patted the pockets of his plaid shorts and shrugged.

This customer satisfaction was for the pits. I fished

around my console until I found a few dollar bills, then held them out to the Steddelbeckers.

Darlene snatched the bills from my hand and scowled. "Guess this'll be enough."

Gee, you're welcome.

I leaned against the car and watched them step onto the curb, cross the sidewalk that ran before the building, and approach the soda machine apprehensively, as though it might spring to life and steal their money. Well, my money.

A door in a nearby building opened, and Todd emerged. He was studying the screen on his smartphone and didn't look up until he reached his truck. When he spotted me, I gave him a little wave.

He lowered the phone. "You still following me? Waiting to plant that evidence?"

Here I thought we'd moved past that, but apparently not. "I'm working. How about you?"

"None of your damn business," he said.

Testy, testy. "Have the day off?" I persisted. Why else wasn't he at work on a Tuesday afternoon?

"I don't have to answer your questions." He yanked his truck door open and hopped inside, slamming the door and starting the engine. But instead of driving away, he sat there, texting.

Fine. I didn't want to talk to him anyway.

I glanced over at the Steddelbeckers, but they seemed to be arguing over what kind of soda to purchase. From the looks of it, they might be there a while.

As I tried to think of something more to ask Todd, I heard a truck horn. I looked toward the sound and saw Crusher motoring across the lot toward me. He made a U-turn, pulled up near the building, and leaned out the driver's-side window, gesturing to me to join him.

The Steddelbeckers were still in the middle of what appeared to be a Pepsi versus Dr. Pepper debate. I trotted to Crusher's truck.

He ran a hand through his blond hair. "I don't know how you found out about my practice, but I definitely appreciate the show of support, especially with this being my last day and all."

I jerked my head toward the Steddelbeckers. "Actually, I'm here to look at some tractors. So are you heading back to San Diego tomorrow, or are you off to another monster truck rally?"

"Home to San Diego. I don't want to compete again until I've signed some deals. I'm not giving my kind of talent away for free."

How quickly commercialism entered the picture. But after losing sponsors before, Crusher probably wanted to lock them in while he could.

Crusher flashed that grin that could thaw a walk-in freezer. "I figured I'd practice that trick a few more times to make sure it was perfect before I head out tomorrow. Why don't you skip the tractors and come watch me?"

Not a bad idea. If he was heading out in the morning, this might be my last chance to get some insight into his knowledge of Bobby Joe. Plus, it might be fun. I glanced at the Steddelbeckers, who had apparently settled on their drink selection and were now trying to feed a dollar bill into the machine. Gordon had only said I needed to drive them to the fairgrounds, not babysit them once we got here.

"Let me show those two where the tractors are located, then I'll break away," I told Crusher.

"Great, that'll give me time to suit up. See you at the track." He drove toward the other end of the lot.

I returned to the sidewalk, glancing at Todd's truck as I went by. He was still engrossed in his phone and didn't look up. Or else he pretended not to notice me.

At the soda machine, I took the dollar bill from Darlene and stuck it into the slot. The dollar disappeared.

"Guess I smoothed that out for you," Darlene commented.

After we'd inserted more dollars and purchased their drinks, I walked the pair behind the building and into a fenced area. The large enclosure was full of dusty tractors, parts, and plow equipment. Not much to look at, from my perspective, but I saw Darlene smile for the first time since I'd met her.

"Look at all these treasures. Why, I feel right at home."

"Yup, yup," Horace said. "Best part of the trip, by far."

If I'd known they liked tractors so much, I could have left them here all weekend. "Guess you two have lots to look at. I'm going to run over to the arena for a few minutes."

Horace and Darlene showed no response as they fondled a fender together, so I headed back across the parking lot, which was at least the length of a football field. With the sun beating down, I felt like I was crossing the Sahara.

By the time I found an open gate outside the arena and stepped into the dirt enclosure, Crusher was already dressed in his jumpsuit, helmet in hand. His monster truck sat in the middle of the circle. He must have parked his regular truck around back.

"I can't wait for you to see me practice."

His enthusiasm was contagious, and I couldn't help but smile. "I really enjoyed watching you at the rally on Saturday night."

He reached out and took one of my hands in his. I resisted the impulse to pull my hand away from this unexpected gesture.

"I'm not used to girls who don't fall all over me," he said. "The way you ran away after our date, you made it pretty clear you're not into me."

"It's not you, it's me," I blurted out, then winced. This wasn't even a breakup, and it still sounded trite. "What I mean is that I'm already seeing someone, someone I care about." Even if we butted heads sometimes.

Crusher released my hand. "I was hoping for one more chance to impress you with my trick, but I guess I'd be wasting my time."

Ugh, I hated turning guys down, especially when I'd only gone out with Crusher for information. "I'd still love to see you practice." As an added bonus, that'd give me more time away from the Steddelbeckers.

Crusher offered another smile, though it wasn't as radiant as the others, and donned his helmet. He climbed into the truck cab, and a moment later, the engine roared to life. The truck lurched into motion and sped across the dirt. I watched as he did a series of jumps, followed by a doughnut, amazed at the difference my new perspective made.

When I'd been sitting in the stands on Saturday night, watching the trucks perform had been much like watching them on TV, only louder. Down on the floor, level with the enormous truck, the experience was downright terrifying. Those giant inflated tires could squash a man flat without even slowing the truck down.

After another doughnut, Crusher drove to the far end of the track and sat for a moment. Was the big trick coming? Was he psyching himself up?

As I watched, the truck raced forward, gaining speed as it approached the ramp. I waited for him to ease off the gas as he went up the incline, but he never slowed down.

The truck went airborne. It soared to impossible heights for such a heavy machine, then dropped back down and landed with a heavy bounce. The truck tipped on two wheels and fell over on its side, then onto its roof.

The momentum carried the truck forward a few yards before it rolled back up on the other two wheels. After a moment, the truck righted itself completely. I wasn't a monster truck fan, but even I felt my mouth drop open as I watched.

Crusher braked and killed the engine. He jumped from the cab and removed his helmet, his gaze never leaving my face as he trotted toward me. He was obviously waiting for me to rip off my clothes and throw myself on him. But my amazement had turned to confusion. That trick seemed so familiar. Where had I seen it before?

Crusher clapped a hand on my shoulder. "Well, what did you think? That's the best trick you've ever seen, right?"

I nodded slowly, still searching my memory archives. "I can see why the scout was so excited. It's just that I've seen that somewhere. Only in drawing form. It was at . . ." I slammed my mouth shut before I could finish the sentence.

I'd suddenly remembered where I'd seen the sketch. On Bobby Joe's desk the night I'd searched his room. So why was Crusher the one performing the trick?

33

Crusher's grip tightened on my shoulder. "This is my special trick. It belongs to me. Only me." His voice took on a pouting tone.

Had Bobby Joe stolen the drawing from Crusher in hopes of perfecting it himself, or had Crusher taken it from Bobby Joe? Bobby Joe was the dead one, so the odds were pretty good that Crusher was the thief. And possibly the killer.

I needed to get out of here.

"You're right," I said, trying to come up with a plan as I spoke. "I saw a similar trick somewhere, but it was nowhere near as cool as this one. You're definitely the king of monster truck tricks."

I stepped to the side and turned so Crusher would have to let go of my shoulder. Maybe it was my imagination, but I'd swear he was eying me like a fox would eye Berta and the other chickens.

"Thanks for letting me watch your practice. It was fun," I said. "I should find the Steddelbeckers now. They're going to wonder why I've been gone so long."

Crusher stared at me so intensely that I had to force myself to break eye contact and stare at the dirt.

"It's my trick," he repeated. "Mine."

"Of course it is. And you did a great job with it." I backed toward the exit, watching Crusher for any sudden moves. He seemed more confused than anything, and I used his uncertainty to slip through the gate, careful not to walk too fast and spook him.

Maybe I was off base. Maybe Crusher performing Bobby Joe's trick had nothing to do with Bobby Joe's death. But Crusher seemed to need this sponsor deal pretty bad. Bad enough to kill for it? He certainly over-reacted when I mentioned having seen the trick already. I needed to find the Steddelbeckers and get back to the spa, so I could pass this information on to the police.

I stopped at the edge of the lot and looked across the expanse of asphalt to where my car waited, baking in the sun. Todd must have left while I was watching Crusher, because his truck was no longer parked near mine. Darlene and Horace were still looking at tractors, since I didn't see them either. They'd be sure to kick up a fuss when I insisted we return to the spa, but what choice did I have?

I heard footsteps and knew I'd hesitated too long. A cough came from directly behind me, and I jumped as I whirled around.

"Crusher, aren't you going to practice some more?"

"Why are you so nervous?" he asked, ignoring my question. "I haven't done anything." The way he said it left no question that he had, indeed, done something.

Well, crap.

I tried to rearrange my face to appear innocent, but

I'd lost all control of my facial muscles. I'm sure my expression shouted my panic.

I tried for the bluff. "I don't know what you're talking about. I'm late, that's all. The Steddelbeckers will want to go back to the farm soon."

He reached up and brushed at a strand of my hair. I flinched when his fingers grazed my temple.

"No, something's up," he said. "You're acting funny. Maybe you're not the cool chick I thought you were."

I held up my hands. "I don't know what's happening here, but I need to get back to work." I had a sudden flashback to four days ago, when we'd been in this exact same position, only then I'd been trapped in his cabin. Why hadn't I noticed how scary he was? How could I have been so easily blinded by his charming smile?

"You're not leaving until I figure out what you know. Do you think Bobby Joe did this same trick?"

"I've never seen any of Bobby Joe's tricks." At least that was the truth, and my voice held conviction.

Crusher jutted his face toward me, as if trying to peek inside my thoughts. "I hope you don't think I killed Bobby Joe. I couldn't have. I went to bed early, like I always do before a rally, like I told you."

Only he hadn't gone to bed early. He'd been at the fairgrounds the night Bobby Joe was killed. Ashlee mentioned how she'd been tempted to flirt with him to get back at her straying boyfriend. How could I have missed that before?

"Yes, I remember," I lied, my mind screaming that I needed to run, to get the hell out of here. "I know you'd never hurt Bobby Joe." I clutched my St. Christopher medal, a source of comfort. "Now excuse me. I have to find the Steddelbeckers before they make a scene."

Before I could move away, he grabbed my arm. A jolt of fear seared my insides.

"You don't know what the last couple of years have been like," he said. "I lost that sponsor deal and gambled away everything I made and then some. All these guys keep chasing me, wanting their money, and I don't have it. But this is my big chance to make it all right. Get everybody off my back." He grabbed my other arm, pulling me close. "I can't let you ruin this."

Almost by instinct, I brought my knee up to his groin, using every ounce of energy I could muster. Crusher released his hold and doubled over with a grunt.

I placed both hands on his head and shoved. Hard. He fell to the pavement. I turned and sprinted across the parking lot, knowing my lead wouldn't last. I aimed for my car like a bullet for a target. If I could only throw myself inside and lock the door, I'd be safe. My feet pounded on the pavement, my car a seemingly impossible distance away.

I wondered if Crusher was chasing me, but I didn't dare take the time to look. I'd swear the parking lot had doubled in length and my car was now two football fields away instead of one. I felt drenched in sweat, the smell of the heat on the asphalt heavy in my nose. My sides heaved, and I gasped for air as I closed the gap between myself and my Honda.

Behind me, an engine fired up, the sound growing louder. This time, I glanced over my shoulder and saw my worst fears materialized.

Crusher swung out of the gate in his monster truck, the giant boulder fists painted on the hood ready to pound me. The noise grew to an excruciating level as he hit the gas and bore down on me.

I faced forward, refusing to watch Crusher advance. If the truck ran me over, I'd rather not see it coming. My car was only a few feet away.

I lunged and grabbed the door handle.

Locked.

No time to dig the keys from my pocket. By now, the truck engine was so loud I was surprised my brain hadn't shattered.

Abandoning the car, I jumped onto the curb and looked back. Crusher's truck was headed straight at me, only yards away. I crouched before the front fender of my car as he launched the truck onto the curb and squealed to a stop. I was lucky he hadn't decided to flatten my car with me in front of it.

I stood up, ready to run to the nearest building, but then froze. The Steddelbeckers were headed my way, halfway between the tractors and my car.

They were still a good thirty feet away, and I flapped my hands at them like a panicked chicken. "Go back! Get out of here!"

Horace put a hand to his chest and looked behind him like I might be yelling at somebody else. As I opened my mouth to shout again, I heard the truck door open. Crusher was coming.

I raced to the Steddelbeckers and grabbed Horace's shoulders. "We have to hurry. I think Crusher killed Bobby Joe. He's after me now." I glanced back and saw Crusher running full steam in our direction.

Horace said, "What the . . ." as Darlene asked, "Who's Bobby Joe?"

I gestured to the dumbfounded Steddelbeckers as I fled toward the tractors. "I'll explain later. Come on." Maybe I could hide them behind some machinery and go for help. With Darlene's bad leg, she couldn't possibly outrun Crusher.

When I reached the entrance to the tractor area, I stopped. Darlene and Horace stood in the same spot. Crusher had almost reached them.

"What are you waiting for? Let's go!" I shouted at them. They still didn't move. Then again, I wasn't even sure Crusher had noticed them. The fury on his face as he stared at me made my body turn cold all over, never mind the scorching heat.

He reached the pair without slowing. Horace stepped in front of Darlene as if to protect her.

Crusher pushed him, and Horace stumbled back.

"Outta my way," Crusher snarled.

As he started past Darlene, she stuck out her cane. Crusher's shin smacked the wood. He pitched forward into the dirt. I held my breath, but only for a second. He was on his feet almost as soon as he'd fallen, gripping his injured leg.

Crusher glared at Darlene. "You're next, old lady." He limped forward a few steps and then broke into a run.

I darted inside the enclosure, no clear idea as to where I was going. Metal loomed up on all sides as I ran among the tractors; some missing tires, others missing cabs, all in disrepair. I rounded a John Deere and slumped behind the giant wheel to catch my breath.

For a moment, all I could hear was my own gasping. As my breathing slowed, I realized I couldn't hear anything else. Where was Crusher? Waiting for me to come out? Or had he given up and gone after the Steddelbeckers?

Only one way to find out. I shifted to a crouched position and lifted my head to peer over the rubber.

Crusher stood directly on the other side of the tire, a crowbar in his hand. How had he gotten so lucky as to find one of those?

Our eyes met. He raised his arm and swung at my head. I ducked back down as the bar hit the metal fender, the sound reverberating in my brain.

I ran, knowing he must be right behind me. I darted between two tractors, then around a plow, the sight of the menacing blades spurring me on. I turned another corner and lost traction in the loose dirt. I slipped, missing a rusty engine block by inches.

As I regained my balance, I felt Crusher's fingers brush the fabric of my shirt. The contact gave me another rush of adrenaline, and I sprinted forward, turning this way and that until I was completely disoriented. I was lost in the maze of tractors. Footsteps pounded behind me, and I zigged behind another huge wheel. Running wouldn't work forever. I needed a plan. And a weapon.

The ground around me offered exactly zero strips of metal or shards of glass. Too bad I couldn't stumble over a crowbar like Crusher apparently had. Maybe I could find a weapon in one of the cabs. Or I could lock myself inside. But then what?

I ran to the nearest tractor that had a cab, but the steps were missing.

Son of a gun.

Muscles protesting, I heaved myself up on a tire, reached over, and seized the handle. I jerked open the door and dragged myself inside, just as Crusher grabbed my ankle. I yanked out of his grasp, pulled my legs under me, and fumbled the door shut.

I checked all around the interior but spotted no loose objects, nothing I could defend myself with. The cab was bare. I pressed down on the horn. No sound. I looked out the window and sucked in my breath.

Crusher was already up on the tire, crowbar still in hand.

The lock! I'd forgotten to lock the door.

As I reached to slap the lock down, Crusher grabbed the handle and pulled. The door opened. The sight sent a surge of panic through me. I grabbed the interior handle and yanked it toward me. The door slammed shut.

Before I could lock it, Crusher pulled again. The door eased open a crack. I couldn't afford to take one hand off the handle to lock the door. Besides, he could always break the window with his crowbar.

That left me one option. I shoved open the door with both hands. The door smacked Crusher in the face. He lost his footing, but hung onto the handle for what seemed like forever. Then he fell to the ground with a thud. The crowbar landed in the dirt to one side.

I had to get that crowbar. I jumped down from the cab but stumbled on my landing. As I scooped up the crowbar, Crusher staggered to his feet. I swung the crowbar and struck his temple, shuddering at the sensation as the metal connected with flesh. He fell back onto the dirt and moaned.

Clutching the crowbar, I stood over him. "Stay down. I don't want to hit you again." But deep down, I kind of wanted to.

Crusher raised his hands. "All right. You win."

The man had lied before. I wasn't taking his word on that.

I pulled my cell phone from my pocket and hit the ON button, ready to call 911. Nothing happened. I hit the button again.

The battery was dead.

I glanced around, unsure of my next move. I couldn't exactly march Crusher out of here on my say-so, crowbar or no crowbar. Then again, I couldn't leave him here while I went for help.

A "tap-tap-tap" sounded from behind me. I risked a peek, keeping one eye on Crusher.

Horace and Darlene rounded a combine harvester and headed toward us.

"You got him," Horace said. "And here we were fixing to help you." I was almost offended by his slightly amazed tone.

Darlene lifted her cane. "This should be registered as a deadly weapon." She poked Crusher's leg with her cane. "Old lady, my eye."

I held up my phone. "Can you two go call the police? My cell's not working."

Darlene waved her own cell phone at me. "Already did."

Even as she spoke, I could hear the wail of approaching sirens. I allowed myself to relax a notch, and even grinned.

When I got up this morning, I never would have guessed that hours later, the Steddelbeckers would help me catch a killer.

A NATURAL MURDER

34

A short time later, an ambulance had carted Crusher off to the hospital with a police escort, and I was telling my story to Detective Palmer for the four hundred and fifty-second time. Okay, maybe it was only the third time, but it felt like more. I was ready to go home and sleep for twelve hours straight, so that I'd be ready for yet another yoga interview in the morning.

"Are we about done here, Detective? I'm bushed."

He flipped through his notes. "Another minute. You really put yourself in danger here. You should have let the police handle it."

"For the last time, I didn't realize Crusher was the killer until I was already alone with him at the track. Otherwise, I most definitely would have called."

"Uh-huh."

The detective didn't sound convinced, but I meant it. I'd let trained professionals with guns handle lunatic killers over me any day, no problem.

"All right, I need to interview Mrs. Steddelbecker," he said. "You can go, and I hope I don't see you for a long while."

"You won't. I'm all done with this murder business."
Especially now that my sister's name was cleared.

I watched Detective Palmer walk over to Darlene,
who leaned on her cane and waited for him. I wasn't
even sure he'd introduced himself before she started
talking. I could hear her words as she practically shouted
at him. "Imagine, a killer staying right next door. We
could have been murdered in our sleep. My daughter-
in-law will never hear the end of this. She's just lucky
I'm so handy with my cane and was able to take down
that Crusher fellow."

Horace patted her hand while Detective Palmer
shuffled back a step.

Darlene pointed in my direction. "And her . . ." she
began.

I sighed, wondering what complaint she might have
this time.

"That one's a spitfire. You should hire her on your
police force."

What was this? Was Darlene complimenting me?

She faced me. "If you ever visit Wisconsin, we've got
a room waiting for you."

"Um, thank you," I said.

Darlene turned back to Detective Palmer. "Now who
do I talk to about suing that Crusher fellow? You wouldn't
believe the emotional distress I've suffered."

I rose from the curb, still a bit unsteady, and saw a
silver Volvo speed across the lot and brake hard near
where I stood. Jason leapt from the driver's seat, shirt
halfway untucked, wrinkles obvious.

He rushed over and swept me up in a bone-crushing
hug. "Are you all right?"

I'd managed not to cry up until now, but the concern in his voice started that telltale burning along my

eyelids. I swallowed. "Yeah, I'm more shook up than anything. I can't believe Crusher killed Bobby Joe."

I started trembling as I recalled the struggle in the tractor graveyard. Jason led me to his Volvo and eased me down into the passenger seat.

He squatted next to me, one hand on my knee. "It's all over. You're safe."

My mind tried to convince my body that Jason's words were true, but I couldn't stop shivering. "At least the whole town will know that Ashlee didn't kill Bobby Joe."

Jason squeezed my knee. "The whole town already knew that," he said.

"But once word gets out, people will also know that Crusher was staying at the spa. They already think the place is cursed. No one will ever stay there again."

Jason stood and draped an arm over the car's roof. "Are you kidding me? The spa is the safest place in town as long as you work there. That's two killers you've caught now."

"You're nice to say that. Are you buttering me up so I'll tell you everything that happened for your newspaper article?"

Jason chuckled. "I can gather enough information from other people without making you answer questions." He lowered his arm. "Now I have to spend this evening writing up the story so it's ready for tomorrow's edition. And you need to go home and recover."

I felt a bud of disappointment bloom. "Guess we should postpone that dinner. On the condition that you let me know everything you find out from the police, of course."

"Deal." Jason glanced at his watch. "Tell you what. If you're feeling up to it, how about coming by the newspaper office at seven? If I haven't finished the story by then, I should be close. I can give you all the dirt."

"I'll be there." I rose, and Jason offered his arm for support. I felt strong enough on my own, but I leaned on him a little anyway.

"I called Ashlee on my way over," Jason said. "She'll be here any minute to drive you home."

I started to protest, and he held up a hand. "I know you're a big strong grown-up, but you'd be doing me a huge favor if you'd let someone else drive you home. You can always pick up your car later."

It might be nice to lean back in the passenger seat and let someone else take control, even if it was my driving-impaired sister. "As a favor to you," I said.

Together, we surveyed the parking lot full of cop cars. Jason had mentioned that an officer was posted at the entrance, so at least I didn't have to deal with any curious bystanders.

As we watched, a bright red car veered into view, a dust cloud billowing behind. I didn't need to see the driver to know it was Ashlee.

She bounced over a pothole and sped across the lot. Just when I thought she'd launch the car onto the sidewalk, much like Crusher had, she cranked the wheel, tires squealing, and slammed on the brakes. The car shuddered to a stop.

"Maybe you'd be safer driving yourself home after all," Jason commented.

"It's not so bad if you close your eyes."

Ashlee got out of the car, slammed her door shut, and practically bounced to the curb. "Sorry it took me so long to get here," she said. "I wasn't sure if there'd be a photographer for the paper, so I had to fix myself up first."

Indeed, now that she'd reached our spot, I could see freshly applied lip gloss, eye shadow, and blush. She'd even taken the time to curl her blond hair. Glad to see her sisterly love had made her rush right out here.

Ashlee peered at me. "You don't look so hot."

"Thanks. Let's not forget I was fighting for my life, and your reputation."

Ashlee smoothed down my hair like Mom did when she was trying to calm me. "But, you're okay, right?"

If I didn't know any better, I'd swear her voice held a hint of concern.

"I will be."

Jason gave my shoulder a squeeze and stepped back. "I should really get going on this story. I'll leave you in the capable . . ." He paused and looked at Ashlee. "I'll leave you in Ashlee's hands, and hopefully see you later."

He offered me a smile, then headed toward a cluster of officers, his reporter persona already taking over. He'd shown restraint by not pestering me for an interview, but he'd get all he needed from his police sources.

Ashlee grabbed my hand and yanked me toward the car. My head snapped back from the force, and my neck yelled at me.

"Come on, get in. I want to hear everything that happened while I drive you home."

"Not much to tell," I said as she let go of my hand and I made my way to the passenger side. "I finally saw that great trick Crusher did and recognized it as the one Bobby Joe had sketched out in his room. I'm not sure, but I think Crusher killed Bobby Joe so he could claim it as his own."

Ashlee was already halfway in the driver's seat, but she popped back out and looked at me over the roof of the car. "He killed my boyfriend over that stupid roll thing? You gotta be kidding me."

"He made references to owing money. With all his previous sponsors dropping him, he must have thought this was his big comeback chance. Then he could pay off the debts and start his career over."

I bent down and settled into the seat. Ashlee took her place behind the wheel.

She shook her head, tears appearing in her eyes. "It was a pretty cool trick. No wonder Bobby Joe wanted to surprise me with it. He knew I would have been so proud."

I dug a napkin out of my pocket, in case those tears started to fall. "At least we've caught his killer. And now everyone knows you're innocent."

Ashlee perked up and started the car. "That's true. And now I can start dating again. In fact, I already lined up a date for this weekend while I was driving over here. He just finished a tour in the army. Well, he got kicked out early, but that sergeant was being a butt. Clyde had every right to hit him."

I groaned at my sister's taste in men, or lack of taste, and laid my head against the seat. I closed my eyes as Ashlee slammed her foot on the gas pedal, and we zipped out of the lot.

At one minute to seven, I pulled into the *Blossom Valley Herald* parking lot. After a quick nap that afternoon, I'd retrieved my car with Ashlee's help, then spent the rest of the time sitting in the recliner under Mom's watchful eye, repeatedly assuring her I was okay. When she offered to reheat last night's cabbage rolls for dinner, I declined. After the day I'd had, I planned to pick up a big, juicy cheeseburger after I met with Jason. And fries. And a chocolate shake. She checked with me another six or seven times, then finally departed for her dinner with Lane. I found myself actually looking forward to hearing about the details of her date when she got back. As long as it didn't involve any kissing. Or hand-holding.

The lobby area was dark when I entered the single-story building, but I could see a light down the hall and headed toward it. I found Jason hunched over his desk, typing furiously. When he looked up and saw me, he stopped.

"Dana, I'm almost finished. How are you feeling?"

"I'm sure I'll be sore tomorrow, but right now I feel great." The Advil had a lot to do with that, along with seeing Jason.

He resumed typing for a moment before he stood. "Follow me." He led the way past the other desks, the monitors all dark, their users gone this late in the evening.

As we walked, my stomach emitted a growl that sounded like a fighter jet in the quiet room. I clapped a hand over my belly as Jason chuckled. "Sorry," I said.

"Actually, that's a good sound."

He stepped to the side of a doorway so I could enter first. I found myself in the newspaper break room. On a small round table, two takeout containers and a bottle of wine waited.

"I took a guess that you'd like chicken parmesan," he said, sounding a little bashful. He offered a half shrug.

"I love chicken parmesan." Good thing I'd decided to wait for that burger and fries.

He pulled a chair out for me, and I sat down. He grabbed some silverware and napkins from a nearby drawer and sat across from me, passing me a takeout carton and accoutrements before pouring us each a glass of wine.

I took a sip, savoring the tangy flavor. "Has Crusher talked at all?"

"The cops can't shut him up," Jason said. "Apparently Bobby Joe kept hinting about some great move he was working on. Crusher decided to spy on him that night, and when he saw the trick, he knew he had to do it himself. He's up to his eyeballs in gambling debt, and the loan sharks are losing patience. A couple even followed him up here."

I remembered the man who'd visited the spa and the one who'd yelled at Crusher after the fireworks show. Guess they weren't old buddies after all.

"So he saw Bobby Joe's trick, then grabbed the nearest tailpipe and crushed his skull?" I asked. It all seemed so unnecessary.

"Not exactly. Bobby Joe caught Crusher lurking around and confronted him. They got into a blowout. Bobby Joe must have realized Crusher would try the trick himself. Crusher swears Bobby Joe took the first swing and he grabbed the tailpipe in self-defense, but we'll never know for sure."

"Either way, what a total waste." I shook my head as I cut off a piece of chicken, added some spaghetti with marinara sauce, and popped it in my mouth. Definitely better than a burger.

"Agreed, but the man was desperate. He even took an iPod off Bobby Joe's body, said he was worried it'd have pictures of the trick on it or something. The cops say it didn't even belong to Bobby Joe."

"No, it's probably Ashlee's." I thought of the photos Ashlee had put on there of herself in risqué poses. "Did you get a look at it?" I asked.

Jason took a sip of wine. "No, it's already tagged as evidence and locked away."

Ashlee would be glad to hear that. At least she didn't have to worry about those photos popping up on the Internet anytime soon. "You know, Todd was at the fairgrounds when I first got there today, and I was almost convinced he'd come back to make sure he hadn't left anything incriminating behind."

Jason sipped his wine. "The cops talked to him after you mentioned seeing him there. Turns out his boss is participating in a job fair next weekend and sent Todd out to see about table space and such."

"Man, I had that guy figured all wrong." I took another bite of spaghetti.

"Everyone makes mistakes. You were trying to clear your sister's name."

I swallowed my food. "Did you ever find out where Maria was that night?"

"Turns out she really was at home. She knew Todd was out, so she lied for him. And since Todd wasn't home, he had no way of knowing where Maria was, so he covered for her." He pointed his fork at me. "I almost forgot. I mentioned Donald's seashell operation to one of my buddies. An undercover cop went out there to make a buy, but there wasn't an ugly seashell magnet in the whole place."

"Tara said he was acting jumpy. Guess I scared him into shutting down. Or he's selling the pot some other way."

"Either way, the cops'll keep an eye on him for a while. Stump, too. My buddy saw him hanging around the station and confirmed he's living in a spare room. He'll probably try to figure out some other way to package the merchandise, but he'll get caught. They both will." Jason wiped his mouth and placed his napkin next to his plate. "But enough talk about drugs and murder. Let's talk about us."

I slowed my chewing, butterflies doing a jig in my stomach. "What about us?"

"These last few days have made me realize how important you are in my life. I don't want to lose you."

My eyes locked with his. "Don't worry. I'm not going anywhere." I thought about my near-death experience and trembled, glad I was still around.

He raised his glass, and I raised mine. Together, we clinked the edges.

"To us, then," Jason said.

"To us."

I took a long, satisfying sip, sealing the toast and its infinite potential.

Tips from the O'Connell Farm and Spa

Being in charge of writing the farm's blog gives me lots of opportunities to learn new things. I've selected some of those tips for your enjoyment.

Cleaning Mirrors and Windows

With so many mirrors to wipe down in the guest cabins and throughout the main house, we find it cheaper and more eco-friendly to make our own cleaner. The main ingredients are water, white vinegar, and rubbing alcohol. I start with two cups of warm water and add a quarter cup each of rubbing alcohol and white vinegar. I mix these together, pour the mixture into a spray bottle, and I'm all set. I always give the bottle a good shake if I haven't used it for a while, and then I'm ready for some shiny mirrors.

Rehydrating with Food

When it's hot outside, you need to stay hydrated. If you're tired of drinking glass upon glass of water, you can always switch to foods with a high water content. The most common foods are certain fruits and vegetables, such as watermelon (or any melon), celery, oranges, grapefruits, tomatoes, and lettuce. Believe it or not, broccoli also has a high water content. As the temperatures climb, make yourself a nice fruit or lettuce-based salad. You're sure to feel refreshed.

Performing the Triangle Pose

While there are many beneficial yoga poses, the Triangle Pose is one of my favorites because of the way it stretches out my legs and spine. To perform the Triangle Pose, stand with your feet about three feet apart and hold your arms straight out to the sides, palms down. Turn your right foot ninety degrees to the right. Turn your left foot about thirty degrees to the right. Take a deep breath. As you exhale, bend to your right so that your left hand is now pointing toward the ceiling and your right hand is resting on your shin or ankle. Hold this pose for up to a minute, taking several deep breaths, then return to standing. Turn your feet to the left and repeat the pose on the left side.

Making Lavender Water

The wonderful smell of lavender can calm anyone's mood and brighten their day. Here at the O'Connell Organic Farm and Spa, we like to spritz a little lavender water in each room to provide that soothing feeling as soon as a guest walks in. To make your own at home, all you need is distilled water, essential lavender oil, and a spray bottle. Fill the bottle with distilled water. Add one drop of essential lavender oil for each ounce of water, and you're all done. It's possible to use actual lavender flowers, but not everyone grows lavender, and I find this recipe so easy.

Caring for the American Flag

Esther likes to always have an American flag waving in the breeze here at the O'Connell Organic Farm and Spa, and during the Fourth of July weekend, we had more than our fair share of flags. If you plant a flag on your own property, it's important to treat the flag correctly. Whenever you carry the flag, hold it up high and make sure it doesn't touch anything beneath it, including the ground or even boxes or items that are sitting on the floor. You should raise the flag at sunrise and lower the flag at sunset, always displaying it with the blue square facing up. If the flag becomes tattered or worn, make sure to dispose of it properly, usually by burning it. You might also check to see if a local organization, like the Boy Scouts, collects damaged flags for proper disposal.

Balancing Priorities

With so much going on in life—what with work, personal time, and everyday tasks—it's easy to become overwhelmed with everything that needs to be done. When this happens, I like to sit down and make a list, then rank each item from one to three. The "ones" are items that have to be done as soon as possible, the "twos" can wait a few days, and the "threes" are things I'd like to do eventually but that I can let slide for a while. Once I've categorized each item, I can focus on the most important ones. Often I'll find that only one or two things need to be done right away, and that immediately calms me. Of course, having my sister involved in a murder threw even my most organized priority list out of whack, but I don't expect that to happen again. I hope.

Making Basil Oil

Basil grows aplenty here at the farm during the summer, and Zennia uses this herb to make basil-infused olive oil. She places six or seven good-size leaves and half a cup of olive oil in a saucepan. She heats the mixture on low for five minutes, then sets the pan aside to cool. After a couple of hours, she pours the oil, leaves and all, in a small glass container and stores it in the fridge. Since the spa fridge is super cold, she leaves the oil out for a few minutes before each use so it can warm a bit. Sometimes she drizzles the basil oil over cubes of fresh mozzarella and adds a sprinkle of salt and pepper. Other times, she tosses some pasta and diced tomatoes with the oil, then adds fresh-shaved parmesan. Either way, it's delicious.

**Please turn the page for an exciting
sneak peek of the next
Blossom Valley Mystery
coming soon from Kensington Publishing!**

1

A gust of wind blew against the canvas canopy, ripping the pole from Esther's hand and threatening to topple the entire contraption. I scrambled to grab the pole and forced it into the base.

"Got it," I told Esther.

She stepped back and wiped a hand across her brow. "Mercy me, Dana. This set-up is harder than I thought."

I glanced around at the nearby stalls along Main Street, where others were struggling to pop up canopies or unfold tables. When I'd first suggested a green living festival to the Blossom Valley Rejuvenation Committee that Esther belonged to, I hadn't anticipated the strong winds that occasionally sprang up during fall here in Blossom Valley. Still, even with these temperamental bursts of air and cooler temperatures, the festival would go on, with the O'Connell Organic Farm and Spa right in the middle of the activity.

As owner of the farm, Esther was hoping this festival would finally draw attention to her bed and breakfast and secure her financial future. After a series of murders in the few months since the farm's opening, business had been understandably slow to pick up, but reservations had steadily risen in the last few weeks, allowing us all to breathe a little easier. As the marketing maven for the farm, as well as the back-up maid, waitress, and animal catcher, I liked to think my ads and daily blog had helped with business, though it was probably the discounts and proximity to Mendocino that had pulled everyone in. As long as people booked a stay, I didn't care why they were there. Unless it was to murder someone.

I finished securing the canopy and stepped over to the plastic folding table to retrieve a handful of glossy brochures from a cardboard box beneath it. I fanned the stack out as I spoke to Esther. "I can't wait to see how many people show up today."

Esther fiddled with a button on her denim blouse. The embroidered pumpkins and fall leaves fit right in with the spirit of the festival. "Heavens, what if no one comes? The farm will get the blame."

"Nonsense. This will be a huge success, and then you'll get the credit. We've been advertising it for weeks." I patted her hand, then reached into the box for more brochures.

"You should get the credit, Dana. This was your idea, and don't think I don't know it. You've saved my bacon more than once."

A cough behind me made my hand jerk. Two brochures skittered off the table and slid to the ground. Gordon, the manager of the farm, had slipped into the booth from the back, dressed in his usual expensive-looking suit and tie, every last black hair slicked into place on his head.

"Yes," he said. "It's good to see Dana finally embracing her marketing role. The festival could be the push we need to ensure the farm's success. As long as everyone works hard and remembers the goal of attracting more guests to the farm."

Gordon had spent the first few months as spa manager snapping at employees and watching our every move, a reminder that he was in charge, even if Esther really owned the place. In recent weeks, he'd adopted a more team captain method that involved pep talks— lots of pep talks—though his abrasive personality occasionally showed through. I usually tuned him out, nodding in all the right places while mentally figuring out what to watch on TV that night or when I needed to get my oil changed again.

I retrieved the fallen brochures and grabbed a handful of pens with pigs on top from the box under the table. I laid them near the brochures, making sure "O'Connell Organic Farm and Spa" was clearly visible.

Gordon picked up a pen. "How much did you squander on these?" He turned to glare at Esther. "Did you approve this purchase?"

Oh boy, here we went.

"Those pens are cute as newborn bunnies," Esther said. "When Dana showed me the picture on the computer, I gave her my blessing."

I grabbed a pen and pushed the pig down. An "oink" squeaked out. "Long after people throw those brochures in the trash, they'll still have the pens. Every time they write with one, they'll think of the spa."

Gordon grunted, which usually meant he agreed but didn't want to admit it. "Let's put them away for now. I don't want to run out in the first hour and not have more when the big afternoon crowds show up."

"Don't worry, I bought a ton of these little piggies, but I can save them for later." I pushed the pig to hear one more "oink," then gathered him up with his other pig pals and dropped them back in the box. You could bet I wouldn't be whipping out the travel mugs until after Gordon left.

He brushed at his jacket sleeve, though there wasn't a speck to be seen. "I have to get to the farm, but I'll check back later to see if you need anything from me." He nodded at the brochures. "Keep those stocked. And where's the photo collage?"

"Next on my list." I almost pointed out that I could have already set it up if Gordon would stop managing me, but then he might launch into another speech about how he was rallying the team for the good of the farm.

"Excellent. Make sure you get that done." He called to Esther, who'd been unpacking a stack of business cards. "Did you want a lift back?"

She straightened up. "Dana, do you need any more help?"

I retrieved the easel from where I'd propped it against the table and popped the legs open. "Now that the canopy and table are set up, I can handle the rest."

She gave me a quick hug. "Thanks again for all your hard work. I can rest easy knowing that you're running the booth."

Gordon placed a hand on Esther's elbow and guided her toward the parking area, clearly in a hurry to get back to work. I finished setting up the giant piece of cardboard with the two dozen pictures of the farm, re-arranged the brochures, and stepped around the table to survey the area from a passer-by's point of view.

A little boring. I reentered the enclosure and re-trieved a handful of pig pens from the box. The pop of pink instantly livened up the white table. I added half a dozen green travel mugs. Much better. Now I was ready for business.

I stood at attention, ready to answer any and all questions from people wandering by. Only there weren't any people. I glanced at my phone and saw it was five minutes after ten. Where were the crowds? The green-living lovers who would flock here and ooh and aah over all the offerings of an organic farm and spa?

After rearranging the brochures again, I clicked the top of a pig several times to hear it oink and turned the picture collage at different angles to see if it changed the viewing experience. Nope. Not that any people had wandered by to look at it.

I leaned over the table to peer down the road, barely able to see past the booth next door. The owner had apparently decided to go with a full tent, rather than a canopy. I stepped around the table for a better look at the street. Rows of tables much like mine lined both sides, all offering different items or services. I thought I spotted a potential customer at the far end, though I couldn't be sure.

Next door, voices reached me as two women came through the door flap in the tent, talking to someone still inside.

"I'll be sure to double-check the stock of sunglasses when I get back to the office," the one with the blond spiky hair with black tips said. A gust of wind blew past right then, lifting up the filmy split sleeves of her blouse and exposing a large tattoo of a panther on her shoulder.

"And I'll get busy tallying those accounts we were discussing. Give me a call if you get overwhelmed," said the older woman in the business suit. Her silver hair was cut in a bob and matched her silver ring, necklace, and bracelet.

The two women headed toward the parking area, and I went back to waiting for my first customer. After ten minutes of keeping busy doing nothing, I looked down the street again. The customer, or whoever I'd spotted at the other end, was gone, and no one else had taken their place.

With nothing else to do, I walked to the tent next door where the women had been to see if I could figure out what they were advertising. The door flap was tied back, and the banner across the opening declared it was the Invisible Prints booth. Miniature wind turbines sat in rows on a table inside. Plastic purple sunglasses with Invisible Prints stamped in yellow lettering on the arms waited on another table next to a slot that held brochures. The cover showed a red barn and a field full of pigs, looking much like the pigs back at Esther's farm. The tag line asked, WHAT CAN YOU DO WITH METHANE GAS? I decided not to think about the answer.

"Come on over and grab a souvenir," a voice said. I spotted a woman inside the tent and stepped into the enclosure. She smiled at me like she practiced that smile in a mirror. Blond and red highlights added depth to her perfectly styled deep brown hair, the large curls cascading past her shoulders. Her makeup looked professionally done, and her business jacket and knee-high skirt were completely out-of-place in downtown Blossom Valley.

I glanced down at my khaki pants and navy blue shirt with STAFF stitched on it and reminded myself that I had to wear my uniform for the farm. I couldn't think up an excuse for my barely brushed dishwater blond hair that I'd pulled back into a ponytail as I rushed out of the house this morning. "Cute windmills," I said. "What are they for?"

The woman picked one up and handed it to me. "Wind power is only one of the services Invisible Prints provides. We're a carbon footprint offsetting company."

Her words sounded like complete gibberish. "Carbon offset what?"

She chuckled like I wasn't the first one to ask that question. "Carbon footprint offsetting company. We help people invest in green energy projects or sustainable resources to make up for all the energy they use in their homes and fuel they burn while driving or flying. The idea is to replace energy and resources that have been used with new resources, thereby making your carbon footprint neutral."

"Interesting." I wasn't sure I completely understood everything she'd said, but her company certainly fit in with a green living festival. I set the windmill back on the table and picked up a brochure from the stand. I stuck it in my back pocket to read later.

"How about you?" she asked. "What business are you with?"

I stepped out of the tent, reached around the pole dividing our booths, and grabbed a brochure of my own to hand her. "I'm with the O'Connell Organic Farm and Spa here in town. We provide overnight accommodations and meals. The chef uses organic fruits and vegetables grown right on the farm, as well as eggs hatched on site and meat provided by local companies." I held out my right hand. "I'm Dana Lewis, by the way."

We shook.

"Wendy. Wendy Hartford."

I'd known a Wendy once, back in school. This Wendy appeared to be my age, and her face had a certain familiarity. Just as I opened my mouth to ask, she pointed a finger at me.

"Did you graduate from Blossom Valley High, by any chance? I used to go to school with a Dana Lewis."

"I don't believe it." I gave her a half hug, memories of the two of us during our middle school years flitting through my mind. We hung out in each other's bedroom for hours, flipping through the teen magazines to find our latest crushes or trying on our mothers' makeup, all the while talking about the future. "What have you been doing these past few years?"

"Oh, this and that. I've been with Invisible Prints for three years now. How about you?"

I thought about how to phrase my answer. We hadn't talked since high school graduation, and I was too embarrassed to admit I'd moved back home after a layoff. "I did some marketing down in the Bay Area for a while, but I moved back in with my mom a few months ago after my dad died."

"I'm sorry to hear that."

The sincerity in her voice made my heart squeeze, and I quelled the tears that threatened to rise. I was once more reminded of what great friends Wendy and I had been during those formative tween years. "Thanks. I can't believe it's been so long since we've seen each other. We really should have stayed in touch."

"I agree. At least we can make up for that time now."

A man in cargo shorts and a tank top stepped into the tent, the brim of his fisherman's hat brushing the tent flap. "What interesting windmills. What do they do?"

Was this an honest-to-goodness festival attendee? I glanced down the street and saw clumps of people stopped at various booths. The awaited crowd had finally arrived.

I headed out of the tent. "Guess I'd better get back to my job."

"We'll catch up later," Wendy said. Her words were the usual thing you'd say when you ran into an old friend, but I found myself looking forward to the idea.

A middle-aged woman in a tie-dyed T-shirt wandered toward Wendy's tent, and I scurried back to my booth. My hands shook a little in anticipation as I straightened the brochures one last time and made sure the picture display sat straight on the easel.

A woman with long brown hair and wearing an off-the-shoulder peasant dress and cowboy boots walked up to Wendy's tent and peeked in. When she saw Wendy was busy, she turned and went back the other way. Fine, I didn't want to tell her about the farm and spa anyway.

The man in the hat left Wendy's booth and moved over to mine. I spent a few minutes outlining the services of the farm, including the new spa features. He took a pig pen and drifted away. Several people replaced him, keeping me busy for the next twenty minutes.

Once the last person had left, I stretched across the table and poked my head out. The street had cleared again, leaving only a couple of women who both seemed to be heading for Wendy's booth. The closer one was the same one who'd stopped by before, the one in the cowboy boots and dress. The other, wearing a shockingly loud neon green pants suit, appeared to be in her early forties, though her flawless, cocoa-colored skin made it hard to tell. As I watched, the African American woman sped up and brushed past, leaving the woman in the peasant dress floundering in the middle of the street. Rude. The first woman disappeared from view, presumably into Wendy's tent, while the other hesitated a moment, then walked away.

I bent down to grab a handful of pig pens to replace the ones I'd given away. As I straightened up, a loud female voice sounded from next door.

"Wendy, we need to talk."

I felt a flutter of concern. She must be the woman in bright green who'd been in such a rush to reach the booth first. She sounded furious.

I couldn't hear Wendy's response, but the woman didn't lower her voice at all. "You know exactly why I'm here. I want some answers. Now."

Maybe I should go over there. Make sure Wendy was okay.

I moved toward the gap at the end of the table, but stopped when someone blocked my way.

"Dana, I didn't know you were going to be here."

Forget Wendy. I had my own problem, and her name was Kimmie.